AFORETHOUGHT
◆ BOOK 2 ◆

DEBTS AND DARKNESS

KYRA ALESSY

ALSO BY KYRA ALESSY

THE DESIRE AFORETHOUGHT SERIES

Demons and Debts

www.kyraalessy.com/demonsanddebts

Debts and Darkness

www.kyraalessy.com/debtsanddarkness

Darkness and Debauchery

www.kyraalessy.com/darknessanddebauchery

THE DARK BROTHERS SERIES

Sold to Serve

www.kyraalessy.com/sold2serve

Bought to Break

www.kyraalessy.com/bought2break

Kept to Kill

www.kyraalessy.com/kept2kill

Caught to Conjure

www.kyraalessy.com/caught2conjure

Trapped to Tame

www.kyraalessy.com/trapped2tame

Seized to Sacrifice

www.kyraalessy.com/seized2sacrifice

For more details on these and the other forthcoming series, please visit Kyra's website / join her mailing list:

https://www.kyraalessy.com/bookstore/

IF YOU ARE IN ANY WAY RELATED TO ME

Seriously, I feel the need to put this in every book I write. If you are a part of my family, put this book down.

Don't do it!

If you do not heed this page, never EVER speak of it to me. I don't want to hear anything about this book from your lips.

I don't want to hear that you're surprised that I'd write about dark demon ménage à trois, doctors' exam table sexcapades, hairbrush dicks, and all-around hot monster fucking.

Also (and if you take anything from this page at all, please please let it be this part.) I 110% don't want to know that I've unlocked a new kink *for you*.

NO THANKS!

AUTHOR'S NOTE

J ane, **the FMC in this series is autistic.** The following is a fictional work, but the portrayal of this 'condition' is as accurate as this author can make it and is based on said author's first-hand experiences of autism, both humorous and serious in nature.

If you believe you may be autistic following reading this book, the author suggests reading up on ASD and seeking official diagnosis as many women are not diagnosed until well into adulthood.

If you are autistic, you are not crazy and, although all of us are different, you are not alone.

Triggers in this book include:

Portrayal of autistic meltdowns / shutdowns
Unobtained consent
Violence and gore
Unloving parent
Mild sexual assault to FMC outside harem
Cliffhanger

1

THEO

The house is gone. Sure, there are other places we can go, other properties we own. But that was *our Clubhouse*. My mind is reeling as I follow Korban, keeping up with him even though he's trying hard to leave me in the dust.

Could this really have been Jane? I can't imagine her trying to kill us. But why not? How well do we actually know her? Maybe I've been unconsciously assuming things about her based on the way her brain is meant to work. Maybe it's blinded me. I mean was that medical document even real, or a plant for us to find and make us underestimate her? Is everything we know about her fake?

I try to treat humans and supes equally but, in that same vein, a human can be just as cunning as any supe or fae. I forgot that where Jane was concerned.

I take the next turn as tightly as I can, using my advantage to overtake our enforcer. He gives me a look, a dark smirk that says he's not going to let me win.

It's on, motherfucker.

Even if Jane is guilty, I have to get to her before Korban

does. I have a duty of care. I have no idea what he'll do but if he's even half as angry as I am, he'll take it out on her if I give him the chance and he's very ... *creative*. There are reasons he's feared almost more than Vic and, as far as he's concerned, she tried to take us down. He thinks it was her who planted the bomb that has destroyed the mansion, somehow had a hand in Vic's accident, and Sie getting shot in the street. She'll get no mercy from him.

The truth is, I don't care whether or not she had something to do with the attack on the Iron I's right now. I just can't let Korban torture her for information or kill her in some human-hating rage. My brothers might not agree with me, but I'm a doctor before I'm a member of the Club. When Vic wakes up, we'll decide what happens to Jane, but, until then, I'm keeping her safe, even from my own brothers if I have to.

I throw caution to the wind as I step on it, going as fast as I possibly can down the backroads towards Metro. It's not long before I reach the suburbs. I lost Korban a while back, but he's probably taking the highway. I'm hoping that I know these roads just a little bit better than him since I come through them almost every day on the way to the clinic, which is only a block away from Metro Gen, the main hospital where Vic and Sie will be taken ... if they aren't already there.

Parking my bike outside the side entrance, I leap off and practically sprint through the doors. I know where I'm going, so I don't stop especially when I see Korban in my periphery. He came in via the main door and he's only about five seconds behind me. I hear the elevator ding open, and I run for it, sliding into it and pressing the number three hard.

'Come on. Come on. Come on!' I mutter, rapidly tapping

on the button to make the doors close faster, my other hand playing with the stethoscope in my jacket pocket.

It finally shuts and starts to move. I'm pacing the tiny space like an insane animal at the zoo.

Should have taken the stairs.

Should have taken the fucking stairs.

When the elevator opens, I dart out onto the third floor and make it to the nurse's station just before Kor bursts through the heavy fire doors from the stairwell.

'I'm looking for Alexandre Makenzie,' I say to the nearest nurse, a petite healing sprite whose eyes widen in alarm as Korban barrels up behind me.

'Room 306, Doctor,' she says, staring at Kor and then at me. She lowers her voice. 'Are you okay? Do you need me to call security, Doctor Wright?'

I'm surprised she recognizes me, but I guess she's seen my face around the hospital from time to time. I turn my head, snorting in Korban's direction.

'No need, but thank you ...' I glance at her nametag. 'Harriet.'

She nods. 'I'll take you to him.'

The sprite walks down the hall, looking back once or twice as if she's afraid Korban is going to attack.

'Relax,' I hiss at him. 'We're in a fucking hospital, not the ring. You can't do anything to her here anyway.'

He grunts and falls into step next to me as she leads us to Vic's room.

Vic is laying in the bed, a monitor beeping at regular intervals.

'He's unconscious at the moment,' she says, 'but that's just the drugs we gave him. He's got two cracked ribs and a deep laceration to his,' she checks the notes, 'left leg. Looks like he was experiencing breathing problems when they brought him in.' She tapers off, going silent as she reads. 'He had a collapsed lung, which is why he's still up here, but he's well fed so his healing will be fast. An incubus like him will be okay in a couple of days. We're just waiting on the paperwork to send him downstairs.'

'Where's the girl who was with him in the car?' Korban growls.

'The human? They have their own hospital a few blocks away. I don't know why they didn't get an ambulance to take her there straight from the scene. Anyway, we don't allow humans up here since all the troubles lately.' She says the last part quieter like she's afraid of being overheard. 'I think she asked one of the other nurses where she could get a coffee, so she might be downstairs.'

I frown. I mean I know about the new rules since the Order has stepped up their attacks in the area, but last I heard there were still a few rooms for human patients who ended up here for whatever reason because this is still a hospital.

'Is she okay?' I ask, wondering if anyone has even checked her over.

It doesn't sound like it.

When I turn, Korban is already racing to the elevator.

Fuck that.

I don't wait for the nurse's response.

This time, I book it to the stairs, basically throwing myself down to the second floor. I run through the long hallway, dodging medical personnel and patients alike, to the small coffee shop at the end. The elevator doors open just in front of me and I hear Kor growl a curse as he sees I'm just ahead of him again.

I win, asshole.

I scan the tables for Jane and see her sitting in a corner

facing away from everyone. She has a coffee in front of her, but it doesn't look like she's even had a sip. She's just staring down at it.

I make my way over to her, giving Kor a glance, letting him know that I will start some shit if he tries to force her out of here with him. He might be a better fighter, but this is my arena and 'a doctor being attacked in a hospital' will not go well for him.

She looks up as I get closer and I notice that faint bruises have already come up on her face. Looks like she was bumped around pretty good in the crash.

I bend down to her.

'Are you okay?'

Her gaze is unfocused, but she shrinks back into the chair a little bit as Korban approaches, towering over her. I give him a look and he rolls his eyes, but he takes a step back.

'Jane.'

She looks at me.

'Are you okay?'

She gives a tiny nod of her head.

'Come on.' I get her up carefully and lead her with small steps back to the elevator.

'Why are you being so gentle with her? Half of us are in the fucking hospital because of this bitch,' Kor hisses low in my ear.

'I'm a fucking doctor first,' I whisper back.

We take the elevator back upstairs in silence, and when the doors open and Jane steps onto the floor, all the sprites at the nurse's station look up at her like hungry birds at a handful of seed.

One of them shakes her head and comes over, her white shoes thudding on the floor as she mumbles something.

'I'm so sorry, Doctor. I'll call security right away.'

She turns to Jane, looking angry. 'I told you earlier, you aren't welcome in this hospital. I'm calling security right now. I suggest you leave before they get here. They aren't paid to be courteous to *your kind.*'

Jane steps backward, bumping into Korban and seeming to wither under the angry sprite's stare.

That's not like her. She's not herself, not at all.

I open my mouth, angry beyond words. Whatever the Human Policy is right now, this is still a hospital. No matter the species of patient, they're obligated to heal everyone, but Korban gets there first.

'She's with us,' he snarls, putting a hand on Jane's shoulder and urging her past the nurse.

I stay back for a moment, confident that Korban isn't going to do anything to Jane, at least not right now.

'She was in a car accident. Has a doctor even checked her over?'

The nurse looks surprised. 'The humans have their own hospital in Metro, Doctor,' she says, her tone turning disdainful.

'Did you get her an ambulance to that hospital?' I ask, clenching my jaw.

'That's not in my job description.'

'You're a fucking nurse!'

She jumps at my outburst. 'Yes, *Doctor*, I am a nurse *and an employee of this hospital.* Do I need to call security to have *all* of you escorted from the premises?'

Any pretense of respect she was giving me is long gone and I know she'll make good on her threat, so I make a mental note of her name because I WILL be filing a formal complaint about this.

Jen Prifty.

'That won't be necessary, nurse.'

I move past the angry sprite, ignoring her in favor of seeing how Vic is doing properly and finding Sie, who should be in the ICU somewhere too since he was only just brought in.

But I don't want to spend too much time here. In addition to getting Jane away from these nurses who are now speaking in hushed, snippy tones to each other while side-eying us over the counter of their station, I want to get back to our townhouse and check her over myself.

I want – no, I need – to make sure her head's okay and that she doesn't have any internal bleeding.

I keep my eye on her, watching her movements like a hawk as we enter Vic's room. She rushes over to the bed and peers at Vic who's still unconscious.

'Is he okay? They wouldn't tell me anything, just made me leave as soon as the paramedics brought me up here with him.'

'He'll be okay,' I tell her, and she looks ... *relieved*.

I'll think on why that might be later, but she certainly isn't acting like a saboteur. She could have run when they made her leave the ICU earlier, but she didn't. Was that because she's not guilty or because her knock on the head has left her confused?

'They're letting him sleep it off. What happened?'

'I don't know. We were in the car. There was a screech, maybe the brakes, and I don't know if we hit something ... but then we were rolling over and over.'

'We need to get the police report,' Korban mutters, looking suspiciously at Jane again while he takes out his phone.

'What happened next?'

'When I came to, there were supe cops everywhere and

they were taking Vic away in the ambulance. He was awake and they weren't going to let me go with him. They were going to take me somewhere else, but he made them bring me too, so that I was in the ambulance with him and they brought us here, but when they took us to the ICU, they told me to leave so I went down to the coffee shop because I didn't know what else to do and my phone was in the car ...'

She's rambling and I can tell she's getting distraught. I put my hand on her shoulder and draw her backwards towards me, not really thinking about what I'm doing. I just don't like seeing her upset. She goes along with it, but her body is stiff. I guess without some heavy bass, we're not quite there yet.

Just then, Paris pokes his head in through the door.

'I got your message,' he says to Kor. 'I spoke to my guy in the Metro PD. He's sending me the report on the crash as soon as it's on the system.'

'Good,' Korban says. 'How is Sie?'

'He's in a room a couple floors down. He's a little beat up, but he's healing pretty fast. You know how he hates hospitals though. He's acting like a caged bear. He already told the nurses he's leaving as soon as his shoulder stops bleeding no matter what so he'll be out later today.'

Kor looks Jane up and down with an expression I can't decipher, but it's definitely not suspicion.

'Helps that he fed recently.'

'What the fuck happened out there?' I ask.

Paris shrugs at us. 'We'd just set up the meeting for later today and were heading to the Metro house when a truck pulled out in front of us. They fired on us from the cab. Sie got hit in the shoulder. It could have been worse, but his bike's totaled. I skidded onto the sidewalk and got a little scraped up, but by the time I could get myself together, the fuckers were long gone and Sie was just layin' in the street. I thought he was dead ...'

Korban puts an arm around Paris' shoulder. 'Are *you* okay?'

'Yeah, nothing I can't handle,' Paris replies flippantly.

'There's nothing more we can do here until Vic's awake,' I say, keeping a grip on Jane who tries to move away from me. 'Let's get to the house and figure out our next move from there.'

'And if they try again?' Korban asks, looking at Vic's vulnerable state.

'Even if they do, you've seen how security is here with all the attacks recently. They have this place locked up tighter than an alpha's asshole. Nobody is getting in here.'

'Try again?' Paris asks, his confusion evident.

'Sie, Vic, the house? Are we going to pretend this is anything other than a coordinated attack?' Korban growls.

'No,' I concede.

Paris' neck rolls in Korban's direction. 'What happened to the house?'

'We'll talk about this later,' I say to Korban, and he shuts up, his eyes narrowing on Jane again.

But she doesn't notice, not that that surprises me. She is pretty oblivious most of the time, but I'm worried she's got a concussion, or worse.

'Come on,' I murmur, taking a last look at Vic's strong vitals. 'Let's get out of here.'

The four of us leave, going down to the front entrance where I hand a very spaced-out Jane to Paris since he doesn't have his bike. It's only a short ride from here to the house, but I still have to make myself let go of her.

As I watch Paris help Jane into a cab, I wonder how I'm going to navigate the protective feelings that seem to be emerging for a human who might be out to get us. I can pretend to the others that this is because I'm a doctor, but it's bull and they know it.

Paris will side with Korban on principle, going along with whatever he wants to do with her. I need to keep her safe somehow, but without Vic at my back, that just got a whole lot harder.

Jane

I'M FEELING PRETTY OUT of it as Paris pushes me into the cab and I slide over. He gives the driver an address and we pull away from the hospital. I don't know how long it's been since the accident. I'm a little fuzzy, but everyone seemed to get here really fast and they said something about Vic upstairs.

'Is Vic okay?' I ask.

'Yeah ... he's going to be fine.'

'And Sie?'

'And Sie.'

Paris looks at me weirdly. I let my head fall back to the headrest, closing my eyes.

'Hey.'

I look at him.

'I don't think you should fall asleep until after Theo takes a look at you. Did they check you out at the hospital?'

'I don't think so,' I say, but I honestly don't remember.

He slides closer to me, peering into my eyes.

I rub my hairline, trying to think, but other thoughts keep intruding. How hot Paris looks right now, how he moved on the dance floor with me the other night, how he kissed me in the pantry that time ... did those other things.

'You're a really good dancer,' I murmur softly, then wonder why I said that because I've just been in a car accident and this seems like a weird time to want to have sex.

'I – What? Did you hit your head, princess?'

'I don't know,' I say. 'It all happened really fast.'

I look out the window, trying to ignore my body and focus on the tall townhouses that line the street go by. We stop at a light, and I stare at the crosswalk as a woman in heels strides across on her phone, looking like she's on her way somewhere.

'Where are we going?'

'To our house, babe. Hey, could you step on it?'

'Step on what?'

His arm snakes around my shoulders gently. 'I was talking to the driver.'

I close my eyes again. I can't help it, and before I know it, the car is stopping.

Paris pays the fare and helps me out.

'What's happening?' I ask.

'We're just at our place in Metro. We keep a house here, remember?' Paris says slowly.

I nod as he leads me up a short flight of red, brick steps. This place looks like it was built a while ago.

'Was I in a car accident?'

He doesn't answer me but opens the door and I find myself in a lobby with a shining wood floor and a high old-fashioned ceiling. Stairs wind elegantly up in front of me, carpeted in red. Paris doesn't stop, taking my elbow in a firm but gentle grip and leading me down the hallway, past the stairs into a bright room lined with books and comfy places to sit. I scan the shelves and see that they're not the kind of books that were in Vic's study back at their Club-house mansion. These are mainstream books like best-sellers and stuff. The kind that aren't for show, just for enjoyment.

Paris' touch leaves me, and I lean into him, wanting it back. Theo and Korban are here, sitting together and speaking in low tones. They stop talking when they notice us.

Korban stands and strides to Paris, giving him a lingering kiss on the lips that makes a zing go straight to my core.

I swallow hard. 'That was so hot,' I breathe.

Korban turns on me with a sneer and suddenly has me by the throat, lifting me up onto my tip-toes.

'It wasn't for you!' he snarls so nastily that I whimper.

Why is he so mad at me?

'Kor, let her go!' Paris commands, but Korban doesn't budge.

'It's about time we found out what this human bitch has been planning. I'm not playing anymore, girl! Who are you working for?'

I'm terrified, but his words make me remember that time he caught me in the woods, the way he held me down and touched me, and I can't help the moan that leaves me. He drops me like I burn him and I catch myself, somehow not falling over.

'Kor, listen to me. She's not right. She's been saying weird stuff in the car.'

Theo pushes past them both. 'What weird things?'

'Just whatever comes into her head and she keeps asking the same questions and then forgetting the answers. She just asked me if she was in a car accident. What's wrong with her?'

'Fuck,' Theo says, looking into my eyes closely. 'Fuck those assholes at the hospital for not doing their jobs.'

I frown. 'What's happening?' I ask, starting to get scared. 'Am I dying?'

'No, sweetheart, you aren't dying,' Theo assures me. 'I think maybe you have a concussion. Did you hit your head in the accident?'

I look over at Korban whose face is unreadable. 'I'm sorry if I said something wrong,' I whisper, my chin wobbling.

He looks at Theo. 'Maybe it would be a good time to question her while she's like this. Might get something useful out of her.'

'She's my patient and there's no fucking way I'm letting you interrogate her when she clearly has a head injury.' Theo rolls his eyes and looks at Paris. 'Do something with him. Now. I'm going to take care of Jane the way they should have at Metro Gen.'

Paris takes Korban's arm and then cups his cheek with his large hand, making Korban look at him. 'There's nothing in the fridge and we need to eat some real food. Come with me to get take-out. She'll still be here to question later when Vic's awake.'

Korban heaves a sigh.

'Fine,' he growls. 'Now. Later. I guess it doesn't make much difference. I *will* be making her tell me what I want to know though.'

Korban and Paris leave the room and I hear them go out the door a minute later. Theo surveys me like he's looking for something.

'How are you feeling?' he asks.

'Not really sure,' I say. 'Why was Korban so angry with me?'

I rub my neck where his fingers dug into me and, for some reason, it makes me pulse between my legs.

'Don't worry about him.' Theo's voice sounds strained.

'What's wrong with me? Give it to me straight,' I try a chuckle, but it falls flat.

'Come upstairs. I'll take a look at you.'

'Sure thing, Doc,' I say without a hint of emotion.

He takes my hand and leads me back to the front door where the stairs are. There's geometric wallpaper going all the way up that captures my eyes and refuses to let go.

'Who decorated this place?' I ask quietly, my gaze running along the symmetrical lines with a will of its own.

'That was Paris all the way. He wanted to keep it in 'the traditional style' or something.'

He watches me closely the whole way up the stairs like this is some kind of test.

We reach a landing at the top with a short hallway to the left and right. There's a bathroom in front of me and an elevator. Before I can wonder why we didn't take it, he moves me along.

'The rooms are smaller here,' he says, 'but you can have mine again if you want. I can bunk with one of the others.'

'Doesn't seem fair that I keep taking your bed,' I say, peering through open doorways into bedrooms as we walk past.

He looks back and gives me a once-over. 'You could always let me stay in there with you, princess.'

My cheeks heat. That one was blunt enough for me to understand. The image I get of being in his bed with him as he ... My legs almost buckle with the force of the need that hits me.

What was that? What's wrong with me?

He leads me into a room, and I stop at the threshold when I see it's like an actual doctors' office.

'Do you meet patients in here,' I ask.

'No one from the general public no,' he says, 'but if a member of the Club needs to see a doctor and I'm in the city, they usually come here.'

My eyes fall on the exam table and I close my mouth, remembering the things he said to me about what he likes ... wow, was that only this morning?

I swallow hard and I hope he doesn't notice that I'm suddenly nervous as he draws me into the middle of the room and closes the door.

'Take off your clothes,' he says.

'Excuse me?'

But I want to. I *really* want to. My heart is pounding hard in my chest and my clothes feel constricting.

'Not like that,' he says. 'I need to check you over properly. There's a hospital gown right there. Put it on. I just want to make sure you're okay.'

'How will you do that exactly?' I ask, stomach fluttering.

'Well, I'll have to touch you – with your permission, of course. But don't worry, Miss Mercy, you're in capable hands.'

My eyes widen. He just did *the Doctor Wright voice*. Does he know he did or is that just how he talks to all his patients?

He turns around and pulls a blue curtain across, giving me a little bit of privacy as I take off the clothes that I put on this morning. I slip on the gown. It's the kind that ties at the back, so if I turn around, he'll see my bare ass.

I slide my hands down my body, the cool cotton teasing my skin, my nipples that are rapidly hardening. I need ...

'Doctor?'

'Is everything okay?'

'Can you help me with this, please?'

I turn my body to face the wall, and I hear him pull the curtain open. There's silence and I look over my shoulder innocently to see that he's frozen. His hand is still on the blue material, and he's staring at my naked ass.

I shift on my legs, letting it wiggle a little even as I wonder who this person is who has control of my body because I never do stuff like this. I don't even know *how* to do stuff like this.

He swallows hard. 'What can I help you with?'

'I can't get the ties.'

'That's okay,' he replies, not making a move to touch me. 'Sit on the table.'

I try not to let my disappointment show as I do what he says. The leather feels nice against me, making me shiver.

'This is just like a regular doctor's office,' I mutter as if I've been in one since I was a kid, which I haven't.

'That's the idea. It puts my patients at ease. Can you imagine if it was all dried herbs hanging from the ceiling, incantation books, and potion bottles in a secret cabinet in this day and age? I mean I have that stuff too. I just keep it on the DL.'

'But I saw your Med School diploma,' I say, canting my head at him. 'I thought you were a regular doctor.'

'I am, but I'm qualified to work on supes as well as humans, and that means training in more than one form of medicine.'

'Like what?' I ask, very interested.

'Well, for example, you need a CT scan. It's a great way of assessing internal damage for humans and for supes but getting a supe inside one of those tubes would be a mission and a half. They just don't trust human machines, so a doctor qualified to work with supes has other means of finding out the same information,' Theo explains, producing two gold, button-looking disks. He holds them in his palm.

'What are those?'

'Just a way of me seeing what's going on with that bump on your head without us having to go all the way to the other hospital. They rest on your eyelids. That's it. It won't hurt. All you need to do is lay still and stay awake, Jane. You can do that for me, can't you?'

I nod. 'Yeah, it's just ... I feel so ...' *like I want to tear off this gown and throw myself at you.*

A shudder runs through me at the thought.

'I know you don't feel like yourself. That's why I need to check you out, sweetheart.' He sounds weird and he's definitely doing *the voice*. 'Are you ready?'

'Yeah.'

He shines a small flashlight in my face without warning and I wince.

'Does anything hurt?'

'Yeah, my fucking eyes,' I growl.

He chuckles and puts the light away. 'Sorry.'

'My shoulder,' I say, 'and I feel hot. My head is starting to ache now too.'

I hadn't noticed that before. I touch a spot on the back of my skull and his fingers follow mine, probing the area.

'You've definitely got a bump back here. That would explain it.'

'Explain what?'

'Don't worry, princess. I'll get you all fixed up. Close your eyes.'

I do as I'm told and I feel him place the two disks gently over my eyes. There's silence for a minute and I'm just opening my mouth to ask him if everything's okay when he removes them.

'All done,' he murmurs. 'Just a little concussion as I suspected. You're going to be fine, I promise. Anything else hurt? Your chest? Your stomach?'

I shake my head.

'You're lucky you weren't hurt worse. I heard the car was pretty banged up.'

'I think Vic made sure I was safe.'

Theo gives me a small smile. 'Sounds like Vic.'

'Why would he do that?' I say half to myself. 'He doesn't even like me.'

Theo doesn't answer.

'Lay back,' he orders and I do what he tells me with a sigh.

'Eyes open,' he reminds me when I close them and I nod, keeping my gaze locked on his face.

There's something there – anticipation maybe – and I'm suddenly nervous again, but I can't help the next thing I ask.

'When you were talking about the exam table before, was this the one you meant?'

He turns away and runs a hand through his hair, pulling it a little like he's frustrated. 'Actually, I was talking about the room similar to this one back at the Clubhouse.'

'Here,' he gets an old-school thermometer out.

'Is that for under my tongue?' I ask.

'Well,' he says, 'I could get my rectal one out if you want.'

My eyes widen, and everything below my waist contracts. He's just playing with me, right?

'No, thanks,' I say quickly, afraid I'm going to blurt out an 'Okay!' instead.

He smiles like he has no idea what's going through my head and I'm sooooo glad he can't read my mind. He puts the thin tube under my tongue and I try to relax as he raises my arm and begins to move it this way and that, making it hurt.

I give a small cry.

'I'm sorry,' he says. 'Looks like it's a little bit sprained. It'll take a few days, but it'll be fine. I'll give you some painkillers. How about your ribs from before? Are they still aching?'

I shake my head. 'No, they didn't really hurt much after that pill you gave me last time. Can I have another one of those?'

He looks rueful. 'No can do. They're a pretty powerful fae concoction. Even supes can only take 'em once in a blue moon. Too much fae stuff has consequences for all of us. Bad ones usually.'

He puts my arm back down and then takes the other one, doing the same thing.

'That one's fine,' I mumble.

He hushes me. 'Just keep that thermometer in your mouth, Miss Mercy.'

His fingers trace my collarbone, down one side and up the other before pressing my sternum over the hospital gown.

'Does that hurt?' he asks.

I shake my head and he moves his fingers down, feeling my stomach, tapping at it here and there. I shake my head again at his inquiring look and he moves down to my lower abdomen.

My thighs squeeze together and I try to keep my breathing level as he goes lower.

Do I really want him to do something now?

Yes. Right now!

Whatever was starting with Vic was interrupted and

although I'm hurting and I think I might be in shock or something, I need this like I need to breathe. I've never felt such desire for anything before, never had such a demand flowing through my body. It's like sexual overdrive. How can I want that when my body is killing me from the accident?

Oh.

He's using his supey power on me. Why would he do that to me *now*?

I wince a little and pretend it's from his fingers pushing gently into my stomach, trying to swallow the emotion that's rising up like a spring tide to drown me. Is it right to feel betrayed right now?

If it is, I know that it's stupid to feel this way. I'm an on-call girl now. It makes sense that they'd use me whenever they need to, regardless of whether I'm physically sound. But the feeling doesn't go away even when I apply that logic.

Tears come to my eyes and I blink them away. A whimper pushes its way past my lips though and Theo stops what he's doing like he cares.

'What is it? Did I hurt you?'

Yes, I want to say, but I don't.

'Just my stomach,' I mutter instead, wishing he'd stop touching me now.

'Okay.'

He sits me up and an intense wave of arousal hits me, making me want to grab him and pull him to me. I swallow hard and watch him do the same.

'You're injured,' he whispers like he's trying to convince himself of something. 'Not in your right mind.'

Then why are you using your voodoo on me?

He takes a step back as my fingers grip his biceps hard. If he doesn't do something first, I'm going to start begging him to fuck me.

He pulls away with a curse and snatches a vial off the table, filling a syringe with the quick and precise movements of a doctor who knows what he's doing.

'What's that?'

'It's something we supes use. It's safe for your concussion and it'll help with the pain,' he sticks my arm with it before I can react, 'and it'll put you out for a little while.'

What?

Panic courses through me.

'But—'

'Don't worry. It'll make you feel better.'

My eyes are already starting to close and I feel him ease me carefully to the exam table so I don't fall as my limbs go limp.

'I'm sorry, Jane.'

2

KORBAN

Paris and I pick up some takeout and are on our way home, walking down the street.

I glance at him. My burning fury is smoldering now, but it's not cooling at all. I'm going to get my revenge on that bitch if it's the last thing I fucking do and I'm in for the long game just like she is. It's obvious she's been playing us from the start. Theo's thinking with his dick. He can't see her for what she is, and he's made it clear he won't let me do what needs to be done. But as soon as Vic's back, I know *he* will.

I grab some beers from the corner store, then we head back to the house. In my periphery, I notice Paris giving me a look I know all too well.

'Are you okay?' he asks.

'No, I'm not okay,' I hiss. 'This is bullshit. I want to know who she's working for. Is another clan moving in on our turf? Or is it the shifters, the fae, the covens, the Order? It's only been a few hours and it's already driving me crazy! We have ears everywhere. Why didn't we know this attack was coming?'

I run my hands through my matted hair and I know I could use a shower but first I'm going to go downstairs and beat the shit out of the pads until I can barely move.

'Whoever is stealing our shipments are probably the same ones who tried to strike us down. We need to root them out. We need to hit them hard and fast, make them pay. An example needs to be set and we should start with Jane. We can use her to help us find them,' I say, letting Paris know that I'll call for his support if it comes to a vote later.

But Paris' look is blank. 'Jane?'

I scoff. 'Yeah. C'mon. Not you too! There's no way she's not in on this.'

My phone buzzes in my pocket and I see it's Vic. Relief courses through me. We have our moments, but Vic is part of my family and I was worried about him even though they said he was going to be fine.

'You're awake.'

'Yeah, came to a little bit ago.'

'They letting you out soon?'

'Should be. My ribs are already knitting back together and my breathing is better.'

'Does he know what happened?' Paris asks me.

I open my mouth to ask Paris' question, but Vic must have heard him because he answers it.

'Last I remember, the wheels were skidding and we were rolling. That's it. Afterwards, Jane was in the ambulance with me. They won't tell me anything here. Is she with you? Is she okay?'

'She's fine.' I barely keep a snarl contained. 'She's with us at the house.'

'Good.'

Vic sounds so fucking thankful. How does this girl have

an entire clan of incubi wrapped around her finger? I'm definitely going to need Paris on my side, that's for sure.

'As soon as they discharge me and Sie, we'll head to the townhouse. Make sure the meetings are set up.'

I frown. I would have thought he'd have something to say about the Clubhouse burning to the fucking ground, and my stomach sinks. He doesn't know yet.

'Have you spoken to Sie at all?' I ask carefully.

But he must hear something in my tone because there's a pregnant pause. 'No.'

I take a breath. Best get it over with.

'After you left the Clubhouse, there was an explosion, a fire.'

There's silence on the other end of the line. I wince and feel Paris' hand on my shoulder, giving me the strength to continue. I slow my pace because we're almost at the house and I don't want Jane overhearing this conversation. She won't have the satisfaction of knowing how much she's hurt the Club and, more specifically, Vic. That house was his mother's. There were reminders of her all over it.

'How bad?'

'Look, we can talk about that—'

'Tell me how bad!'

I grit my teeth, almost able to feel his power through the phone even though that's impossible.

'The house is gone, Alex.'

'The on-call girls okay?' His voice sounds strained.

Of course that would be his next question. Some might think his concern for them was just because they were our source of food, but I know Vic better than that. He cared about them – cares about humans more than he pretends.

'We couldn't get to them.'

'Fuck,' Vic breathes on the other end of the phone. 'Is there anything left at all?'

'I don't know,' I say truthfully. 'We left as soon as we got the calls about you and Sie. The house was still smoking.'

'Jane.' He hisses her name.

'Looks that way,' I say.

Maybe this won't come to a vote after all if Vic is already sure about her involvement. But why is he? My eyes narrow. He's been keeping secrets from us.

'Don't do anything,' he says. 'Let her think she got away with it. She's going to pay for this. Don't tell the others anything yet either. We'll discuss it later.'

The call ends just as we arrive at the house, and I put my phone away as I open the door. Paris goes straight to the kitchen to plate up dinner and I take the stairs, heading for the clinic. It's empty.

Letting out a harsh breath, I go down the hall to Theo's room and, as I suspected, I find them. They're in the bed, Jane curled up asleep next to Theo.

'What the fuck?' I practically snarl, though, for some reason I keep my voice low as if I don't want to wake her and that pisses me off even more.

He rolls his eyes. 'Back off. It's been a long fucking day for all of us. We'll talk about it when Vic gets back.'

'Fine,' I mutter, turning to go.

'Wait.'

I look back as Theo extricates himself from the bed slowly, leaving her in the middle of it on her front.

'When will you next need to feed?' he asks.

My jaw clenches as hunger rises up in me at the mere mention of it.

'Soon.'

'It's going to have to be her,' he says, looking back at her sleeping form. 'We don't have any contingencies in place. But give her at least until tomorrow. That bump on the head today did a number on her.'

Fuck. I need to go down to the gym and hit something.

'Fine,' I grate out again.

'I know you, Kor. Can you be trusted not to kill her when you do get hungry enough?'

'Fuck you, Theo,' I sneer, but my eyes gravitate towards her. '... Paris will be there.'

I take one last look at Jane before I turn around and leave.

I go back downstairs, intending to go straight to the basement gym off the garage, but I catch sight of Paris sitting alone on the livingroom couch and sigh. It *has* been a hard day for all of us. I can always pummel something later.

I sit with Paris and we eat in silence, watching TV and relaxing as much as we can right now. I crack open a beer and put my arm around Paris' shoulders. He leans against me, the warmth of his body comforting me.

'I'm glad you're okay,' he says quietly and I squeeze his thigh, giving him a kiss on his temple.

We're finished eating our dinner and it's getting late. Theo made an appearance a little while ago, grabbed a plate, and then headed back upstairs saying he was beat and going to sleep in Paris' room, which means Paris is with me tonight.

I capture his gaze. 'I'm hungry.'

He nods. 'Me too. What do you want to do?'

I snort. Like there's even a choice. As much as I don't want to get in bed with the enemy ...

'We've only got one on-call girl. Get her.'

Jane

'JANE,' someone whispers and I snuggle deeper into the pillow with a groan.

'Leave me alone,' I mutter.

'Jane.'

This time it's more insistent. Someone shakes my shoulder gently.

I open my eyes, groggily peering up into Paris' face.

'What is it?' I ask, turning over onto my back and blinking up at the ceiling. 'Where am I?'

'The townhouse in Metro. Remember?'

'Yeah.' I sit up. 'Whose room is this?'

'Theo's. Are you feeling better?'

'I think so,' I say, rubbing my eyes and I'm not lying, but it's relative to how much pain I was in earlier. I'm exhausted and feel like I got run over by a truck.

Paris glances towards the door and then back at me. He looks a little sheepish. 'Uh, so the thing is, Jane ...'

'Yeah?' I yawn.

'We ... Kor and I ... we're hungry.'

I frown in confusion. 'Weren't you guys going to get take-out?' I ask out loud, wondering if I dreamed that happening. My mind is clearing, but it feels like it's playing catch up.

'No, Jane. I mean, yeah, we did, but ... You don't understand. You need to wake up. We're hungry. We need to feed.'

My eyes snap open as I realize what he's talking about. '*Oh!*'

'Come on.'

Nervous, I stand on legs that already feel like Jell-o.

'But I—'

He hushes me. I look down and realize I'm back in my

clothes. Wasn't I in that weird hospital gown before? Being in Theo's clinic comes back to me in full and I gasp.

'Theo drugged me!'

Paris shrugs. 'He's a doctor,' he says as if that explains it.

He urges me down the corridor to a closed door and I pull back a little, getting more scared with every step. Feeling my resistance, he turns around.

'I'm sorry, Jane, but you signed up for this,' he reminds me.

Yeah. For Shar. I can do this. I have to.

I let out a breath. 'I know ... but both of you? At the same time?' I ask, my voice coming out a little shaky.

His lips form into a thin line. 'It's for the best, sweetheart. Trust me.'

He opens the door and pulls me into the room quickly, so there's no more opportunity for me to voice dissent.

The lighting is dim, but I can just make out a hulking shadow on the bed, facing me.

'Tell her to get rid of the clothes,' Kor says and I shudder.

His voice. He sounds like he doesn't want this at all. Maybe I should ... I turn towards the door just in time to see Paris turn a key with an ominous click. My eyes flit to his, and I turn back around to the bed, stepping closer. My hands cross over me to pull off my sweater but then they stop and it feels like I can't make them move.

'Do you want me to do it?' Paris asks and I shake my head, my arms pulling jerkily at the fabric.

I want to do it myself, keep some semblance of control, but I'm equal parts frozen and shaking like a leaf. After watching me struggle for a few moments, Paris takes over. He strips me of my outer clothes methodically. Ruthlessly.

And then I'm standing in just my underwear in front of two demons.

'Bring her closer.'

I take an instinctive step backward, feeling like I'm about to be devoured, but Paris takes me by the scruff of the neck, gently but firmly pushing me toward Korban until I'm standing at the end of his bed.

I get a good look at the other incubus who hasn't moved at all since we came in. He's lounging over the covers in some faded jeans and an unbuttoned shirt, looking like a model on a photoshoot. I feel like a light breeze might come from nowhere to ruffle his hair any second for the prime shot.

I almost roll my eyes, but I'm much too nervous for that. Instead, they dart around, but inevitably end their journey back on the man in front of me. His chest is on display, giving me a good look at the many tattoos that decorate his muscled torso, and I swallow hard, my body feeling like it did with Theo in his examination room.

I'm terrified, but I want this, *them*. It's undeniable. This must be the lull I've heard about. So this should get easier, right?

My breath hitches and I press my thighs together as Paris' lips graze my shoulder and I feel rather than hear the sound of approval that comes past his lips. His hands skate down my arms and lift them up, putting my hands on top of my head.

'You have to do everything I say just the way I say it,' he mutters. 'Promise.'

'I promise,' I whisper, my voice weak and monotone.

My emotions are what are too much to handle right now and I need them to check-out. I need to feel nothing to continue.

'You don't touch Korban.'

When I don't say anything, his hand comes to my chin and jerks my ear towards his mouth. 'Tell me you understand.'

'No touching. I understand,' I gasp.

'Leave your hands where they are until I say,' he orders.

I nod jerkily.

In front of Korban, Paris' fingers run down my body to my thighs and back up again. They graze over my tummy and up to my chest. My bra goes slack and he eases my arms off my head for a moment, the straps sliding down. The bra drops to the floor and he places my hands back on my head.

My bra gone, Paris' hands cover my breasts, weighing them in his hands. Calloused palms worry my nipples, making them pucker and my abdomen clench.

I let out the breath I've been holding as he kicks my legs apart just a little, his hand going between them over my underwear.

'Take them off her,' Korban says low.

I look away from him as Paris tugs them down over my hips and they fall to the carpeted floor next to my other clothes. I shiver under Korban's gaze even though the room is warm.

'This is different, huh?'

I twist my neck to look back at Paris, and it takes me a second to realize he isn't speaking to me, but to Kor, who nods.

I wonder what he means, but then I'm hit with a surge of desire so strong that I feel like my knees are going to give out and all coherent thoughts are swept out of my mind. It's all I can do to keep still, to keep quiet.

Paris' hands leave me.

'Stand next to the bed and let him touch you but, remember, your hands don't move.'

I nod slowly, still scared, but the other feeling is rapidly making the fear sink into the background and I'm actually thankful that they're using their power to make me want it. I walk slowly around the bed to where Korban is.

He stares at me, his eyes flicking up and down my body, but he doesn't move. Is this some kind of test? I squirm under his intense perusal but he just watches, doing nothing else. Perhaps he doesn't want this. Perhaps he doesn't want *me*.

I turn my head to look behind me at Paris in askance, but as I do Korban's hand comes out fast, grabbing between my legs roughly. I rise onto my tippy toes and let out a cry as I jump back, my arms coming out in front of me involuntarily.

Paris is there in an instant, pulling my hands back to the crown of my head.

'Remember what I said,' he growls harshly, pushing me back towards Korban.

This time, when Korban touches me, he's gentler, his fingers part me as he feels me, but the damage is done. That need that was taking hold of me is long gone and now I'm just scared they're going to hurt me for shits and gigs.

Tears come to my eyes and I wish they'd either turn up the supey charm or get this done already.

His eyes dart up to mine and he looks … puzzled maybe, like something isn't quite right. I mean, it's not, but I wouldn't have expected him to notice that.

He looks to Paris as if he needs some direction though he was clearly in charge a minute ago.

'Relax, princess,' Paris says. 'You're going to like the things we do.'

I try to do as Paris says, looking away from them and closing my eyes, pretending that I've done this a thousand times before, that I'm experienced and not totally freaking out.

Kor slides a finger inside me and I stifle a shocked sound.

'She's wet,' he says.

I feel Paris behind me, his hands skating over my body before I feel his finger enter my pussy as well. He takes it out, but almost immediately, he begins working it into my ass. I buck slightly, making a noise as it eases into me and I'm impaled on both of their hands.

I'm breathing fast and my heart is thudding in my chest. It's too much! I screw my eyes closed even tighter and my body tenses.

'Is she coming already?' Korban asks, sounding confused.

Paris is quiet for a second or two.

'No,' he says finally. 'She's scared.'

'They aren't usually scared anymore by now. This isn't going to work.'

'She's not usual. I have an idea.'

Paris doesn't remove his finger but his hand snakes around me and he picks something up off the bedside table.

A moment later, music sounds through the room. Loud. Thumping. It's a lot like the club music from when we danced before.

I make myself focus on it because I need to get through this, and my muscles begin to unlock.

He throws the remote down on the bed and his hand comes around my waist again, holding me as he impales his finger deeper into me.

The need is coming back now, making me want more

again and I open my eyes to stare at Korban who's now standing in front of me, the shirt gaping down to his abdomen.

Not really knowing what I'm doing, I lick my lips as I take him in and his eyes shoot to my mouth. It makes him want more too because his finger pushes into me hard, almost raising me up off the floor. I whimper as his other hand comes to my throat and I wonder if he's going to choke the life out of me. I don't say anything and I keep my hands where Paris told me to leave them.

Kor presses the sides of my throat. Not too hard. I can still breathe. But it makes me feel a little lightheaded before he eases his grip.

He crowds his body closer to mine. 'You're going to be a good girl for us, aren't you, Jane?'

His words make me moan aloud and I find myself nodding, but I have no idea what being a good girl for them is going to entail. Will they tell me the rules or will they assume I know them?

But before I can start getting anxious about that too, he locks eyes with Paris again and I'm walked closer to the bed. They use their fingers to move me where they want me.

What am I doing here? Why did I think I could do this?

My eyes dart away from the scene again, and I'm breathing hard. I wasn't made for this. I inhale deeply, my head swimming.

'Hey,' Paris says low next to my ear, 'what's wrong?'

'I—I just...' I don't know the words to say. I can't explain. 'I can't... Please just do your thing like you do ... like you do with the others,' I beg like a little bitch, but I can't help it. I don't even care what I sound like right now.

I glance back at Korban, who's standing in front of me and try to just breathe. I feel like I'm going to hyperventilate. He's staring at Paris. They're speaking to each other with their expressions, but I don't know what they're saying.

'Close your eyes,' Paris says.

I do what he says on a shaky breath, wondering if this is how they do it, if I'm going to get that euphoria soon that will leave me staring out into space like I saw Monique that first day.

I didn't want that before, but I'd give anything for it right about now.

'Listen to the beat of the music. No one's going to hurt you. We're going to make you feel very, very good, princess. I promise. Okay?'

I'm skeptical because there's no way I'm getting even close to coming when I'm feeling like this, but I give a small nod and try to relax, distancing myself further from what's happening. They aren't going to hurt me. Paris promised and he might be a lot of things. *Strike that.* He definitely *is* a lot of things including an arrogant douchebag, but he hasn't lied to me, I tell myself.

The truth is I have to believe him or I'm going to freak the fuck out even more and no one wants that.

Just get it done.

I open my eyes to find Korban sitting on the bed. He looks at me for a long second before he lays back. His finger disappears from my body and I realize he was moving it inside me gently this whole time. A whimper leaves my lips. I want it back. I'm out of my depth, but my body does want what happens next. I just have to listen to it instead of my brain.

I give in to the music, listening to the rhythmic bass as I'm propelled forward without warning. I teeter and collapse, straddling Korban in my attempts not to touch him anywhere. But my hands automatically go out to break my fall and land on his hard chest.

Oh, shit! I touched him! Fuckity, fuckity, fuckity fuck!

My eyes widen as he tenses all over. He stares up at me, and I don't know what I'm seeing on his face at all. Is he angry? I can't tell.

I fumble around like an idiot, trying to pick myself up while moving my hands off him at the same time as quickly as I can, but he pulls me back down with a sound of impatience and puts my hands back on his pecks. Then he raises my hips and lines me up with his cock, not breaking eye contact with me once. But instead of it unnerving me like it would with anyone else outside this fucked up little circle of supes, I find it oddly comforting.

My mouth opens, my breath stuttering as he lowers me down, filling me. I let out a high-pitched, feminine noise. The defined muscles of his abs undulate as he picks me up at the same time as he pulls out and then thrusts back in hard. I let out a scream at a pitch I didn't know my vocal cords could even produce, my eyes rolling into the back of my head at the sensation of his body inside mine. Paris' fingers move in and out of my ass in time with Korban's determined thrusts.

I didn't know it could feel like this!

Paris' other hand comes around to my breast and kneads it, capturing the nipple between his fingers and pinching. I let out a scream as I come without warning, tears leaking from my eyes. My arms give out and I fall onto Korban's chest, my cheek laying against his thudding heart. He hasn't stopped pounding into me and his pace is getting harder and faster. It's almost painful, but it's a good kind of pain. I want it. I need it. I come again hard, my body shaking and still they don't stop.

Paris adds another finger, stretching my ass and hitting a sweet spot that makes me scream as the waves of pleasure crash and don't stop this time. I don't know how long my body is taut, suspended in pleasure, but when it finally ends, my entire body goes limp, sated in ways that I could never ever have imagined.

I'm realize I'm lying on Korban's chest, half-comatose and basking in the aftershocks still humming through me. I'm dimly aware that I didn't follow the rules. I feel Korban pull out followed by a rush of liquid. I'm lifted up and see Korban in my hazy vision, leaning over me as he lays me back. I'm breathing hard. The pounding of the music dissipates as one of them turns it down. Paris is in front of me and, at first, I think he's going to fuck me now too. I don't think I want him to. I can't take anymore tonight. But I can't even utter a sound right now let alone talk straight.

But all he does is open my legs and spread me, looking down at me. He shifts to stare at Korban.

'You came in her.' He shakes his head. 'But you've never …I don't get it.'

He says more words, but I don't listen. My body is pleasantly exhausted and I'm feeling very relaxed all of a sudden. I close my eyes and drift into sleep, curling up in Korban's bed where it's warm.

3

VIC

I check my watch again as I wait for Sie. I'm trying not to pace. It feels like I do that all the time these days. I rub my thigh over my pantleg. It burns a little from where the glass gouged it in the crash, but it's practically healed, and my chest and ribs are just giving a twinge now and then.

The nurses are ignoring me as I rap my fingers on the counter of the nurse's station. I've been in this hospital for over twenty-four hours now and I'm itching to leave. I need to get back to the Iron I's, figure out what the fuck is going on, and deal with a certain female human who duped us.

I underestimated Jane and that's on me. Carrie and the others are dead. That's my fault too. I should have protected them better. But really I'd lay their deaths squarely at Jane's door. She was the one who blew up the house and as soon as I get out of here, I'm going to wring her duplicitous little neck.

Sie comes walking out and I greet him with a hug.

'All done?' I ask.

He nods, looking surprised. 'Everything's fine. All healed up,' he says.

I stare into his eyes, searching for a lie, but for the first time in a long time I see my friend, my brother, looking back at me.

Yesterday he was on the brink of madness. Today he's bright and clear as a sunny, summer's day.

Fuck.

That means that I was right. There's something about Jane that has brought Sie back from a place that few incubi return from.

'You feel better.' It's not a question.

He nods. 'I'll be even better once we're out of here.'

I nod because he hates this place. Hospitals put him on edge and I know why.

'That's not what I meant,' I say.

'I know.' He looks uncomfortable. 'But I do feel better. I hadn't realized how far gone I was. I want you to know that. I'm sure the changes in me must have been ... difficult to keep under wraps.'

'Difficult, but not impossible,' I say with a grin. 'There might be a few weird rumors about you for a while though. I had to get pretty creative to explain away some of your actions.'

'Look. Alex,' Sie gives his head a shake as he combs his fingers through his shock of dark hair. 'This is going to sound crazy, but I think it was—'

'Jane.'

'Yeah,' he says, brow furrowing. 'How did you know?'

I let out a breath. 'I just had a feeling.'

'I want to thank you for contracting her despite what I said. You probably saved my life.'

I give him a nod, but inwardly, I'm worrying. I was

hoping that Sie's newfound mental stability after feeding from Jane was just a coincidence. As glad as I am that I'm not going to have to put a bullet in my best friend's brain, it complicates things because it means I can't just get rid of her. She's a snake in the grass who tried to end us, but Sie needs her and, not to be callous in the wake of the other on-call girls' deaths, but Jane is also now the only girl any of us are legally allowed to feed from until we can find and vet some new ones, which will take months.

It looks like we're going to have to keep her around a little while longer. All we can do is make sure she can't screw us again. Her being officially contracted to the Club makes things a bit easier. It means that even though her plan was a failure, she won't be able to give us the slip. She doesn't know it but signing our contract old-school with her blood means there's nowhere she can hide from us now, even if whoever she's working for does find a way to extract her. The old ways really are the best.

She's also got far fewer rights than a free human and that gets me to thinking. Maybe we can get what we need out of her while still getting our revenge on her at the same time.

I mull over that as I leave the hospital with Sie. I haven't bothered to let the others know we're coming, so there's no car waiting for us outside. We take a cab because it's pouring with rain and we spend most of the short ride in silence, each of us thinking about our own shit. I idly wonder how many of us have working bikes after last night. Can we even be considered a motorcycle club right now? Theo and Kor's were saved, but I'm guessing mine was in the Clubhouse garage when it burned, and Paris and Sie's are fucked from the attack.

'Your bike was totaled, right?' I ask.

He nods. 'And most of my others were in the garage at the Clubhouse.'

I wince. That probably hit him hard. The man loves his bikes more than anything else besides the Club and he had some nice classics in his collection.

'Are you going to start again?'

Sie shrugs. 'Don't know yet. I think I worked on them a lot to keep my mind focused. Maybe I don't need that anymore.'

We pull up to the house. I pay the cab fare and we go up the steps. The door isn't locked because nobody fucks with us in this city. Well, they didn't used to. I make a mental note to talk to Paris about beefing up security here as we go inside and I heave a sigh as soon as I'm over the threshold. It's nice to be in my own space again. At least I'll be able to relax in relative comfort later. Right now though, I need to talk to the others.

There's a yell from the kitchen and I roll my eyes as I hear Theo shouting. Some things never change even when we're at our lowest. A pang hits me square in the chest as I think about all that's different since yesterday. The on-call girls being gone is bad enough, but what state is the Clubhouse likely to be in? I already made the calls for my people to find out what can be salvaged and start the repairs. I should go there myself, but, to be honest, I can't stomach it. I know it's just a house, but my first memories were in that place, of a mother who loved me, of countless summer afternoons spent with her during the vacations from the boarding school my father insisted I attend, of her final days when she would let me read to her while she rested. Anger flows through me at what Jane has done and I push it down. She'll get what's coming to her. She's going to wish she'd never set foot in our bar, never dangled that pretty orc stone in front of us.

That's a point. We're going to need to sell that as soon as we can if we want to rebuild the Clubhouse and keep those fae assholes from darkening our doorstep in the next few days demanding their money.

Sie stays in my shadow as I move down the hall to the back of the house into my favorite room. It's cozy in here, but large enough to comfortably accommodate all five of us and almost every wall is lined with good books from floor to ceiling. We find Korban and Paris standing side by side in their usual united front. Theo's here too and he looks mad as hell. It takes a lot to piss Theo off like this so even I'm wondering what Paris and Kor did.

'I said to you to give her time. I gave her something to keep her out because she wasn't in her right mind, but I turn my back and you're both on her inside a minute!'

Korban snorts and Paris throws his hands up in the air. 'Who else are we going to feed from? The other girls are smoking corpses!'

I hear a gasp and see Jane standing in the doorway to the kitchen. She looks good, considering all that's happened. Her bruises have already faded substantially and she's moving around pretty well. I survey her. She doesn't seem overly hurt from the crash, and something in me uncoils. Was I that worried about her?

Yes, I was.

And that's a problem. I'll need to get rid of these protective feelings when it comes to her or doing what I have to do for this club is going to be very difficult.

'Carrie and the others are dead?' she asks, her brow furrowing as her hand covers her open mouth.

Kor shakes his head and scoffs.

'Yeah,' he says, 'your human pals were killed in the fire.'

'What fire?'

Damned if she isn't a good actress. Either she really doesn't know anything about this or she's taken a ton of acting classes to prepare for this little mission.

'*What fire?*' Korban mocks, growling low. 'The fire that put my—'

I give him a look and he shuts his mouth. I don't want her to realize that we suspect her of anything yet.

'There was a fire at the house,' I say instead.

'We tried to get them out,' Theo says.

'Sure,' she says faintly, her face now blank.

'Hey,' Theo moves towards her and takes her shoulders. 'I'm sorry. I promise you, Kor and I both went in there and I tried to get them out, but ...'

'They were trapped,' she mutters.

'How do you know that?' I ask her, wondering if she'll give herself away so soon.

'No fire exits in the basement,' she mutters without looking at me.

I see Theo wince.

She turns away and leaves the room without a word. Theo starts to follow her, but I call him back.

'We need to talk.'

Theo's shoulders sag. 'I see.'

He thinks he knows what's coming, that I'm going to tell Kor to take her out in the woods and put her in a shallow grave, but that couldn't be further from the truth.

He closes the door and Paris pulls out his phone, doing his thing to make sure no one can listen in.

'She didn't seem like she had any idea what happened,' Theo mutters.

'It was definitely her,' Korban rasps. 'I say we get rid of the bitch now.'

'Easy for you to say,' Paris mutters, crossing his arms. 'You're feeling full. What about the rest of us?'

Korban shrugs. 'You were there. You could have fed properly from her if you'd wanted instead of just snacking.'

'It would have been too much for her without a lull.' Paris glances at Theo. 'It *was* too much for her.'

Theo gestures at the door Jane disappeared through. 'I fucking told you to wait—'

My eyes narrow. 'Quiet. All of you.'

The room goes silent as I sit down heavily.

'We can't get rid of her,' I say to Korban who opens his mouth to argue, 'because, one, she's the only on-call girl we have. Two, she somehow made Sie come back to himself when we all know he was on borrowed time, and, three,' I take a breath. I should have told them this as soon as I saw that photo of them together. 'She's Foley's daughter.'

Theo, who's staring at Sie with a smile on his face as he realizes our brother isn't on the edge of insanity anymore, twists towards me, his expression falling.

'Foley? As in Don Foley?'

'The lieutenant the Order?' Sie asks, his jaw working.

I nod, keeping my eye on him. If anyone has cause to hate Foley the most, it's Sie.

'Guess we know who she's working for,' Korban mutters. 'Shit!'

'How *do* we know this?' Theo asks me.

I keep my grimace off my face. 'Because there was a picture of them together in the file.'

'I didn't see one.'

'I destroyed it.'

Korban begins to pace the room. 'You knew about her?'

'Not until I saw the photo. I suspected, but Sie was interested in her and I thought she might be able to help him. His mental health was … *is* more important. Also, I thought, as I still do,' I glance at Sie to gauge his reaction, 'that we can use her.'

'She almost killed all of us!' Paris explodes.

'Keep your damned voice down,' Kor snaps. 'Humans' senses are weak, but they still have fucking ears.'

I stand so I'm level with Paris. 'I set a trap to catch her in the act of spying for them, but she moved before I could slam it shut.'

I look away, the submissive move so uncharacteristic of me that I see surprise on more than one of my brothers' faces.

'I underestimated her and the Order.' My lip curls in anger. 'It won't be happening again.'

I glance at Sie again. He's not saying a word, not giving away his thoughts.

'If we can't get rid of her, how are we going to make her and the Order pay?' Korban asks.

'First things first. As I said, there's a trap that's yet to be sprung.' I say, my eyes training on Paris. 'Have you gone through the Clubhouse feeds from before the explosion yet?'

'I've started working my way through them, but it's slow going. There's a problem with the servers.'

'Focus on my study from the past couple of days. See if she went in there alone at any point during the last forty-eight hours before the fire. I left some information for her to feed to whoever she's working for. If she found the papers, we'll soon know if her friends are the Order or someone else.'

I turn back to Kor. 'As to your question, she's the Club's now. How do you suggest she be punished for her crimes?'

Korban snorts. 'Not by living in the lap of luxury with us, getting everything she wants handed to her on a platter, *gifts* from the Club she tried to destroy.'

I pretend not to notice his look of recrimination at Paris that could be construed as jealousy as I survey them all.

My brothers. *My clan.*

'She's shown us how shrewd and devious she is since the day she hired us with that orc stone,' I say. 'We need her for now, but we aren't going to give her the opportunity to hurt this club again. We won't be letting her out of our sights. Wherever we go, she comes with us. That means she'll need to look like she belongs with us. Paris, get her whatever clothes she needs. She isn't going to be allowed to show us up any more than she already has.'

'What kind of stuff?' Paris asks.

'That's your department,' I say with an impatient huff.

'I mean, do you want me to get her the kind of stuff I did before? Because she hated everything enough to throw it all out in the hallway ...'

That gives me pause. I should say yes, start her torment with the very clothes we make her wear. If those articles Theo sent me were anything to go by, her senses are delicate. She'll hate every miserable second she's dressed. But I decide against it.

'No. Take her with you and buy her clothes she can wear out with us that she's also comfortable in. She needs to appear calm and collected while she's around other supes, not fidgety and losing her shit like she was at *The Circle*.'

'Are you seriously suggesting she just lives here in the house with us, wandering around freely?' Korban growls low.

'No.' My lips curve into a smile. 'But we are demons, my friend. I think we're qualified to make sure this place is a hell fit for a human like her.' I close my fingers around the neck of the hefty, crystal decanter that sits on the table and take out the glass stopper. 'I suggest we feed from her as needed, since we have no other girls right now, but,' I pour myself a healthy dose of scotch and sit back in the chair. 'As the lull doesn't seem to work on her, we all need to make sure she wants it *the human way*. No forcing her. We're fucking incubi,' I mutter. 'If we can't seduce a human female without our power then we have no business being the most dominant clan in the region.'

I ignore Kor's snort. He knows I don't mean him, but I do glance at Paris and raise a mocking brow. 'If you need some pointers, ask one of us.'

Sie and Theo chuckle, and even Korban smiles as Paris scowls. 'She liked me playing with her well enough last night,' he huffs.

Theo makes a sound of anger. 'You said yourself it was too much for her and, as I tried to tell you last night, she wasn't in her right mind after she hit her head. Hell, she was trying to seduce *me* while I was examining her. That's not like her at all. As far as I'm concerned you both took advantage.'

Korban rolls his eyes. 'She's an on-call girl. We didn't take advantage. We made her do her job.'

'Made her?' Theo's voice is low, threatening.

'You know what I mean.' Korban rolls his eyes. 'Not like that. She was happy enough to have a rough, incubus cock making her scream for more.'

Theo takes a step towards Korban, a gallant knight defending his Lady's honor. He's further gone than I thought.

'You sonofa—'

Korban raises himself up to full height, his glamor fading and showing us the beast beneath. Thick, black horns rise from his skull and his skin turns an iridescent red. His forked tail swishes, almost taking out the table behind him. He grins, showing sharp fangs and his now solid black eyes glitter.

'What are you going to do, white knight, go head-to-head with me? Think I won't beat the shit out of you just because we're friends?'

'Shut the fuck up. Both of you,' I growl.

They quiet again as I down my whiskey. 'I suggest you stop goading each other. Look around. We have more important problems.'

Korban nods, looking sheepish as his demon side recedes, and Theo mumbles an apology.

I give Theo a hard look. 'You need to rid yourself of these feelings you have for her.'

Advice I need to take myself.

'Any *feelings* I have are within the confines of a doctor and patient relationship,' Theo grinds out and then glowers at the derisive noise Korban makes at his statement.

'There is no 'relationship' with her,' I clarify. 'Also, don't any of you let her know that we suspect her of anything.' I give Korban a pointed look. 'Trust me. Be nice to her, make her lower her guard.'

I stand. 'Court's adjourned. I'm going to shower the hospital off. Try not to do our enemies' work for them while I'm gone, huh?'

I go upstairs slowly, my leg aching and my breathing a little labored. Clearly, I need a few hours' more recovery time. A part of me is tempted to find Jane and finish what I started in the car, but I need to get myself together first. I can heal up the old-fashioned way. I have reserves.

I see Jane sitting on Theo's bed through his open door as I make my way to my room. She looks lost.

Speak of the devil. Hope you're making the most of the comfort of the main house, girl, because I'm ripping it away very soon.

Her gaze locks on me as I walk past.

'Wait.'

I turn back, wondering why I'm even humoring her.

'Do you think Theo and Korban really tried to save them?' she asks me quietly.

I regard her with a frown. What does she care? Maybe the other humans were collateral damage and she's trying to ease her guilt.

'Yes, I do.'

I tell her the truth though I don't know why. I should give her the rest, all the gory details that I've heard so far. Monique and Julie were found in the bathtub by fire crews putting out the smoldering ashes. They'd closed themselves up in the bathroom, trying to escape the smoke. Their arms were wrapped around each other. Carrie's charred remains were half-way up the stairs as she tried to get out of the inferno. All of them died of asphyxia.

But I don't tell her.

'Theo's a doctor first and foremost,' I say instead. 'He doesn't care whether a person is a supe or a human. He tries to save everybody. He's always been like that. Kor would have helped him because he takes Club duty seriously.'

She gives me a small nod. 'I'm glad you're okay ... and I wanted to thank you.'

'For what?'

She gives me a half smile. 'There's no way I would have survived that car accident if you hadn't made sure I did.'

I give her a once-over and continue on down the hallway, wondering how I'm going to feel when this girl gets what's coming to her because, for the first time, I don't think I want revenge on the person who wronged us. Maybe she is a victim in all this.

I let out a harsh breath and steel myself against these thoughts of mercy. She made fools of us all, played her part in trying to take us down. The MC is what's most important. It doesn't matter what she says, doesn't matter if she seems like she's telling the truth. She's a fucking liar and she's very good at it.

I just have to make sure I'm better.

Jane

I woke up naked in my room this morning, my body feeling pretty energized and better than it has in a long time.

I try not to think about last night. It's like it was a dream, something that wasn't quite real, but the soreness between my legs is proof that it did happen. I'm confused though. I thought after the first time was done, I'd feel better about it because I'd know what was coming. But I don't.

I can't help the feeling that I'm missing something, that there's something big going on around me that I just can't see and I don't like that sensation at all. It's like a tiny alarm bell, but I have no idea where it's coming from, or what it's warning me about.

Maybe it's the changes of the past few days catching up with me and keeping me on high alert. It seems like as soon as I begin to relax, something else happens to throw my head into turmoil. But as I think on it, I know that it isn't just that.

I have a nasty feeling in my gut that the rug is going to be ripped out from under me very soon and everything I think I know is going to be proved wrong. This has happened to me more than once in my life and it's overdue. I hate the stomach-curdling confusion of my world turning on its axis, but I have an inkling that this is probably going to be worse.

It's not going to be like the times when I thought people were my friends at work or at school and they turned out, well, not to be; using the things they found out about me while I trusted them to hurt me or make fun of me later. That stuff was bad enough.

But I already know these demons aren't my friends, don't I? So it's going to be something else. But what? Not knowing is making me feel like I'm going to vom, so I break out my shiny new headphones. I thought they might be lost in the crash, but my bag was by the bed when I woke up and my beautiful, *beautiful* headphones don't seem damaged, thankfully.

I lean back in the bed and close my eyes, putting on something to take my mind off my impending doom. But I keep thinking about their little meeting downstairs in hushed voices. I shouldn't have gone looking for them, but if I hadn't, I don't think they would have told me what happened to Carrie, Monique, and Julie.

Vic practically promised me that Theo and Kor did go in to save them, but is that true? I know as well as the next human how cheap our lives are. There are jokes in the supe community about how fast we breed. We're worth less than nothing to them. I need to make sure that I look after myself here because no one is going to do it for me.

My phone pings, and I see a text from Shar. It's a selfie of her and the kids on the beach and I allow myself a smile. It reminds me again who I signed the contract for. I didn't have a life. I didn't have anything, but Shar did and still does because I'm here and as long as she's okay I guess I don't really matter.

I heave a sigh and get up to go back downstairs. I can't stay in my room all day. I'm not going to be like those girls at the Clubhouse who stayed in their little dungeon until they were summoned only to die down there like forgotten chattel. Fuck that. I'm as real as the Iron Incubi and I'm not going to let them pretend that I'm nothing more than a convenient meal when they get peckish.

In the deserted kitchen, I grab myself a glass of water and check out the pantry. I haven't eaten since yesterday, so I'm pretty much starving to death. I rifle around, looking for nothing in particular until I find two boxes of cereals nestled on the bottom shelf– *THE cereals* – and I can't help my silly grin of anticipation as I pour myself a bowl. Before I start my cereal-eating routine, though, I hide the box ... and the other one too for good measure. Just in case.

'That's for trying to use your supey mojo on me yesterday,' I mutter to myself as I remember being on Theo's exam table.

After grabbing the milk out of the fridge and finding a spoon, I sit down at the small table and frown as I look out of the small window over the rooftops of Metro. I miss staring at sprawling gardens while I eat.

I'm not sure I really like this house, I decide. It's a lot smaller than the mansion and I liked the airy feel of the high, old-fashioned ceilings it had. I'm not complaining. At the end of the day, I was living in a shoebox apartment not long ago. I guess I just got used to all the space of the Clubhouse really quickly.

That's not to say that this house is tiny. It's not at all and I guess the dull, ambient noise from the street outside is kind of relaxing. It reminds me that there's a whole world out there. It's not just me all by myself even if I am effectively a lone sex slave now.

I eat my cereals, basking in their deliciousness, the texture of them just perfect. Even the temperature of the milk is everything I wanted it to be and it puts me in a very good mood.

I'm about to get up when a guy I don't recognize shuffles into the kitchen and I jump. He gives me a once over but doesn't really say anything. He's human. He brings in some shopping bags full of food and puts everything away. He doesn't look at me or talk to me but I feel his gaze on me more than once.

'Hi,' I say, glancing up from my bowl.

'Hi,' he mumbles.

He doesn't look like any of the Iron I's non-supe members who I saw briefly at the Clubhouse while I was there. Maybe he's one of the human prospects.

'Are you one of the Iron I's?' I ask directly.

He stares at me and there's something in his face that makes me draw back.

'No,' he says almost inaudibly. 'I just bring the groceries and stuff.'

He leaves the kitchen without a word and I stare at his back as he goes.

That was weird. Was it weird? Maybe it wasn't weird. I mean I don't socialize much for a reason, after all. I finish up and put my bowl in the dishwasher. As I turn to leave, Paris appears.

'Ready to go?'

I stare at him for a second, not able to help thinking about the last time I saw him and he had his fingers in my ass, but now he's standing here in the kitchen acting like everything's the same as it was yesterday. I shake my head a little. I guess this stuff is normal for sex demons.

'Ready to go where?' I ask.

'Shopping, sweetheart.'

I give him a practiced look to show my displeasure, my spirits plummeting (Yes, I actually rehearse expressions in the mirror sometimes. Don't judge me. They don't come naturally to some people!). I can only imagine what actual, physical shopping is going to be like with Paris. If the clothes he bought me last time are any indication, I'm in for a hell of a morning. Ugh, and I was feeling so good after my cereals too.

I start towards him.

'Sure,' I say, but I haven't been able to muster up the enthusiasm in my tone to even pretend to echo his excitement.

He gives me a grin and puts his arm around my shoulders that makes me tense for a second. 'It'll be fun. I promise.'

I give him a skeptical look. 'It's definitely not going to be fun,' I say. 'Can't we just do it online, or something? Do I really need things?'

'No, we can't do it online. Yes, you need things. This is Metro and you,' he points at me, 'are part of the Iron I's. Last time was my bad. So let's do it right. That means going to some actual stores.'

'Okay, but where are the Goodwill places here? I mean

not for underwear though,' I add hastily because I always make sure my underwear is new and my bras are good quality even if I have to save for them. 'I always get bras and underwear from nice places.'

'You know they're all made in the same factories, right?' he says, walking away from me like he has no idea he just blew my tiny mind.

I follow him down the hall.

'No way! That's bullshit. You can't tell me that a bra that costs three times more than another brand is made in the same building. They feel totally different. Bad bras suck smelly ball sacks. I bought one exactly one time,' I put a finger up to emphasize my point as he looks over his shoulder at me, 'and it made autistic me shrivel up and die inside. I got rid of it the same day. If I could have burned it, I would have.'

'Strong words coming from a woman who came to us wearing one that was basically a rag,' he teases. (I think.)

'That's only because it was an old one,' I huff. 'It was just a little past its prime, that's all.'

'I don't think they have Goodwill here,' he deflects ... *and clearly lies.* 'I'm talking about nice stores for the nice stuff.'

I roll my eyes. If his idea of 'nice stuff' is what he bought before, I am going to be in hell the entire time I'm here.

'This is going to be like that scene in *Pretty Woman*.' I perk up at the thought. 'Are we going to get pizza?'

He laughs and I can't help my smile. 'Yeah, if you want to.'

'Okay, I'm sold.'

I grab my shoes from by the door and we go outside. It's a little chilly and I shiver, wondering if he's going to make me ride on the back of his bike.

I turn back. 'I don't have my earphones.'

He stops me with an arm around my middle, pulling me back against him. 'Do you need them all the time?'

I frown. 'No, but the sound from your ...'

'We aren't taking my hog.'

He turns me around and I see there's a sleek, black town car waiting for us at the curb in front of the house. He opens the door for me and I slide into the matching seat. I'm met with the scent of leather and new-car-smell.

Paris opens the other door and gets in next to me.

'Are you okay?' His eyes look me over.

I frown, not really understanding why he cares after yesterday ... and last night, I guess. I'm a little surprised that he's bothering to ask.

'Yeah,' I say quietly.

Bullshit alert!

But I'm pretty sure now that he and the others can't read my mind, so, hopefully, he won't call me out on it.

'I know that it was kind of sudden with me and Kor, and you weren't a hundred percent. I'm sorry.'

Oh, no. He wants like a heart-to-heart or something. What if he wants to talk about ... feelings?

'It's fine, I'm fine. I understand that's why I'm here.' I say quickly, swinging away and looking out the window, hoping that's the end of our talk because my mind is already going blank at the threat of an intimate conversation that I haven't prepared for.

Thankfully, he doesn't say anything else about it and the rest of the car ride is quiet, but I can feel him watching me, looking for something. What, I have no idea, so I can't even pretend to give it to him.

It's a bright day and I keep having to shield my eyes from glints and glares. We get out at a street with some nondescript shops, names I don't recognize, but everything's clean and nice; upmarket and there's hardly a human in sight.

That's how you know you're in swanky-land in this world. Technically, the law says humans are allowed everywhere, but if I was walking this street by myself, I have no doubt a supe cop would materialize and politely invite me to haul my mortal ass the fuck back to human-town.

'Come on,' Paris says, ushering me into a distinguished looking building.

We take an elevator all the way up to the top and when the doors open, it looks like the ladies' wear section of a very, very nice department store from the movies. One of the price tags for a shirt hanging to my right takes my breath away and I don't look at anything else.

From what I saw of the other girls' clothes at the Clubhouse, I doubt any of them had *anything* bought for them from a store like this. They're dead and I'm shopping. I'm such an asshole.

'Are you sure you want to shop here? *For me?*' I ask.

He gives me a look but doesn't say anything as he ushers me into a private dressing room the size of a penthouse hotel suite.

A store assistant comes out of nowhere. She's petite with short dark hair and a nametag that says 'Hannah'. She greets us politely and, when she looks at me, I don't feel like I'm something living on the bottom of her shoe.

Hannah looks human, but she's not, not fully anyway. She's part something else that I don't think I've come across before. I'm still trying to figure it out as Paris gives her instructions that I'm not listening to, and she bustles away.

Paris turns to me, watching me watching her as she darts around, picking out clothes for me.

'She's only half human,' he mutters and I nod.

'What's the other half though?'

'Pixie.'

I'm surprised.

'I thought they had wings,' I murmur, scanning the smooth lines of the blazer she's wearing.

'They can hide their wings if they need to, but,' he stares at her for a second, 'I don't think she has any. Poor girl.'

'Is that bad?' I ask, fascinated.

'For her I imagine. Pixies love to fly. Being a half-breed is bad enough, but if you only take on your *human* parent's qualities ...' He glances at me ruefully. 'No offence.'

I snort.

'A pixie not having wings ... well it's sort of like if you were born without an arm. You can get along just fine, but everyone can see you're different.'

I look away, wondering if he understands the implications of what he just said *when it comes to me*, but thankfully Hannah, the half-pixie, returns with a pile of clothes in her arms and he doesn't say anything else about it.

He just sits on the couch as I go into the changing room and start trying the many, many items Hannah has brought me. I suppose they're going to dress me up like a doll, but, as the material floats against my skin, I have to concede that this doll's clothes are going to be pretty fucking fine. These are nothing like the awful clothes that appeared in Theo's closet. There are fabrics here I've never worn before, soft and cool next to my skin. If this is what having money means then I really need to up my game because being a waitress is never going to get me nice things like this!

'Are you going to come out?' Paris calls from outside.

Feeling a little self-conscious, I open the door to show Paris the first thing I like. When I step out of the changing room, his eyes move over me and I frown as I try to work out if he's pleased by what I'm wearing.

'Is this okay?'

'Oh, it's more than okay,' he mutters, staring at the bright, halter-neck sundress that clinches in at my waist with a thin belt and flares out at the hips. It's so different than something I'd ever choose for myself, I can't help twirling in front of the mirror.

'It doesn't need to be black?' I ask.

He grins now. 'That's just while we're out at meetings and stuff like that. Other times you can wear what you want.'

'What I want?' I echo.

'Yeah,' he says, 'unless Vic says something different. That goes in the 'yes' pile.'

I nod and go back in to try on the other things, but they either don't fit as nice or I don't like them. Then, I put on a black dress that I like the look of. It's longer than the one they made me wear before. I show him that as well and he nods his head.

'We'll take that too,' he says. 'You can wear it tonight.'

'Tonight?' I ask.

'We have somewhere we need to go.'

I frown at his cryptic response.

'Why am I coming?' I ask. 'None of the others ...' I trail off.

His eyes spear me. 'Maybe we just want to make sure you're safe after everything that happened.'

I nod like I believe him, but somehow I know he's lying, or at least not telling me the whole truth. I go back into the dressing room, changing into my clothes, pretending we're friends just hanging out and he's not a lying demon who wants to feed from me while we have sex.

'So, are you and the other Iron I's full incubi?' I ask as we leave, grasping for a topic of conversation because the silence between us feels awkward.

'It doesn't work like that for us. There are no half-incubi.'

'At all?' I ask, taking in what he's saying and trying to understand. 'So, like, your kind never have kids with humans? Ever?'

He shakes his head. 'No, I mean my mom was human. All of our moms were.'

'What? So then you're all half-human, right?'

'No. Like I said, it doesn't work like that for us. All incubi have human mothers and incubus fathers.'

'Where are your mom and dad?' I ask, a vague scene of him sitting around a table with his family at the holidays coming into my head.

'My mom was hired to have me. Once I was born, she gave me to my father and left with the cash.'

My eyes widen. 'Oh,' I reply, not sure what to say to him in this situation. 'What about your dad?'

'He's dead. Got killed in a fight with a shifter over a bar tab.'

'I'm sorry.' *That's what you're supposed to say, right?*

He shrugs. 'Hardly knew him to be honest. Vic took me in when I was in my late teens. The Iron I's are my real family.'

I nod and turn to look out the window, shielding my eyes from the sun again.

'Here.'

A black, rectangular box falls into my lap. It's a glasses case. I give him a confused look.

'They're for you.'

I open the box and stare at the contents, tears coming to my eyes for some reason.

Sunglasses.

I turn towards him, not sure what to say *again*.

'T-Thank you,' I stutter, putting them on.

He shrugs again and doesn't say anything.

I frown because a 'thank you' isn't enough compared with how his consideration has made me feel.

'You're very good at gift-giving,' I say, giving a small sigh because that's not it either. 'I love them.'

'I noticed you don't like the sun in your eyes,' he says.

'Photosensitive,' I mutter and he nods.

'I know. I read it online.'

I cant my head at him. 'Online?'

He shifts in his seat, looking away. 'Theo sent us websites so we could read up about ... you know ... anyway one of them said that light sensitivity is common.'

I blink. Theo sent them websites on autism?

'Well, thank you ... for reading up on autism,' I say, not sure what to think.

He doesn't say anything else and we pull up to the next store. Things progress much like at the last one, with a polite sales associate making me feel at home and finding me clothes to match my body shape and preferences.

The next one is the same and, by the fifth, I'm retailed-out and the thought of trying on one more thing makes me feel exhausted. When I tell him as much, he has the driver take us to a restaurant. I look out the window as we pull up and can't help a laugh.

'We're actually getting pizza?'

He grins back. 'I promised you pizza. I'm just sorry we couldn't do it the way they did in *Pretty Woman*.'

'That's okay. Pizza's pizza,' I say.

'Well, that's what I thought, so I figured you'd forgive me. You sure you still want?'

I nod my head vigorously, my stomach growling. 'I definitely still want!'

We go inside and it's just a normal sort of place, which makes me relax up a little after the hoity toity stores we've spent the morning in.

'The pizza here is amazing,' he says. 'Once you go *Gino's*, you never go back.'

When we get inside, the hostess approaches. 'Two? Did you book?'

Book? I glance at Paris. Maybe this isn't a normal pizza place after all.

'Nope,' Paris says, not looking the least bit apologetic.

'I'm sorry, sir, but if you haven't got a reservation, it's going to be probably an hours' wait.'

'Oh,' I say, a little disappointed. 'It's okay. We can go somewhere else.'

Paris tuts at me, rolls his eyes, and locks arms with me.

'I'm an Iron I,' he announces. 'We don't *go somewhere else*.'

He gives the hostess an indulgent smile as she splutters at his words.

'I'm sure I can find something for you, sir!' she says, practically falling over herself to grab one of the other staff members and whispering to him frantically while she gestures at tables.

We're led to a corner booth a minute later and Paris just shrugs when I give him a questioning look.

'People know us,' he says, like that explains everything.

'When Shar told me to go to the local MC for help, I just figured you were a motorcycle gang in Welford. I didn't realize you guys were like kings of the World, or something.'

He chuckles. 'Hardly. The Kings of the World operate out of Cali.'

I laugh in spite of myself. 'If you guys are so well known here, why was your Clubhouse out in the middle of nowhere? How do you do all your business stuff?'

'It's not that hard these days,' he says. 'A lot of people work remotely. Our jobs aren't all that much different. Besides, most supes like to be out in nature when possible. Metro has green spaces, but it's not the same as acres of national park.'

I nod like I know what he means, but to be honest, acres of forest doesn't sound even a little bit fun. It must show on my face because he chuckles.

'I'll show you,' he promises and I'm struck by how nice he's being to me.

I don't want to wonder why. What does that say about me? But I do. Does he want something? It can't be to sleep with me. I'm a sure thing.

Wow, I am actually in Pretty Woman right now. Like, minus the previous sex work, a best friend who spends our rent money on drugs, and knowing how to drive a Lotus Esprit.

The waitress comes and I order a pie, deep dish with extra cheese and pepperoni. When it comes, I can hardly contain myself, cutting into it with gusto and moaning at the flavors, the textures.

'This is so good,' I say with my mouth full, trying and failing not to stuff my face.

I look up for a second and I see he's watching me, eating his own pizza slowly.

'What?' I say, suddenly embarrassed.

I'd forgotten myself. I sit up straight and try to go a little slower.

'Sorry,' I mumble. 'I forget social mores when I get excited.'

He takes a massive bite of his pizza.

'Hadn't noticed,' he garbles and it makes me laugh.

There's a look on his face that I haven't seen on him before; something that looks *real*, an actual, fond expression that I mimic because this is quite a nice moment.

It's easy to forget with him, I realize. His laidback charm slips through my defenses and I need to be careful.

We finish up and leave, and he takes me back to the house.

When we get inside, three of the guys are in the living room and Paris sits down close to Kor who puts his arm around him. It's adorable, but I try to ignore it. Last night I think I said something and Korban was very upset with me. I can't for the life of me remember what it was, but ...

'Where's Theo?' I ask, noticing he's the only one not present.

'Probably out at the clinic,' Paris says.

Sie nods.

'He's usually there if he isn't here. It's sorta like his day job,' Paris explains.

'I didn't know he works at a clinic,' I say.

'He hasn't been putting in so many hours since you arrived, so you probably wouldn't have noticed,' Korban grates out.

He has an expression on his face that I can't decipher, but I get this feeling deep inside that he can't stand me. That he thinks I'm a spoiled brat. That he thinks I'm a liar.

Whoa, brush that human chip off your shoulder, Jane.

'Who does he see? Supes?' I ask, ignoring the weird thoughts.

'Anybody who can't pay.'

I can see that about Theo.

'That's really nice,' I say.

Paris gets back up from the couch and comes close. 'I'm nicer,' he says. 'Right, Vivian?'

I grin. 'I don't know if you can class getting a girl a pizza in the same vein as giving medical attention to people in need.'

Paris grins at me. 'To close to call,' he says, giving me a wink.

I give him a wry smile in return. 'Yeah, okay. It was really good deep dish.'

'What time we going out,' Paris asks over his shoulder.

'Ten,' Vic says. 'Make sure she's ready.'

'Where are we going?' I ask, trying to get at least a little info on the evening ahead.

Vic ignores me. 'Did you get what she needs?'

I frown. Why is he acting like I'm not even here? Rude.

Paris nods. 'It'll all be delivered this afternoon.'

'Good.'

Korban stands up and pulls Paris closer to him.

'Go and wait in Theo's room,' he orders me and I'm taken aback by his command and his tone, and something else rolling off him that makes me recoil.

Hatred.

But Paris just chuckles and shrugs off Korban's arm. 'We have some Club stuff to talk about, princess,' he explains lightly.

I'm shepherded from the room before I can say anything and the door closes in my face, locking instantly.

I stare at it for a second, my formerly good mood falling down a few notches.

'You're not a part of them,' the nasty voice in my head says again. It's getting more annoyed every time. *'Why would they*

want someone like you for anything other than sex? Maybe not even then since you suck so royally at it.'

Fuck you, inner voice. Stop kicking me while I'm down. Also, I know all that, so shut up.

But, if I already know, then why do I feel so sad?

I go up to Theo's room as directed. I sit on the bed, putting on my earphones and my favorite playlist. Lying back, I stare at the ceiling.

So they don't want me around. So what? I've never needed anyone before and I sure as shit don't now. If they want to be assholes, fuck 'em.

But that damned voice asks me if I can really do this for three years. The idea of it depresses me. I thought I was good at being by myself. Maybe I was.

But I keep getting glimpses of something more with these demons and it's rubbing my nose in how completely isolated I've been. How solitary my life is. How alone I will always be.

4

PARIS

Spending time with Jane was fun today and the realization makes me feel a little weird. I don't think I've had *fun* spending time with her kind since I was young and my dad didn't care if I played with the human kids from school. But that was before my incubus side kicked in. After that, Vic took me into the Club and I left my old life behind. I expected it because that's how it is when we reach sexual maturity, but I actually don't think I've spent any time with humans since then ... except for the human prospects sometimes, I guess.

I didn't think Jane would like shopping with me. She definitely wasn't looking forward to it and she doesn't seem overly materialistic. I could tell she was worried that I was going to buy things she didn't want too. But once we both understood the parameters, she was getting into it like a kid with carte blanc in a candy store. If I can show her the perks of spending a little extra, then I know I can get her on board. We can also stick to the stuff I know she'll dress in while we move away from her go-tos of jeans and tank tops. That's not to say I don't like the clothes she dresses in. Jane looks hot in everything, but that's not going to work all the time in our world.

I hear the door and Theo answers it. He comes into the room a minute later.

'How much did you fucking buy?'

I shrug. I probably went a little nuts, but that's how I do things.

'I had it all laundered too, since that was part of the problem last time,' I smirk.

I don't tell him that they used my soap to do it. Every single piece of clothing, down to the socks, smells like me. But Theo notices a second later. His nostrils flair and he rolls his eyes.

'If you think that's how you're going to get her to want you, you don't understand human females.'

I shrug again. 'We'll see.'

I don't reiterate that she wanted me well enough yesterday because it turned out he was right about what he said. I don't really understand what was happening last night, but while Korban and I played with her, she flitted between arousal and fear. Yeah, Korban was able to feed, but it wasn't the way it usually is ... maybe that's why Korban was so different with her, letting her touch him, *finishing inside her like that.* But she was into it even without the lull. I know she was and she seemed happy enough after she'd come a few times.

Earlier today though she was colder, distant, bordering on anxious. She thawed a little as the day went on, but I don't really know how to ask her what the problem is. I don't want to think we took advantage of the state Theo says she was in but ... I run a hand through my hair. Maybe we did.

Kor walks through the room and we lock eyes for a

second. He gives me a wink. In contrast to Jane, he's in a great mood today, and I can't help thinking that it's not just because he fed properly for the first time in weeks but maybe it was *who he fed from*.

I've noticed he can't take his eyes off her. It wouldn't usually be all that interesting, but when she touched him last night, he didn't lose it. In fact, he seemed to like it.

I've seen him break humans' fingers in the street after they accidentally brushed against him. But not Jane. I feel something inside of me and I wonder if I'm jealous. It's just a little but it's there and I don't know how to feel about that either.

I glance at Vic. He's sitting in the corner reading, lamenting the loss of his study I imagine. He doesn't really have a space like that here except for a small desk in his bedroom, which he never uses.

'What's going on with the house?' I ask.

He doesn't look up. 'Surveyors have been there all morning. They're getting me a report later today.'

'I'm sure your father's ties will work to your advantage,' I say with a grin. 'He'll

want you back in your estate projecting old money strength as soon as possible.'

Vic snorts. 'Have you found anything on the feeds?'

'I have a program running through it all now. It should be done within the hour.'

I turn a chair towards him and sit down. 'What are we going to do about Jane?'

'What do you mean? We've already discussed this,' he answers. 'She'll do what she's meant to do and she'll come with us wherever we go while we're in Metro. I'm not letting her get the upper hand again. At the end of the day, I'd love to get rid of her...'

He pauses and I wonder if that's true. I've noticed Vic watching her as well and he protected her in the car during the accident. That doesn't sound like a demon who comes from a incubi line that the supe, fae, and human communities all nickname 'Vicious'.

'But,' he continues 'right now we need her.'

I nod. 'I know that, but—'

'Where is her punishment, he means.' Korban booms from the kitchen. 'It's not sending a great message: Try and kill us, humans, and we'll let you live with us rent-free and make sure you have everything your heart desires besides.'

Vic rolls his eyes in Kor's direction, takes off his glasses, and pinches the bridge of his nose. Then he pins me with a stare. 'We're getting to know her weaknesses.'

He said something like that before.

'What does that actually mean?' I ask, hoping Kor doesn't interrupt again because that wasn't what I was trying to ask Vic at all.

He gives me a sly smile. 'Let's just say she won't be sleeping in Theo's cushy room during her stay in Metro like she expects.'

He goes back to his book. 'Make sure she's ready to go out later,' he says absently.

I frown as I get up, not liking what Vic is saying at all. But I realize that I haven't taken the clothes that were delivered earlier up to her. Everything is still in clear plastic in the dining room. Most of it can wait until tomorrow, but I specifically wanted her to wear that black dress from that first store tonight. It's perfect.

I grab the bag from the pile and take it upstairs. She's in Theo's room, laying on the bed, staring up at the ceiling. Music's blaring through the earphones I got her and a pleasant sensation winds through me. She likes my gift.

When she notices me, she sits up looking a little alarmed.

I glance up at the corner where I know the hidden camera is. Does she know it's there? My guess is no.

She takes off the earphones and looks at me expectantly. 'Your clothes are here.'

'Already?'

I put my hands up. 'Iron I's,' I say in way of explanation.

I throw the small bag on the bed next to her. 'That's for tonight. Don't worry about shoes. You can wear your flats. They're already in the closet.'

She takes out the dress slowly. The fabric is soft and I see her hands move over it, feeling it. She looks like she's recalling trying it on in the dressing room and I stifle a smile that quickly turns into a frown as something about what Vic's been saying clicks. This girl is led by her senses. That's what Vic meant by us knowing her weaknesses. What does he have in store for her and why don't I want her to suffer after what she's done?

'Do you want to put it on?' I ask, pushing away all thoughts of what her punishment might be.

'All right.'

She looks almost longingly at it and I know she's remembering how it felt. I don't think she's ever worn anything beautiful in her life and, for a girl who clearly enjoys the finer things deep down, that's almost as sad as the half-pixie with no wings.

She bites her lip as she thinks about it and then stands up.

I'm tempted to tell her I'll turn around and she can do it here in the room. Give Theo a little show to get him back for when he feasted on that pussy over the feed and I couldn't do anything but watch and lust. Last week, I would have done it without hesitation, without remorse, but it feels wrong after the time we spent together today.

I don't say anything and she goes into the bathroom, shutting the door. I chuckle a little because I've already seen her body and she knows it, but I leave her to her faux modesty and I wander around Theo's room.

I see her phone on the side and a message pops up from her friend, who Vic *actually* flew to Hawaii and bought a house for. To be honest, I thought it would be a trick. I figured he'd just pay the woman to say whatever he wanted her to, but nope. Sharlene Kempinsky and her three children are living practically on a beach on the main island. That should have been my first clue that Jane wasn't going to be an ordinary on-call girl.

The bathroom door opens and I step away from the phone as the subject of my thoughts comes out. I don't want her to think I'm snooping.

She comes into view and my eyes move over her. Her fingers are worrying the black fabric, hands moving over it, up and down her own body. I know for a fact that she has no idea how hot she looks right now. The dress itself is sophisticated and quite modest really compared to what we had her wear to *The Circle Club*. It's longer, coming down to her mid-thigh. It looks even better out of the fluorescents of the department store.

'What do you think?' she asks a little shyly.

I swallow hard. 'It looks good. *You* look good.'

She doesn't say anything, just goes to the mirror on the inside of the closet door and gazes at herself.

'It's so comfortable,' she says, sounding surprised.

'A lot of things are when you don't shop at consignment stores.'

She gives me a look at my poking fun at her.

But then while I'm fucking watching her, she pulls the shoulder strap up to her nose and inhales deeply.

'It smells good,' she mutters and I literally go weak in the knees.

She doesn't seem to realize what the scent she's enjoying is, *but that's all me, princess*. Theo and Korban can move over with their little body wash games. I'm in the lead now and I'm not ashamed to say that my dick is just about to explode in my pants.

I turn to leave.

'Thank you,' she says. 'I had fun today.'

'Me too.'

I turn back. 'Look, about last night ...'

She looks away immediately and I see a shadow pass over her face before she locks it down.

'I told you. I know what I'm here for,' she mutters. 'I'm sorry if I wasn't as into it as your on-call girls usually are.' She looks up. 'You can lull me next time. Don't take this the wrong way but I'd actually prefer it if you did. I find this stuff – sex, I guess – difficult.'

I frown. She doesn't know. No one's told her our lull doesn't work on her. *Fuck.* If Vic hasn't, then it's for a reason and I can't be the one to ...

I wish my lull *would* work on her, not so I could get what I want, but so that she doesn't have to feel the way she's feeling.

But I nod like I'll do what she's asking and I see relief in her eyes.

I'm a fucking coward.

I leave her room, not looking back, not really knowing what to do with myself. I don't usually have a problem with keeping my feelings in check. I don't actually catch them. I don't understand where they're coming from, but I don't like this at all.

I go down a couple of levels, using my key card for the restricted access to the garage. She can't get down here. No one besides us five can. There are some old bikes lined up by the wall and, just off to the side are two doors. One leads to the gym and, beside it, the other one goes to the cell.

It's cold down here and pitch black when the lights are off. I go into the second room, turn on the light that hums, and stare through the bars. We don't have anyone locked up down here right now, but I'd bet good money that this is what Vic meant.

Is he going to throw her down here? Keep her in the damp and the dark for us to feed from until her contract is up or until the Club doesn't need her anymore?

I stare at the dirty mattress on the floor, the uneven cement, and the waste bucket. I don't want to see her in there. With all her sensory shit she'd probably lose her fucking mind. I guess that's the point. Will Vic and the others care? I don't know, but the thought of her alone down here, miserable and cold, makes me want to take her away from here to somewhere this club can't hurt her.

But that's impossible.

Sie

SHE LOOKS MORE relaxed with us tonight. She's not fidgeting nearly as much as she usually does when she's nervous. I've been watching her since I got out of the hospital yesterday, afraid I'd hurt her the other night when I lost control of my needs, needs that are a thousand times more manageable since having her on the gym floor of the Clubhouse.

But she seems okay and she didn't run screaming when she saw me, so maybe it wasn't as bad as I remember it being for her. I hope that's the case because I realize now how close I'd been to losing it for months. She fixed whatever it was that was destroying me however inadvertently, and I don't want to have caused her pain while she was helping me ... even if she is Don *Fucking* Foley's daughter.

I still can't get my head around that. How can this girl be related to that piece of shit? If I knew where he was, even Vic wouldn't be able to stop me from hunting him down and gutting him after what he did. I try to think about something else before my mind begins to remember all the reasons that I hate that that asshole is still breathing.

I don't want to admit it, but if we can use Jane to get to him, I'm all for it. Revenge has been the only thing keeping me going for a very long time.

Fuck. Dark rabbit hole.

I turn my attention to the present before I slide down into its depths. My shoulder aches. It's still healing from the shooting, but at least they got the bullet out before the skin grew over it because I know from personal experience that extracting one from a partially healed wound is painful as hell. It's well on the way to being completely repaired though and, thanks to Jane choosing me as her first demon fuck, it should be completely gone by tomorrow.

The car is quiet and Jane sitting between me and Vic, her hands folded in her lap. Her dark hair is up in a ponytail the way it usually is and I know that Paris is probably already thinking of lining up some kind of stylist or something for her since we'll probably be in Metro until the Clubhouse is rebuilt.

The black dress she's wearing looks nice too, I think as I shift to look out the window, so I don't keep staring at her.

I wonder if Vic's even bothered to tell her where we're going right now, or if he's using it as the beginning of the punishment he's promised. Will it offend her delicate human sensibilities? I suppose that'd be the point. Maybe it'll be interesting to see what Foley's daughter can take, I think callously.

The trip through the heart of Metro is quick because it's almost ten on a weeknight. Jane doesn't say anything the whole way. She's not the most talkative on-call girl we've ever had, but even she seems quieter than usual and I eye Korban. I know he fed from her last night. I didn't get into it with him, but he should have waited. Yesterday was hard for all of us, including her. He could have put it off for a day.

I let out a breath, frustrated at the direction of my thoughts. Why do I care if yesterday was hard for Jane? This was all her doing, wasn't it?

I'm trying to stay objective, but I'm finding it difficult to believe she pulled the figurative (and literal) trigger on us. The little human double agent is about as far from a spy-movie fem fatale as she could get. But maybe that's her strength because we did underestimate her.

When we're nearing the club district, Vic turns his head to speak to Jane directly for almost the first time since we got back from the hospital.

'You stay with Sie at all times,' he orders. 'Do you understand?'

'Yeah,' she says almost sullenly and I hide an involuntary grin that splits my face.

Vic's hand will be twitching at that tone. I'll bet he wishes we weren't in the car so he could dole out a little physical discipline.

Jane, completely unaware of how close she is to getting a spanking from our president, yawns next to me.

'Are we keeping you up?' I drawl.

She looks at me with surprise and I realize I haven't actually spoken to her since I was pounding her into the mat the other day.

'I'm not really much of a night owl,' she replies quietly.

I chuckle, inordinately glad she's actually speaking to me because it probably means I didn't force myself on her the other night ... even though I don't want anything to do with her if I can help it.

'You'll get used to it,' I say, but my mind is in turmoil.

I'm not hungry. I don't need to feed tonight so why am I basking in her attention? Why can I not stop thinking about her?

We pull up at a glitzy club with a line out the door and she's looking at it curiously, clearly thinking that that's where we're going.

After I help her out of the car, I ignore her puzzlement as we walk across the street to a nondescript entrance. She takes a look over her shoulder at where the music is coming from.

'Not tonight, princess,' Paris says to her, 'but we can grind on the dance floor again soon if you want.'

Her eyes widen a little as she looks at him and she turns back around quickly.

Vic pushes a button and then shows his face to the camera positioned above the door. It clicks open and he takes a step forward, but at the last second, he turns to me.

'You keep her with you every second,' he reiterates.

I give Vic a single nod, putting my game face on. I'm the human's bodyguard and I take that shit very seriously.

We go through the door, over a subtle, magickal

threshold that checks us for weapons. I left my gun in the car, so we're not stopped. We make our way down a long hallway. I keep one eye on Jane who's walking next to me and I see Paris doing the same. He wants to see her face when she finds out what this place is too.

We turn the corner and go through a mesh curtain, which I guess was magickal because we can suddenly hear loud dance music that we couldn't before. Jane looks surprised as her eyes take in a massive disco ball, a round stage and a pole for the ladies here to make use of when they dance.

Her eyes are wide, but she doesn't look missish though it's clear what kind of establishment we've brought her to. If anything, she looks intrigued and her eyes are pretty much glued to the flecks of light reflected off the mirrored ball slowly turning in the middle of the room.

What I wouldn't give to see her shaking that ass on one of these poles, I think to myself. Not here where everyone could see though. *In private.* I swallow hard. What the fuck is going on with me? I need to get my head on straight.

'Supes only. You know that, Vicious,' a bouncer says, coming out of the shadows and gesturing to Jane.

Vic smirks. 'Gonna be hard to hold that meeting if we turn around and leave.'

The big shifter holds his ear for a second, clearly getting instructions. Then he nods and retreats back to the wall as the hostess, Fiona, approaches. She's dressed in a black sequined dress, sparkling like a jewel. She looks radiant and healthy, almost *alive* tonight. She gives us a smile that's welcoming. 'They're waiting for you in the back room.'

Vic smiles. 'Looking good, Fi. New benefactor?'

She gives him a coy smile. 'Ada does let me out some-times,' she purrs, but then she sees Jane and her expression shutters. 'No humans.' She casts an angry look at the bouncer who shrugs apologetically and taps his ear. She shakes her head a little.

'Be careful with your *human* whore, incubus. There's a reason they aren't allowed in here even if Ada seems to think it's fine.'

With a flourish, she turns and stalks back to the bar, saying something to the barman who pours her a very *crimson and viscous* drink from an elaborate carafe.

We move across the room, Jane walking slowly behind us as she gawks like a tourist. I take her arm in a gentle grip and urge her along with me.

'You heard what Vic said. Don't go off on your own in here. It's dangerous, little human.'

Jane looks up at me and gives me a nod, but her eyes leave me immediately to trail after the dancers in their glittering outfits and I almost smile though I'm a little bewildered. Humans are known to be a little more ... *prudish* as a rule. She must know what this place is, but she still stops and stares at the main stage as one of the dancers is flitting around a pole, a smile erupting on her face.

'Wow,' she breathes as the graceful female effortlessly inverts and moves into some kind of elaborate spin that defies gravity.

'Come on,' I say, catching up to the others who are disappearing into one of the private rooms at the back.

We follow them. The room is dark and I make sure that Jane is still right next to me. This isn't a normal brothel, after all. The patrons here can be very wily and dangerous, which is why usually there are no humans, neither male nor female, allowed.

We sit down on the long, round sofa. There's a small table in front of us with a pole in the middle but there are no dancers in here now, not while we talk business. A tray of champagne is in front of us. Only the finest. I take one of the crystal glasses and hand it to Jane because I can tell she wants one.

She sits with a murmured 'thank you' and I plant myself next to her, my arm draped behind her in an overt and protective gesture that the three fae dressed in bright silks on the other side of the table won't miss *or mistake*.

OURS!

Their eyes move over Jane with interest until they realize she's human. After that, they ignore her completely.

'Torun. Thank you for coming,' Vic says.

'You asked for this meeting,' Torun, the one in the middle murmurs, clearly in no mood for pleasantries. 'What do you want, Alexandre 'Vicious' Makenzie, President of the Iron Incubi?'

Vic doesn't take a drink, but he sits back, spreading out a little bit, giving the air of indifference that we all do, except for Jane who's making herself appear as small as possible and looks ready to bolt at any moment. We'll have to talk to her about that. She needs to project strength in the supe world. It has an effect on how the entire MC is perceived and if our enemies think we're weak since the attack, they'll start moving in like jackals.

'No doubt you've heard about the latest shipment.'

'We have,' Torun acknowledges, 'and also your rash of *very* bad luck recently.'

The other fae chuckle.

'Indeed,' Vic says.

'I hope you're not here to blame us.'

Vic doesn't look at Jane, but I know where his thoughts are.

'Never crossed our minds,' he says. 'In fact, we have a

pretty good idea of who's behind it and we should be retrieving our lost property from them very soon. That's what we're here to talk with you about.'

'Interesting,' Torun says, looking intrigued.

This time, Vic does look Jane's way. He gives me a look and I whisper in Jane's ear. 'Do you want to see some more of the club?'

She glances around and nods.

We leave, going back out into the main bar area. Though it's only been five minutes, there's a remarkable difference in the atmosphere. The place is busier and, not only that, there's an aura of excitement that wasn't in the air before.

I frown as I look around. Maybe there's a show tonight. It's midweek so it shouldn't be this energized in here without reason.

Jane doesn't seem to notice the change, her eyes moving around, taking in girls giving lap dances, the ones serving drinks, and the clients sitting around tables. Some are by themselves, nursing drinks. Others are in increasingly rowdy groups, flipping gold coins onto the stage, or tucking them into the girls' clothes and hair. Dollar bills don't fly here. Every one of these guys is a supe, and they're all much richer than your average human.

I overhear two of the waitresses talking not far away in hushed voices.

'What's going *on* in here tonight?' one asks her friend.

The other one is looking around and shaking her head. 'No clue. I haven't ever seen it so wild, not even on Jello-fight Night. Go tell Fi. She might want to speak to Ada, call in some more bouncers or something.'

I frown, but Ada's been in charge here for as long as I can remember. She knows her business, so I turn my attentions back to my charge, keeping one eye on the riffraff beyond her.

'Do you like this place?' I murmur, leaning against the wall outside the door.

I'm crossing my arms, making sure I look as imposing as possible to anyone who'd dare approach. It's not difficult. I'm easily the biggest supe in this place except for maybe the lone dragon shifter in the corner by himself who looks three sheets to the wind.

Our human doesn't answer me right away as if she's not sure if it's a trick question, or not.

'I've never been anywhere like this,' she says. 'I mean I know what this place is, I'm not an idiot. I wouldn't want to work here or anything.'

I cant my head, and she's clearly afraid she's offended me because her eyes widen.

'Not because of ... you know ... *the job they do*, but,' she looks wistfully at the stage where there's another girl doing a floor routine. 'The way they move is hypnotic, don't you think?'

'I suppose,' I say softly, my dick feeling anything but soft in my pants.

Her moving like that for me would be much more interesting than the show going on in front of us.

'Why don't you try it?' I ask.

She laughs and tilts her head to the side as she stares at the show. 'Uh ... I don't think my hips do those things.'

I step very close to her, crowding her against the wall. 'Takes practice,' I murmur in her ear, wondering what I'm doing but not seeming to be able to halt my seduction of her.

She jumps a little and I curse myself for scaring her. But

then I smell the unmistakable, fruity scent of lust coming off her over Paris' soap.

Making a snap decision that's completely out of character for me, I grab the handle of the door next to me and throw it open. I don't know where it leads, but I'm a hundred percent sure there's no one behind it.

I grab Jane and pull her inside with me, closing us into a dark room that smells of Windex.

I roll my eyes. Of course it's a fucking supply closet, and not a private room with a couch. That'd be too easy. But I turn my attention to the little human in front of me. Her mouth's open and she's breathing hard as she's looking up at me.

'What are you doing?' she asks.

I don't answer her. Instead, I kiss her, my tongue invading her sweet mouth as I pull her off her feet and wind her legs around me. My hands are all over her and she seems to like it, undulating against me with a moan.

Oh, those hips can move, I think as I push her dress up out of my way.

She's gasping against me as I lick down her neck and bite her collarbone gently. Her breathy sounds turn needy. She wants this as much as I do. I thought I'd imagined it last time, but this is exactly how I remember it ... and her.

'Is this okay?' I breathe, just wanting to make absolutely sure.

Her hands slide into my hair and she puts her cheek to mine.

'Yes,' she whispers and then kisses me hard.

With a low growl of pleasure at that amazing word, I unzip my pants and I don't wait. I move her underwear to the side and bury myself inside her in one, deep thrust. The sound that comes from her makes me want to rip her dress off and worship her body in ways I've never even contemplated with a human. She feels so fucking good!

I brace myself against the door with one hand, holding her with the other as I pound into her hard. Fast. Every move of me inside her feels like the most sensual caress I've ever experienced and I'd love to fuck her like this forever, but we're on a time schedule so I find my release faster than I'd ideally like. She bucks against the door as my seed floods into her. She cries out as she comes and power fills me to the brim. Fuck, I thought it was a fluke before, but this girl and me make magick.

Literally.

I let her down, something niggling in the back of my mind as I rearrange her dress. She's looking a little dazed as I open the door.

'Jane?'

'Huh?'

'Are you okay?'

She smiles at me dreamily and I wonder if this is how she feels the bliss the other humans get from us.

Then I hear glass breaking and shrieking from the main room and I thrust Jane behind me as I step out into the club. The frenzied scene in front of me has me banging on the door where Vic and the others are still having their meeting with the fae.

There are bottles flying across the room, clients fighting over girls, others chasing each other. There's a veritable orgy by the bar and Fiona is standing on the wooden counter, spraying cold water on people while frantically yelling into her walkie-talkie.

Paris opens the door. 'What's the prob—'

'We need to get out of here,' I yell.

The Iron I's and the fae come out a second later just in time to see the supe cops swarming in.

'Fuck,' Toran says, putting a portal link on the door to the closet I was just in with Jane.

He and the other fae go through the door immediately and when I see inside for a brief moment, it's not a closet, but a completely different room. The last one gives me a mock salute before he closes the door and they're gone.

I open the door to see if we can escape that way, but the portal is already severed and all I find is the same closet on the other side.

'Fucking fae,' Korban mutters. 'Let's get the hell out of here before the cops notice us. I don't want to get locked up tonight.'

Fiona jumps off the bar, punches a guy in the face, and then breaks a bottle over another's head as she beckons us.

We make our way across the room, keeping a still-dazed and very languid Jane in the middle of us as we force people out of our way. Fiona opens a door next to the bar and slips through. We follow her into a dark corridor that leads down some steps.

'The cops didn't see you,' she says, 'and they don't know about this exit.'

'What the hell happened in there,' Theo asks, looking back over his shoulder to make sure no one's following.

'I have no fucking idea,' Fi mutters. 'I haven't seen a lust rush like that in a very long time. If I didn't know any better, I'd swear it was ...' She gives herself a shake. 'That's impossible.'

'What is?' Paris asks.

'Doesn't matter,' she said impatiently. 'Follow the tunnel north and it'll take you to the river. I need to go back before

Ada comes down, loses her shit, and kills every last fucker in there including the cops.'

Vic nods and Fiona turns back, her sequined dress somehow looking as pristine as ever.

We follow the tunnel that looks like an old sewage duct and Paris lets out a laugh. 'Never a dull moment, huh?'

We all chuckle and I grin in the low light. That kid always has something to say.

We emerge out of some bushes by the river as Fi said we would and I'm buzzing. I feel like I could climb a mountain, swim against the current of the Styx out of the underworld itself if I needed to.

I freeze mid-step, almost falling over and a coldness settles over me as I realize what was bothering me in the club. What's been bothering me since the gym now that I think about it.

I stare at Jane, walking behind the others like she's a normal, run of the mill human.

But, she's not.

I have to be wrong, but if I'm not, we're fucked, the Club is fucked, and Jane is as good as dead.

5

JANE

The tunnel from the strip club lets us out in, as far as I can make out, the middle of freaking nowhere. None of us have phone reception, which strikes me as weird. I mean, we're literally in the middle of the city, but the guys don't bat an eye about it.

I shiver and Theo hands me his jacket without a word. I accept it with a grateful smile and we start walking, keeping to the road that runs parallel with the river.

I keep glancing back at Sie as we make our way out of this weird part of Metro. He just fucked me against a door in a closet and I wanted him to and it was the hottest thing ever.

I hope he didn't hurt himself so soon after he came out of the hospital. I suspect that his shoulder where he got shot is hurting him. I don't know why I think that's the case, but I want to ask him if he's okay.

But he doesn't even glance at me. It's like I don't exist anymore and it's so dumb, but it hurts my feelings. He got what he wanted from me *again* and now I'm not worth anything just like last time when he left right after.

I let out a slow sigh. When did I become so sensitive?

'Who were those guys that you met with?' I ask, trying to take my mind off things that are making me depressed.

'Just some fae,' Theo murmurs.

Even I know that clandestine meeting with fae aren't a good thing, no matter if it's with other supes.

'What for?'

He shrugs, giving a non-committal sound. 'It's just what we have to do sometimes. Supe stuff. Nothing to worry about.'

I sigh as we walk. They never give me any real information and it's frustrating because if I'm not explicitly told things, it's not like I can infer all that well and when I do try, I almost always get it wrong.

'Look,' Paris says, 'it's just Club stuff, princess. That's all. You'd be bored out of your mind if we discussed it with you.'

Don't worry your pretty little head over man business, princess. Just service us when we need you.

I roll my eyes. Does he even know what he sounds like sometimes? I don't respond to his platitudes, and we walk in silence. My feet are already hurting even in my flats and I'm infinitely glad I don't wear heels even if I did feel totally underdressed in the presence of the hostess in her glitzy dress and five-inch stilettos. I'll bet her feet would be destroyed right now if she were here.

I think back to the strip club that, now that I'm mulling it over, was probably a high-end brothel too. Everything was so colorful and, weirdly, I really liked it in there, which makes me feel bad because sex work is exploitative, right? Maybe the girls in there didn't want to be there at all. I mean, they all seemed happy enough and the tips looked AMAZING to waitress me.

Maybe I could get a job in a place like that the next time

I move on, but, like, a human one. It would have to be as a waitress though because, with the greatest will in the world, I could never be able to dance like those girls, and I'm finding it hard enough trying to please these guys sexually. I can't even imagine the abject failure I'd experience trying to satisfy even more than that on a daily basis.

We move for a good twenty minutes in the dark through what looks like the most deserted part of town, all derelict warehouses and dilapidated apartment blocks. Most of the streetlights are broken and the ones that do work flicker like ominous candles.

We're sticking close together with me in the middle, Vic and Korban in front, Theo and Paris beside me, and Sie behind and I'm glad they're with me because wherever we are, it's feeling more and more like we shouldn't be here.

'What is this place?' I ask out loud. 'This isn't Metro.'

Vic looks back at me, his eyes flicking to Sie and I wonder if Vic knows what he did in the strip club.

'What makes you so sure?' Sie asks.

I cast a furtive glance back at him, my core clenching again at the memory of that closet, the way he kissed me, held me up and ... I push the thoughts away.

So not the right time!

'It's ...' I grope for the right words to answer Sie's question, but can't come up with anything better than, 'It's *wrong* here.'

'She's right about that,' Paris mutters.

'This is Metro,' Vic says, 'but most humans never see this part of the city. It bleeds into the fae realms.'

I look up sharply, wondering if he's fucking with me. Every human knows the fae worlds and ours never cross over. It's very hard to get back and forth between them. The fae have always been adamant about that.

'That can't be true,' I argue.

'You'd know best.'

I narrow my eyes at him. 'But I've never even heard of this place. This entire section of Metro looks like it's been abandoned for years.'

'Not completely.' Korban mutters, stopping in his tracks.

I strain my eyes to see what he's looking at. 'What is i—'

'Be quiet,' Sie hisses in my ear.

I shut up and stare through the darkness at where they're looking and I see an animal loping across the street. It's eyes are red and glowing like a cheap Halloween decoration. It stops and sniffs the air, turning to stare at us and I feel like it's focusing solely on me, which is ridiculous.

Korban takes a step forward, emitting a low growl that makes me go weak in the knees. Why does that sound make me melt?

He twists around to stare at me, his eyes *changing* just for a second and I take a step back, bumping into Sie.

Is that Kor's demon?

My body's contact with Sie's instantly makes me feel secure and my reaction confuses me. Only a few days ago I was terrified of Sie even looking my way. Now, when he's around me, I'm not scared at all. I get this warm feeling like I'm the safest I'll ever be, which I know sounds great in theory for a human playing in the supe world, but I don't think I like it because it makes me realize how unprotected I've felt since dad disappeared and how it's not going to last.

The creature turns and runs down an alley.

'Where there's one, there's fifty,' Theo murmurs and we start moving again, faster now.

'What was that?' I ask, my heart beating fast.

'Hell hound,' Sie answers me.

I can feel him finally looking at me, and I get this sensa-

tion that he's upset about something but I'm probably imagining it, wishing for a link between us, any kind of
connection no matter if I have to make one up.

Pathetic.

I don't look back at him again.

Gradually, the streetlights get better as we follow the
road and I can see that people actually live in these buildings. We arrive in something that resembles civilization, and
Vic checks his phone.

'Cells are working again,' he mutters as he texts
someone.

His phone buzzes almost immediately. 'Corner of 89th
and Main.'

We turn left and keep going until we get to some traffic
lights. There, I see two cars waiting.

I get in the second one, assuming that Sie and Theo will
get in with me, but when the doors slam shut, I'm sand-
wiched between Vic and Korban instead.

I get this feeling of anger and resentment, of malice
tinged with righteousness aimed directly at me.

It's coming from Korban, but I'm imagining it right? But
why would I? It's not nice. It's terrifying. I don't want a
connection like that with anyone.

Alarmed, I look up at Vic as I try to make myself as small
as possible and wonder where these feelings are coming
from, who they're coming from because maybe I'm not
inventing them at all.

Vic looks down his nose at me.

'As if I'd let you out of my sight now,' he mutters and I'm
struck again with how cold his tone is.

'Have I done something?' I ask him, looking for a straight
answer, a reason, but he ignores me like he didn't even hear me.

Maybe he didn't. I tap him on the arm and he looks down at me again.

'What?'

'I asked if I've done something wrong.'

He rolls his eyes and casts a look at Korban.

'Stop talking,' Korban says, his voice menacingly quiet, 'or I will find another use for your mouth.'

My eyes widen at his tone as I try to work out what he's actually saying and then I look at the floor, my heart humming in my chest and my stomach bottoming out.

Does he mean what I think he does?

The human driver glances at me in his rearview mirror, catching my eye and I think I hear him laugh. I won't be getting any help from that quarter if Korban decides to make good on his threat, not that I'd expect any, I guess. There's a reason why the supes and the fae are so easily able to lord it over us humans even though we have the superior numbers and it has nothing to do with their strength or magick. We're easy to keep divided.

We pull up at the back of their townhouse, the other car just behind us, and Vic opens a cavernous garage with his phone. Its right underneath the property, sort of like a basement I didn't even know was there.

We go inside and I look around. It's huge. There are bikes down one end that look old or maybe the word is 'classic'. The floor is the same as the garage in the Clubhouse was with that thick, buttoned rubber that car showrooms always seem to have.

The elevator opens and I go to step inside, but I'm hauled back by my ponytail.

My eyes clench as I grab it close to my head, squealing loudly in shock more than anything.

'What the fuck?' I yell, twisting around, too wrung out for anything even resembling bullshit.

I find Vic with my long hair wrapped around his fist, and I clench my jaw as he pulls harder, tears coming to my eyes. *Involuntary* ones!

What the fuck is going on now?

'Did you think you were just going to stay in Theo's room?'

I frown through the pain, not really sure where he's going with this because, yes, I did think I was staying in Theo's room ... mostly because they told me that's where I was staying.

'Do we have to do this?' Theo asks and my eyes cut to him.

He looks away immediately.

'Yes,' Vic says through gritted teeth.

'On-call girls don't live in the main house. They stay in the basement until they're needed,' he sneers.

His hand leaves my hair and I take a step back, but he grabs me by my forearm tight enough to bruise and hauls me across the garage through one of two doors I hadn't noticed.

It holds a cell with bars on it, an old, dirty mattress, and a bucket. I look back at them with wide eyes, shaking my head vigorously.

I stare at Theo. Did he know that Vic was going to do this? Did Paris? Of course they did. I look at the others' faces. None of them meet my eyes except for Korban.

They all knew.

NO! They can't leave me down here!

Vic lets me go and Kor opens the door to the cell, staring into my face.

He's relishing my fear. I can feel it.

I pull away from him with a cry, but he takes hold of me, pushing me inside hard and the door clangs shut. Vic locks it. The others are looking on, not doing anything. Then they leave without a word, filing out anticlimactically like they haven't just caged me like an animal. I'm shaking my head, not able to believe they're just going to do this ... but then it gets a thousand times worse.

'Wait!' I cry in terror as I see Korban's fingers find the switch on the wall. 'No!'

But he doesn't even hesitate. He flicks the lights off. And before I can say anything, I'm left in the pitch back.

I scream. I can't help it, but then I lock it down.

My breath is coming in fits and starts. It's so dark. *So dark.*

My eyes dart around, trying to find something ... anything to focus on, but there's nothing.

I might as well be locked in a tiny box. I flail, smacking my hand into one of the bars and my screech of pain echoes through the room. I'm crying and my breathing is loud and hard. It's all I can hear. I try to calm down, closing my eyes so I can pretend that there's light around me as I walk slowly around the cell that I only saw for a second. I bang into something that tips over with a clang.

The bucket.

There was a mattress too. I walk forward until I feel it with my foot. It looked dirty. It smells too. I take a deep breath that ends on a sob.

Why is this such a shock to me? They've shown me over and over again what I am to them. This shouldn't be a surprise, but the truth is, as much as my ego would love to say, 'saw this coming a mile off,' I didn't. At. All. Yeah, my gut was telling me something was going to happen, but I had no idea it would be something as awful as this.

How long are they going to keep me down here? What if they forget about me? What if they don't bring me food? What if they just let me die down here?

My breathing is coming hard again, and I sink to the floor, but it's so cold that I bite the bullet and sit on the nasty mattress. But even that doesn't do much good. It's damp and I don't even have the jacket that Theo gave me when we left the tunnel. Korban grabbed it off me as he threw me into the cell.

I shudder, still seeing his nasty smile as he locked me in here, as he turned off the light. It was like I could actually feel what he was feeling. *Again.* Just like what happened with Sie. I'm *sure* I could feel how much he wanted me in the strip club and that his shoulder was hurting afterwards. I haven't noticed it with the others, but Korban and Sie are the only ones who have actually slept with me. *Fed off me.*

Am I going crazy or is this real? If it is actually happening, why didn't they warn me about it?

Because you mean nothing to them. Why would they care if some dumb human can read their feelings?

It's probably bull anyway. A human girl feeling supe emotions? *Please!*

I start to shiver. Why did they lock me down here? What did I do? Was it because I wasn't into Kor and Paris enough the other night? Did I do something wrong in the club? How long is it going to be before I really start freaking out?

I'VE BEEN DOWN HERE for a while, but I have no idea how long. I haven't needed to pee in the bucket yet, but I am holding it. It's like, if I use it, this is happening. I am actually down here.

I'm hearing things. I can feel things too, but I don't think they exist. It doesn't stop me from scratching at my skin where I can feel crawling though.

I think my brain is freaking out. Sensory deprivation messes with your other senses.

I saw a documentary.

I'm sitting in the middle of the nasty mattress, hugging my knees because I'm freezing. For all I know roaches live in the mattress and that's what I can feel. There's a sound of dripping every few seconds.

Drip.

Drip.

Drip.

Drip.

DRIP.

DRIP.

My hands are covering my ears but I can still hear it and now I know why the guy in *The Tell-Tale Heart* confessed to the police he was a murderer when all he could hear was the beating heart of the man he'd killed. Maybe Edgar Allen Poe was autistic because he definitely knew the power of an incessant noise. I haven't even *done anything* and I want to confess it if it means I never hear this sound again.

I know it's ridiculous. It can't have been more than a couple of hours, but I think I can safely say that I'd never hold up under torture. Thirty seconds of plate scratching or nails on a chalkboard and I'd be throwing my fellow soldiers under the bus.

I cried at first but my tears have dried up for now. I feel numb and I'm thankful.

Have they broken me this easily? The truth is that, yes, they might well have because there are a lot of things they could have done that wouldn't have been as bad as this. They chose something they knew would be the worst thing for me. They're using my diagnosis against me, to torment me, punish me. I guess I'm naïve and stupid AF, but I never thought they'd be so cruel.

Something clicks and there's a two-second delay before the fluorescents above me flick on. I cover my eyes as the light blinds me and by the time I can see, Vic's standing in the doorway. I dry my eyes, hoping that he can't see how upset I am.

He doesn't say anything, just stares at me like I'm an exhibit in the zoo.

Finally, I can't take it anymore. I stand up on wobbly legs and go to the front of the cell. To be honest, I don't know what to say. I don't know what question to ask first. He saves me the trouble.

'Stop looking at me like a wounded bird. You know why you're down here,' he states, his tone so cold it makes me shiver even more.

Bedroom Vic. Business Vic. This is another Vic. I've seen glimpses of him since he came out of the hospital. *Mean Vic.*

So I should know why I'm down here? I look away because I do know. It's obvious. I'm a shitty on-call girl and this is my punishment. I could beg. I could say that I'll do better, but it would be a lie.

I go back and sit on the mattress, pretending defiance that I don't really feel.

'I don't know why you wanted me to sign,' I say miserably. 'It was obvious from the beginning that this wouldn't work.'

Something passes over his face, but I don't even try to work out what. I don't give a shit what the hell he's thinking or feeling. The truth is I have no fucking idea what motivates these demonic motherfuckers.

But that's not quite true now. At least not where Sie and Korban are concerned.

Then I have an errant thought that chills me. What if they don't protect Shar and her family anymore?

He turns to leave.

'Wait,' I cry. 'I'm sorry!'

I throw my dignity onto the dirty mattress even though it pains me. Shar and her family are more important than that.

I hurl myself at the cage and grip the bars.

'I can do better,' I plead. 'Please. I'll do anything. I'm sorry. Please!'

He turns back and looks me up and down. 'Anything?' he asks and warning bells go off in my brain, but I nod my head.

'Anything.'

He scoffs at me and comes forward with a key in his hand, and I think he's gonna let me out but then he pulls a Theo and draws it back.

He leans down so his eyes are level with mine.

'I can already have anything from you that I want. We all can. You're going to stay down here until one of us needs you,' he says. 'You won't be coming upstairs until then, *maybe not even then*. Might want to stay on the mattress, Jane. It gets pretty cold down here.'

He turns off the light again and, when he closes the door, I can't help the whimper that bubbles up from my throat.

He wanted that, I realize now. He wanted to hear me beg. It amused him.

I scrunch my eyes up and curl into a ball on the mattress, tucking my legs under the dress. It was a nice dress, but it's not the best when you're a prisoner in a cold, wet basement. I clutch my arms and curl tighter, trying to think warm thoughts.

I try not to cry, but all I can hear is that fucking drip over and over and over.

I scrunch up my face and scream into the darkness, but that doesn't make me feel any better. I want to sleep so badly, but I can't. I know that any 'normal' person could just *not focus on it* but I can't not. All that exists for me now is dark, cold, and that fucking sound. It's not long before I feel things crawling on me again and I start scratching at my skin hard, no longer caring if I hurt myself.

A little while later there's a click as someone flicks the switch on the wall. The door closes before the light comes on, but at least I'm not in the pitch black anymore. There are scratches all over my arms and legs, but no bugs. I put my head in my hands, still more miserable than I've ever been in my life. These demons are going to be the death of me, but maybe I have one ally up there.

Theo

'I NEED TO FEED.'

Vic glances up from where he's sitting, doing work at the table in the living room, basically to gatekeep the garage, making sure none of us go down to Jane without his say-so, I'm pretty sure.

'Do it then,' he says, not seeming to give a shit that it's been days and he hasn't let her upstairs even for a moment.

I finally convinced him to let me cook her some dinner, but he said he would be the one taking it down. He brought it back up the morning after, uneaten. I'm not ashamed to say that I'm worried about Jane … and about Vic. He took the attack on us and the destruction of the Clubhouse personally and he's making Jane pay for it, though she was likely not the mastermind behind it.

His temper has been going through the roof since she's been in the cell. It seems like he's having trouble controlling his power. He hasn't said anything directly to me, but I wouldn't expect him to. It's my job to notice when something isn't right with a member of the Club, even if that member is Vic. He's clearly not himself. But I need to look out for Jane too.

'I'm not doing it down there,' I say to Vic.

I practically see our president grit his teeth as he looks up at me and I make an effort not to reach into my pocket to start messing with my stethoscope. They know when I'm doing it and they know it means I'm nervous.

'I meant what I said to you. You bring her up here and anything happens, you're responsible. You feed and then you take her back if you really can't do it in the cell.'

He rolls his eyes and goes back to what he's doing. I don't let the frustrated growl that I want to let loose emerge from my throat as I leave the room.

I go upstairs to my bedroom and make sure everything is ready for her because I *am* bringing her up here, and I'm not throwing her back down there as soon as I've used her like she's a piece of trash.

Fuck Vic.

The truth is that I don't even need to feed. I just can't bear the thought of her down there any longer.

I start the water running in the tub so that as soon as I bring her up, she can get warm.

There's a knock at my door and Korban waltzes in without waiting for an invite. I haven't seen him for a couple of days. I'm not sure what mission Vic sent him on, but he looks like shit.

'Where the hell have you been?' I ask.

'Undercover,' he murmurs. 'I need to ask you a question. The girl downstairs ...the on-call girl.'

'She has a name.'

He shrugs and I resist the urge to backhand him across his smug face.

'She have one of those things,' he taps the top of his arm, 'like the other girls got when they signed?'

'You mean an implant?' I ask. 'So she doesn't get pregnant?'

'Yeah.'

I pause. I actually don't know. I should know. I'm her fucking doctor, but I'll bet she's never even been to a gyno.

'No, she doesn't yet, but all of us are carefu—'

I see it in Kor's face, but I pretend I don't. To say I'm surprised is an understatement. I know for a fact that he's always been incredibly careful never to even chance getting a girl pregnant. To be honest, I assumed that, due to his past, he couldn't *finish the business* with them for it to happen.

'When will you need to feed next?' I ask carefully, trying to gauge what he's done and when because it might already be too late, even if it was just the other night.

'I won't need to for a while,' he says, pretending he doesn't care. 'I just wanted to make sure.'

He turns and leaves and I let out a breath, adding trying to get Jane back on my exam table to the mental list of things I need to do to make sure she's okay. I don't know how her birth control could have slipped my mind, but I guess with everything that's been going on I was going to drop a ball somewhere.

Helluva ball to drop though.

I hear Kor's heavy footsteps receding down the hall and his door shutting, and I don't waste any time. No doubt he's going to shower before he goes to see Paris after getting back from wherever he's been.

Knocking on Paris' door, I don't wait for him to tell me I can come in before I push it open.

He's sitting on his bed, watching something on his laptop. He puts on the screensaver as soon as he sees me and I act like I didn't notice.

'Kor just came to see me. He asked me if Jane is on birth control. Is there something I should know?'

Paris runs his fingers through his hair. 'Shit. I didn't even think of that. Yeah. The other night when we ... well when Korban fed he ...'

'Spit it out,' I order, my hand in my pocket, forefinger tapping on the white pad of the stethoscope like a tiny drum.

'... he finished inside of her.'

I don't bother to hide my confusion. 'I thought he couldn't, that it was one of his triggers.'

'That's what I thought too, but he did it and he didn't bat an eye. He's never done that before, not even close. As far as I knew, he couldn't because of—'

I put a hand up. 'I know.'

'He's told you?'

'Enough. I've inferred the rest.' I glance at the laptop, the screen still blank. 'You're watching her, aren't you?'

Paris winces. 'Yeah.'

'How is she? What's she doing?'

'I don't know. She hasn't moved from the mattress in hours. I thought she was asleep at first, but her eyes are open. She's just staring into nothing. She only moves to cover her ears sometimes.'

'Fuck. We can't leave her down there. She's probably freezing to death.'

'Vic won't go back on what he said. You know that, don't you? Maybe he's right. He has a plan and as soon as he knows Sie's really okay, he won't care how it ends for her. You can't either. You need to distance yourself.'

I scoff at Paris' words. 'So do you. You think no one noticed how you two were acting together after you went shopping the other day?'

'I like her. I can't help it.' He heaves a sigh and changes the subject. 'I finally came across the footage that Vic wanted. A lot of the files on the server turned out to be corrupted, but I was able to find some of it in the mess and restore it, which is why it's taken days instead of hours.'

'Is that normal, for so many files to be damaged like that?'

Paris shakes his head. 'It looks like it was a cyber-attack. Luckily, I'm very good at what I do and I was able to save most of what we need.'

I glance at the laptop, wondering what Paris has found. 'Have you shown Vic yet?'

'No. I just found it.'

'Show me.'

'You aren't going to like it,' Paris mutters, but he pulls up a video.

I watch the file, showing a grainy Jane entering Vic's office.

'She goes in and then looks at the paperwork on the desk that Vic left for her to find.'

I watch as she picks something up, staring at it. I can't see her expression clearly, but she isn't smiling. She doesn't look excited. If anything, she looks upset. I watch as she turns off the light and leaves.

'What did she find?' I ask. 'What did Vic leave out?'

'Just info on a shipment that doesn't exist.' He closes the file.

'That was the night I found her crying in the hall and the timestamp shows it was just after this. I know what this looks like,' he says, 'but I don't buy it.'

I nod, glad that I seem to have Paris on my side. 'Vic wants her to be guilty. He wants retribution for the house, the attacks, and the shipments, especially now that it looks like it was Foley. Who better to take it out on than the man's daughter?'

'Fuck,' Paris says again. 'He'll say this was a ploy, that he left the documents there and that's clearly what she looked at. But why would information on a shipment have upset her like that?'

'I don't know ... unless ...' I shake my head. 'The day after, she knew that we were aware of her diagnosis. What if that's what she found, the papers Vic had about her?'

'That would make sense, but if that's all she saw then no one will be there to steal a shipment that doesn't really exist.'

'I'm bringing her upstairs,' I say. 'I know she must have had a hand in the Clubhouse and the other things because of who she is, but this is messed up. We've never treated any other humans this way.'

Paris lets out a half-amused sound. 'I guess you could argue that no other humans have tried to end our entire MC either, but it's true. Something doesn't smell right. I guess we'll know soon enough though. Vic told me the fake shipment was meant to be delivered to the warehouses tomorrow night, so if someone shows up to collect it, we'll know it was her and we'll know for sure who she's working for.

I nod, my stomach in knots. *Tomorrow is too soon to lose her.*

'Sie's been acting weird too.'

I look up sharply. 'The same as before?'

'No, not psychotic. More like every time I leave the room, he comes in here and watches her on the monitors. Just stares.'

'They did something in the club the other night,' I say. 'I could smell him on her, but now ... there's something else going on with him and it has to do with her.'

Paris stands up and stalks over to the TV, picking up the remote. 'Vic has been keeping secrets and now so is Sie. I don't know what the fuck is going on with this clan, but ever since this girl showed up, it seems like we're ... I don't know.'

'I do. We're fracturing, but maybe it's been like this for a long time. We just didn't notice it before,' I mutter as I turn around and leave Paris' room.

I check the bath, testing the temperature, throwing in some bubbles, and making sure it's one of the smells that she likes. On the way back down, I stop in the living room.

'I'm going to get her now,' I say to Vic, 'and I'm telling you right now, as her doctor, I'm not taking her back to that cell.'

Vic is annoyingly indifferent to my announcement.

'You won't have to. I'll take her off your hands when you're done.'

'Fine,' I choke out.

I go down in the elevator and flick the switch in the garage. It's so fucking cold down here. Damp. Is Vic really in his right mind? How far will this go? How far *will I let this go*? I'm a fucking doctor!

I go into the back room. She's bolt upright, sitting on the

mattress. She doesn't move, just stares at me as I come closer.

'Are you okay?' I ask.

Dumb question.

Her knees are drawn up to her chest, trying to keep herself warm in the skimpy dress from the other night. She doesn't even have a blanket. Cursing Vic for not letting me down here sooner, I unlock the door.

She doesn't move, but her eyes are accusatory and I don't blame her. In fact, I'm glad I still see some fire in her. I step into the cell slowly in case she thinks I'm there to hurt her, but she doesn't fight me as I scoop her up into my arms.

Her arms and legs are scratched to shit and her fingernails are broken and bloodied. I grit my teeth as I take her to the elevator. She hasn't said a word, but when she puts her head on my shoulder, I'm just about undone. No matter what she did, this is not some hardened criminal, no human terrorist.

'I'm so sorry, sweetheart,' I'm murmur. 'I'm not letting him put you back down there.'

I hear a hiccup and I looked down and see that there are tears on her cheeks. Her mouth opens and I think she's going to say something, but she just lets out a breath and closes her eyes again.

We get to my room and, thankfully, don't see any of the others on the way up. I put her down on her feet and I push her hair back away from her face.

'Do you ... do you want to go somewhere *quiet*?' I ask in case she needs to decompress.

Still shivering, she shakes her head and I lead her slowly into the bathroom where the steaming bath is waiting. She looks down at the bath with obvious surprise.

'Do I smell?' she asks, sniffing her arm.

I put my forehead to hers. 'No,' I breathe.

'Oh. You want to make sure I'm clean before you feed.' Her voice is devoid of emotion.

'That's not it,' I say. 'I don't need to feed. That's not why I brought you up here. That's just what I told Vic.'

She gives a small nod, clearly not believing me.

'Do you want me to go?'

She nods again and I leave her in the bathroom. There's silence for a little while and then I hear the water sloshing as she gets in followed by a hiss of pain as the water hits those scratches.

I was going to give her some time, but then I hear the unmistakable sound of a sob and I'm on my feet and at the door in a second. I hover the threshold, wondering if I should go in. She said she wanted me to leave her alone. I don't want to make things worse.

Fuck what I said.

I go in and find her sobbing quietly into her knees and I kneel down next to the bath, putting my hand on her shoulder.

'Hey, sweetheart, it's okay. Hey.'

She looks at me.

'I'm sorry,' she says.

Is this an admission of guilt?

'Sorry for what?' I ask.

'That I'm such a shitty on-call girl. I'm guessing that's why I was put down there. You're going to take me back when you're done, aren't you? Please,' she swallows hard and her voice breaks. 'It's so cold…' She scratches idly at her skin and I pull her hands away, taking them in my own. '…and the sounds …'

'Sounds?' I ask.

'Drip, drip, drip, drip, drip, drip, drip, drip, drip, drip. I think I'm going crazy.' She looks at me, eyes pleading. 'I'll be better. I promise I'll be better.'

Fuck this. Fuck Vic.

I stand up, needing to get out of here for a minute.

'I'll be right back with some Neosporin and I'll take care of your scratches and bandage your hands, okay?'

She nods.

'Don't do *something stupid* while I'm gone.'

She looks up at me. 'What do you mean?'

'Nothing,' I say, not wanting to put an idea in her head that might not even be there.

I rush to my clinic to grab the things I need. I'm gone for a couple of minutes and, when I come back, I find Sie at the bathroom door, watching her.

She doesn't know he's there. Her head's resting on her knees, and she's just staring at the wall.

'If you're here because you need to feed again, you can't. She's not in any state.'

He ignores me completely. I stare at his back, wondering what is up with him lurking here like a creeper.

He leaves my room without a word and I glance into the bathroom. Jane hasn't moved and I walk in, clearing my throat so that I don't scare her.

I grab the shampoo and lather her hair up, wondering if she'll be okay with this. She closes her eyes, sighing deeply and her shoulders relax, so I continue. I wash her hair for her and then put in the conditioner that I know she likes before I wash the rest of her body with the soap – *my soap.* Her nostrils flare as she smells it, but she doesn't say anything.

I keep my movements as impersonal as I can because I don't want her thinking that this is anything other than what it is, which is me taking care of my patient. At least that's what I keep telling myself.

I finish up, rinse her hair, and wrap her in a fluffy towel, carrying her easily into the bedroom and laying her on the bed. She looks at me expectantly, like she knows what's coming next and I give her a rueful smile.

Instead of doing what she thinks I'm going to do, I tuck her body against mine and turn on the TV. I pick a romcom to keep it light. She soon relaxes against me again and I know this was the right thing. I'm not sure why I want her to trust me ... or maybe I am sure. I feel her body go lax next to me and I know she's asleep. I kiss her on her temple and close my eyes.

I HEAR my door bang open and I'm bolt upright in a split second, quickly realizing that I must have fallen asleep. The TV is blank, the movie long over judging by the sun streaming through the windows.

Vic is in the doorway.

'Time's up,' he mutters, striding forward.

He doesn't say another word, reaching over me and grabbing a very groggy Jane who's still in just a towel. He pulls her into his arms leaves the room without a backwards glance and I'm left in my bed seething with rage. I've never been so pissed off with our president. He might be in charge, but there are rules even for him when it comes to on-call girls. We don't just steal girls from each other's beds. Either Jane is one, or she isn't. He can't have it both ways.

The only thing that mollifies me a little is that I know that he'll make her want it before he does anything. Even Vic isn't so much of an asshole that he'll do something she doesn't want ... but then he's going to take her back and put her in that cell.

Fuck. That.

I grab a bag from my closet and start throwing stuff in; the blanket from my bed, some of her warmer clothes that Paris had delivered ... that I'm not ashamed to admit I relaundered myself so they don't smell like him anymore. I make sure there's everything she might need to make her as comfortable as possible down there.

If Vic thinks that I'm going to let him put her back in that empty cell with nothing but a nasty mattress to lay on, he's got another thing coming.

6

VIC

My jaw tightens as I grab Jane and she goes rigid in my arms, but I'm more annoyed with my own reaction than hers.

I've been resisting staring at the feed from the cell, but that doesn't mean that she's been out of my thoughts.

I don't fucking care about her!

But twice I've been thwarted, and this time I'm going to feed properly. That's all this is. I'm just hungry.

She smells like Theo, but I realized almost as soon as I picked her up, that it's only his soap. He hasn't fed from her. This was a ploy to get her out of the cell against my orders. I frown. How far does his insubordination go? If he's not careful, there's going to be discipline heading his way. Ignoring directives can't be tolerated in a clan like ours.

I carry Jane down the hall and into my room, closing the door behind me. I don't lock it, mostly because I think that'll spook her even more. I put her on her feet and then move away from her, but when I look into her eyes, it's not fear I see, it's anger. She doesn't move, just tries to stare me down as I take off my shoes, and then my socks and unbutton my shirt a little.

Her eyes follow my fingers and I wonder if I need to be more blatant with her.

'Do you understand why you're here?' I ask.

The look of contempt she gives me lets me know that she does and then she sneers.

'It doesn't matter what you do,' she says. 'Feed from me if you want to feed from me, but I'm not going to like it. You're not going to make me want it, asshole.'

I take a step towards her. 'Care to wager?' I ask.

She takes a step back.

'No,' she says, 'I don't.'

Hurt appears in her eyes for a second. 'You think you can just lock me in a cell and, what, bring me up here and make me feel so grateful that I'll just fall into bed with you? Fuck you, Vic, or is it *Alex*?'

She gives me a final look of disgust and turns away, taking those flashing eyes off me.

Wrong move, baby girl.

I'm scooping her up before she understands what's happening, and throwing her on the bed, ripping the towel away at the same time. But if I was hoping for a reaction, I don't get it. She lays there quietly, jaw locked, looking up at the ceiling.

Are those scratches on her arms and legs?

'What the fuck?' I hiss, pulling her arm towards me to take a closer look. Her nails are all broken and the scratches look red and angry. They're on both her arms and her thighs.

'Did you do this to yourself?'

She doesn't answer.

'What is wrong with you? If you think you're going to guilt me into ...'

Her eyes flash.

'You left me in the dark! I could feel things crawling on me. It was unbearable! I didn't do this for you. Not everything is about YOU!'

She goes silent. I see her lips start moving, but she's not saying anything.

'What?' I growl.

'Nothing!' she snarls back.

'Then what are you saying?'

'Nothing to you. I'm counting the stalagmites on the stucco.'

'Do you think that's going to stop you from enjoying it?' I ask with a grin.

'I have no idea,' she says and goes back to counting.

With a growl, I jump on the bed, pinning her but she stares defiantly past me, no fear in sight, and, fuck, it makes my blood heat. When was the last time a human challenged me like this. I don't think one ever has.

I keep a hold of her as I move slowly down her body, taking in her throat, her breasts, her navel ...

'Shall I show you what happens to insolent girls like you?' I murmur, humming a little against her pussy and biting back a smile as she shifts under me.

'No,' she says petulantly and I grin in spite of myself, licking all the way from the pucker of her ass to her clit.

I look up at her expression to see that she's trying very hard not to show that she likes what I'm doing.

'You can pretend all you want.' I rumble. 'I can smell how much you want me.'

She huffs. 'Believe whatever you want if it eases your

bruised, demon ego,' she says with a sweet smile and then gives me the finger.

My palm tingles. I would love to flip her over right now and spank that naughty little ass, but in her current mood I don't think that's my wisest course of action. Instead, I pull her legs apart and begin to lick her. She tries valiantly to pretend that she doesn't like it, that she isn't even feeling it, but she's suddenly very wet and I chuckle, pushing my tongue into her, fucking her with it and then releasing the glamor just from that part of me.

She gasps, her hips rolling when she feels my tongue's sudden change of girth, as it flicks inside of her.

'What are you doing? What is that?' she asks and I glance up to find her on her elbows, looking down at me curiously.

I roll my eyes and push her back down.

'You think too much,' I murmur and her mouth falls open when she sees my tongue. It's black, thick, long, and *forked*.

Her eyes widen.

'Holy shit,' she breathes, and then moans as I suck gently on her engorged clit.

Her hands fist the covers on either side of her, her legs shaking as she bites back a sound of pleasure. I can feel her muscles contracting hard as she comes, but I don't stop even when she tries to shy away. I grip her thighs hard, not letting her escape my greedy mouth.

I ease my motions, letting her pleasure mount again slowly and teeter on the brink. She's writhing, making little mewling noises. She covers her face with a pillow as if that's going to stop me from hearing the pleasure that I'm giving her. I don't say anything though. I'll gloat later. Right now, my tongue plays with her asshole as my thumb rubs her clit gently and she screams my name.

My real name.

The sound of it on her lips makes me groan and I realize I've just come in my pants like a teenager.

Embarrassed and hoping she doesn't notice the wet patch at my crotch, I draw back slowly and let her go. She doesn't move, legs splayed out in my bed. She's clutching the pillow to her chest and staring at the ceiling.

Bet she's not fucking counting now!

Breathing heavily, she peeks at me over the pillow, clearly wondering what I'm going to do next but I get up and go to the bathroom, turning on the shower. I don't need her or the others knowing what just happened, just how much I want her.

I shower quickly, throw on a robe, and come back out. She's sitting on the bed, the towel wrapped around her again.

I grab the Neosporin and coat all the scratches, hushing her when she tells me that Theo already did that.

'Get up,' I say when I'm done, and her face falls a little at my tone.

She heaves a sigh and gets up, wrinkling her face up like she's annoyed with herself.

Yeah, you aren't the only one.

I throw the Neosporin on my dresser and I grab her by the nape of the neck, thrusting her forward in front of me. I haven't fed properly, but I want to even though I don't need to now. That's the problem. It's not hunger that's making me ache to push her onto the bed and take her. It's just me wanting to be with her. To be close to her. To fuck her. Just her arousal has given me enough to sustain me for at least a couple of days. That's going to have to be enough.

I decide in that moment to call Maddox to loan us a couple of his clan's on-call girls. He'll be a dick about it, especially since I went to *The Circle* alone to see him the other night and paid him back for trying to steal Jane by breaking his nose. He'll definitely price gouge me for that, but I don't care.

He's got six or seven girls and at least they'll be vetted. It's not usual. In fact, it's downright weird to request another clan's stock, but we've known each other a long time. He'll say yes.

Jane is causing too many problems in the clan. Her mere presence is dividing us. I'll speak with Sie to make sure he's still feeling a hundred percent, but, with some luck, Jane's not going to be a problem for us after tomorrow night.

I push her gently toward the elevator and she deflates as we draw closer.

'It's just a cell,' I mutter more to myself than to her, letting her go as I feel my hand start to massage her neck in comfort.

Jane

I NEVER UNDERSTOOD what emotional whiplash was until I met this man. Hot. Cold. Sizzling. Freezing. Volcanic lava pit. Glacial crevasse.

I stare at his face, trying to get a glimpse at his tongue but it looks like it's gone back to ... I don't know. Normal? Is that normal or is his demon form the thing that's real? So far, I've only seen Sie when he was trying (and failing) to scare me, again in the gym that first time with him, and then a tiny bit of Korban the other night, and I'm curious. Do they all look the same? I don't remember Sie having a forked tongue, that's for sure!

He sees me staring. 'What?'

'Can I see you?' I ask.

'You're seeing me right now.'

I roll my eyes. 'You know what I mean. The other you. The demon.'

'No,' he growls and I think that I might have upset him.

I let out a harsh breath.

'I miss Bedroom Vic,' I mutter petulantly.

'That's it!' he says and, before I know it, he's pushed a button on the elevator and it stops descending.

He grabs the towel and pulls it away from me again. I gasp, rooted to the spot, trying to get a read on what he's doing because he's scaring me. He turns me around and bends me over, putting my hands on the rail. I realize there's a mirror in front of me that I didn't notice before and I watch, wide-eyed as his hand comes down hard on my ass.

I yelp and try to stand, but he has a hand on the middle of my back, keeping me where he wants me. His hand comes down again, this time on the other cheek.

'OW!' I yell. 'Get the fuck off me!'

'No,' he says. 'You are going to learn your place here.'

'If I'm going to learn anything by this, it's that you're even more of an asshole than I thought!'

All he does is smirk and that pisses me off even more.

'We'll see,' he says, his hand coming down again. 'Stay where you are, or I'll go harder. You're getting ten. Pretty lenient I'd say. Three,' he says aloud. 'The next time I do this, you're going to count out loud for me, baby. Four.'

'There isn't going to be a next time,' I seethe.

'Five.'

My skin under his palm smarts with his strikes and I clench my teeth.

'Six.'

I focus on the floor, not his punishment.

'Seven.'

My lip is wobbling. Fuck, it hurts.

'Eight.'

A tear falls from my eye followed by another.

'Nine.'

One more. Only one more.

'Ten.'

His hands leave me and I quickly stand up straight, wiping my eyes before turning to face him.

Five on each side. At least it's even.

He looks me up and down, his gaze on me somehow making this even more humiliating, but I stare into his eyes as he gives me the towel.

I snatch it back and wrap it around myself. Then, I face the door as he pushes the button and we start to move again.

I don't look at him. Though I'm not looking forward to going back to the cell, I want to be away from him. I sniff.

'You brought that on yourself,' he says low.

I ignore him.

I also try valiantly to ignore the fact that my core is clenching like my body wants more from him now. I didn't like being spanked, did I? I'm so confused.

The doors open and I walk across the wide garage, taking myself to the cell. The lights are on. I pretend I'm not afraid, but, fuck, I want to run away as I get closer and closer to that door at the back. But I won't give Vic the satisfaction of begging him not to leave me down here.

I'm Jane Mercy, motherfucker. I've spent ten years alone, on the run, and most of my friends have been murdered. This dumb cell is not going to break me. You aren't going to break me.

But as I approach the door, my steps falter and I have to make myself continue. Maybe he could leave the light on this time ...

No! Don't even ask him!

I go through the door and halt, my eyes widening when I see the cell. It's been transformed.

'What the fuck is this?' Vic asks from behind me.

I belatedly notice Theo inside the cage.

'I told you I wasn't going to let you return her to the cell the way it was,' he says, his eyes not leaving Vic's. 'It's far from ideal but at least she won't freeze to death down here now.'

My eyes take in the cell properly. The dirty mattress is gone, propped up on the wall outside the bars. In its place is Theo's own from his bedroom. There's a bag of clothes and a ton of blankets.

Vic pushes me into the cell hard enough for me to fall onto the bed and I turn to give him a look of disgust that I don't think he even notices.

'You and I are gonna have a reckoning, Theo.'

Theo gives a single nod.

'But not now,' he says and pushes the cage door shut.

Vic locks the door, his eyes not leaving me.

'You're staying down here with me?' I ask Theo and he nods.

'Have fun in the dark,' Vic calls over his shoulder as he turns off the lights.

I gasp, jumping to my feet as the pitch-black envelopes me and makes some of my bravado evaporate immediately, but Theo is behind me and he pulls me against his broad chest.

'I'll fix it in a second,' he whispers in my ear. 'Focus on me.'

I hear the elevator open and Theo chuckles as a light appears. It's a small camping lantern.

I grin at him, glad he thought of a light along with all this other stuff.

Then, to my shock, he unlocks the cell door, walks across the room, turns the light back on, and waltzes back over.

'I only brought the lantern down in case someone sees the camera feed and comes down to turn the lights back off and steal my key back,' he says.

'Thank you,' I say, but the words don't feel like enough.

I take his hand and squeeze it, wondering if he'll understand that touching someone voluntarily is something I rarely do except with those I trust.

He squeezes back and I'm relieved. He gets it.

'Do we have to stay in the cell if you have a key to get out though?' I ask, staring at the door that leads to the garage – and to freedom – with longing.

'Yeah, and I can't let you go either.'

'That's okay. I can't leave anyway.'

'Why not?'

'My friend Shar and her kids,' I say. 'I need to make sure they're taken care of. It's my fault …'

'What's your fault?'

'Uh, that my stalkers were going to kill her and her kids. I can't let that happen again.'

Theo sits on the bed, watching me.

'Again?'

I sigh, sitting next to him.

'Don't you know all about me from that file? The first one they killed was my mom … well, she wasn't really my mom, but she might as well have been. She was the only person who cared about me after my dad disappeared. They warned me and I didn't listen, so they killed her.'

Theo takes my cheek in his hand, cupping my face and turning me to look at him. 'That was not your fault. You were what, fourteen when that happened?'

I nod.

'You were a kid. This is no one's fault except theirs. Is that how they've made you do the things you do?'

'What things,' I ask.

What's he talking about?

Something passes over his face.

'Nothing,' he says quickly. 'Don't worry about it.'

I frown but change the subject. 'Do we *really* have to stay down here even though we can get out? We can't sneak upstairs just for a little while?'

'Nope. At least, not at the moment. Vic can be a stubborn asshole and his patience is running out. Push him too far now and—'

'You get a beating,' I interrupt.

Theo looks surprised. 'Maybe, but I was going to say he'll lock us both down here, take all the comfy stuff, and make sure we can't get out until he's good and ready, but you can show me your pretty pink ass later if you want.'

He winks.

My eyes widen. 'Do you do that too?'

'Not exactly, princess. Maybe I'll show you another time.'

'If we can't leave, you don't have to stay in the cell with me,' I say even though I'm crazy glad he's here and I would hate it if he left.

'Yes, I do. You're my patient. I'm not letting you stay

down here like that and I'm sure as shit not okay with you spending another night on *Hepatitis Mattress*.'

I shudder as I look at it looming by the wall. *Plotting.* 'Who have you kept down here before?'

'Supes and low-level fae mostly,' he says vaguely and I frown at another response that tells me nothing.

'Here.' He rifles through the bag and brings out some thick socks and sweats.

'Put these on,' he says. He even turns around.

'You've already seen me,' I say.

'I know and there's a camera hidden over there by that pipe,' he says, shrugging, 'but ... I'm sorry about this. I'm sorry about Vic. He has his reasons for putting you down here. He's going through a lot. I know it's not an excuse but—'

'You don't have to explain,' I say, looking down. 'I know I'm not really cut out for this. I'm really bad at it.'

Theo takes me by the shoulders. 'Jane, listen to me. I don't know what it is you think you know, but you're not in this cell because you are a bad on-call girl. You're not. Who told you that?'

'No one. I just thought ... I don't understand why Vic and Korban and even Sie sometimes seem to hate me. And I don't get why *you're* being so nice, or why Paris took me out to buy me things and get me pizza.'

Theo doesn't answer.

'Will you really stay down here with me?' I ask.

'If Vic won't let you upstairs, then yes,' he confirms.

'Your mattress is going to get all messed up on the floor,' I say.

'I'll get a new one.'

Theo gets up and thrusts a paper bag at me. 'I didn't have time to cook you something. I hope you like burgers.'

I nod, my mouth already watering as I sit cross-legged on his mattress and delve into the bag, thanking him for being the best demon ever. I'm starving. I couldn't eat when Vic brought food because I was too upset.

'What's going to happen to me?' I ask between mouthfuls. 'You can't stay down here with me forever.'

He looks grim but doesn't say anything and I stop trying. He's a closed book. They all are ... except Sie and Korban ...

'Ooh, fries!' I grab them from the bag. They're a little on the cold side but I don't care as I shovel them into my mouth.

I glance up at Theo and pat the bed next to me. He hesitates but then comes and sits down. I nudge his shoulder with mine and offer him a fry.

'I'm sorry I stole your cereal.'

'I knew it was you!' he hisses.

I smile. 'Just share it with me properly and we won't have a problem.'

7

KORBAN

I'm standing at the back, pretending I don't care if I see this or not, but really, I'm staying as far as I can from where Vic sits with Paris at the table as they watch the screen. I can smell her on our president, but I can tell he hasn't fed properly. Just the scent of her is enough to make me want her again and that can't happen. It might already be too late. All it takes is one time without protection as the humans say.

I turn my attention to the screen. The quality isn't good, but Paris has already told us that a lot of our files were corrupted. Another part of the attack to add to the list, I guess. I see Jane go into Vic's study. She looks at the desk, finds the dummy papers he left for her, and then leaves.

'Do we need more definitive proof than that?' Vic asks.

As far as I'm concerned, no, but as I survey the others' faces, I don't think they're as sure of Jane's guilt as they were two days ago. Things have changed in the time I was out of the house. I can't tell what Sie's thinking, Paris doesn't look convinced at all, and Theo isn't even here. I look at Paris again and I frown. I thought I could count on his support.

Now that Sie and Theo might be on the wrong side, I'm going to need Paris if it comes to a vote.

I watch Sie, wondering what's going on in that guy's head. He's been lurking around, watching her through doorways, sneaking into Paris' room when he thought no one was keeping tabs on him and staring at her in her cell over the monitors. He's clearly obsessed with her. Maybe he's still batshit crazy, he's just hiding it better these days.

'We keep her in the cell until tomorrow night,' Vic says. 'We can't risk anymore problems from her.'

Vic looks over his shoulder at me. 'I'm guessing tonight's meeting is cancelled?'

I nod. 'There's no need for it now anyway.'

'Why not?' Paris asks, glancing at me.

He's wondering where I've been for the past two days and I'm not about to tell him the details. He doesn't like it when I'm gone. It bothers him when he doesn't know what's going on, but it's better that he doesn't know the things I get ordered to do. Even Vic doesn't know the full extent of what I've been up to this time and that includes my little side quest. I hope he never does find out because I'd have no idea how to explain my reasons when I don't really know them myself.

'Because the Deviant Dogs don't exist anymore,' I tell him.

Paris looks shocked and I'm not surprised. They were the largest shifter pack in Metro.

'What happened?'

'A bomb took out their headquarters last night. Looks like all of their alphas were there celebrating one of their many holidays. Most were killed outright. The rest of their leadership are in the wind. The pack is in disarray. It'll be a long time before they're able to recover. If ever.'

'The Order again?'

'Looks like it.'

'This is insane,' Paris mutters. 'Even a month ago they would never have done anything that bold.'

'Well, their attack on us went so well,' I growl as I leave the room.

I wouldn't be surprised if they had plants in every major supe faction from here to the coast, but I'm not about to say that out loud. Paris worries.

Going back to my room, I take a look at my phone and bring up the feed from the cells downstairs just to make sure she's still there because I wouldn't be surprised if she finds a way to escape.

What I see on the camera makes my mouth fall open. Theo and Jane. Lounging on a … *is that his mattress*?

They're lying on it side-by-side, talking like they're in the fucking *Babysitters Club*. I frown. What is he doing? Even if he did go down there specifically to feed, I would have thought he'd be doing it by now, but again I see that there's something different with Jane in addition to the lull not working on her.

I lean against my bed and think back to that night when she was in this very room, my fingers finding the red thong that lives in my pocket. What is it about her? I haven't been able to fuck a human woman like that in a very long time. Usually Paris has to restrain them or lull them into a stupor so they can hardly move before I can get anywhere near relaxed enough to feed.

When Paris told me Jane couldn't be lulled and freaks at her hands being tied, I thought it would be harder. Actually, that's an understatement. I thought it would be nigh on impossible, but then she was in the room with Paris behind her, naked except for those little scraps of fabric that were soon gone ...

My cock stirs as I think about how she felt while she was on top of me, when she touched me and it felt like a caress regardless of how accidental it was. I panicked for a second, but then something else took its place. I enjoyed her hands on me and I want it again.

'Fuck,' I hiss and get up, going into my bathroom and turning on the shower as cold as it'll go.

I shuck my clothes fast, throwing them in the corner and get into the freezing spray, willing myself to think about Paris and not the delectable girl downstairs. Besides the energy they give us, nothing good can come of being with a human female, I remind myself. They're treacherous. Poisonous. No matter how innocent they seem, they'll turn on you as soon as they have the chance. I think about the footage that Paris was able to get from the Clubhouse before it exploded.

Jane already has turned on us.

One more day and hopefully this will be over. Some of our enemies will be destroyed and Jane will be gone one way or the other. I stare at the tiles in the shower for a long time, trying to convince myself that I don't care what happens to her. She brought this on herself by getting into bed with the wrong people.

I turn off the shower, my lust in check for now at least and I try not to think of her as I dry off and put my clothes back on, but I can't relax. I feel like I'm bouncing around like a pinball in my room. Usually I'd go find Paris, but I know he's busy. I head downstairs and through the kitchen, intending to hit the pads for a while, but, as I go by the door into the small library, I see it's ajar. It's almost always locked because it's a protected space in case of a fire. There are a lot of very old books in there that can't be replaced according to Vic, stuff his family's procured over the years.

I slip inside to take a look, down the small flight of steps and into the tiny room lined with raggedy tomes. By the smell that comes through the dust, I'm pretty sure some of them are bound in shifter skin. None of us particularly like it in here, which is why I'm surprised when I notice Sie in the corner with one of the oldest books in his hands.

He turns a page slowly, his finger running down as he reads. He looks up when he registers my presence and for a second I see something in his eyes. He doesn't like that he's been discovered in here. I'll bet he forgot that door doesn't latch properly unless it's locked.

'Doing some research for Vic?' I ask.

'Not really,' he says. 'Just making sure the books aren't deteriorating since nobody's been in here in a while.'

He slips the book on the shelf casually and walks past me, leaving the room. I look suspiciously at the one he put back and I frown at the title. *A History of the Supernatural.* I take it down and try to find the page he was on but I didn't get a good enough look.

I go back to the kitchen, closing the door to the library and locking it behind me. I hear the elevator ping and wonder if it's Theo coming back up, but it's descending. My eyes narrow. Where's Sie going now? I go into the foyer and take the stairs, emerging in the dark garage. I see Sie's silhouette watching the cell from the door, and I sneak up behind him.

He jumps and I'm surprised. There are few who can sneak up on Vic's Second. He's unfocused.

I look through the door at Jane. So pure. But the worst ones always look the most innocent. They make you lower your guard even when you don't want to. I'm ashamed to admit that I came back down here and turned the light on for her after we locked her in because I heard her whimpering in the darkness.

The things I do for this club ... to humans and supes alike. I torture them when I need to. I kill them. But I can't leave one girl in the dark? I go out into danger to avenge her in secret? What is wrong with me?

'What the fuck are you doing here?' I ask Sie, probably projecting my anger like my therapist says I do. 'Are you really this obsessed with the human?'

'Fuck you, Kor,' he says under his breath, turning around and going back to the elevator.

I sprint after him and slip in before the door closes.

'What the fuck are you doing? Having second thoughts about tomorrow? Vic told me you okayed it. She got under your skin, big man?' I goad. 'You shown her your real face? Your scars?'

'Fuck you,' he says again. 'I don't answer to you. I'm the Club Lieutenant.'

I practically bare my teeth, and I know I've lost control of my glamor, but I don't give a shit.

'Don't you dare! Don't you fucking dare pull rank when you've been a fucking shadow for months. I've been taking care of everything while you've been too out of your mind to do a damn thing to help this club and, what, now suddenly you're better? Taking things in hand? Bullshit. What's this girl got on you? Maybe it's not just her who's a fucking snake.'

I'm thrust hard into the elevator wall, and I push back, but Sie's got a good thirty pounds on me. His forearm across my throat cuts off my air supply.

'Careful, brother. You make an accusation like that, you better have something to back it up,' he hisses with a cold smile. 'Just because I don't fight for the Order anymore, doesn't mean I forgot how and we both know I could kick your ass so bad Paris wouldn't recognize you.'

I'm able to dislodge his arm just as the door pings open, and he strides out as I gasp for air.

'Yeah, fucking run away,' I mutter, but I'm disturbed by Sie's behavior. That's Theo gone and potentially Sie too. I definitely need Paris on my team because although Vic seems like he knows what's going on, this girl is getting inside all our heads.

I find Paris in his room, messing around with his many screens that are bolted to the wall behind his desk.

'What was that earlier?' I ask, not beating around the bush.

'What was what?' he mutters, not looking away from what he's doing.

'When we were watching Jane finding the papers Vic left out, you didn't look convinced. You know she's dangerous to us all.'

The roll of Paris' eyes is enough to make me have to hold back a wince.

Shit. I've lost a lot of ground.

'Look,' he says, his eyes finally coming to rest on me, 'you don't like humans, especially the females. I understand. But there's something else going on here and I think that your biases are blinding you.'

Shit. Not him too!

I step forward and check myself as Paris moves his chair back, a wary look on his face.

'Are Vic and I the only ones in this club with our heads on straight?'

'I just think there's more going on,' he says again.

'There's not. It's pretty cut-and-dry. That human bitch

downstairs is a member of the Order just like her daddy is. They're getting bolder and stronger and more humans are joining their cause every day and now you're all getting behind a female who has already shown us what she truly is. If I didn't know any better, I'd say she'd bewitched you. Maybe she's not human at all.'

'That's ridiculous,' Paris scoffs.

'Is it?' I ask, making myself wonder.

Maybe Sie knows something we don't. He can hardly take his eyes off her. I thought he was obsessed with her pussy, but maybe he's been watching her for another reason. The more I consider it, the more I think it might be true, but what creature could mask as a human so well that even her smell didn't give her away?

'No typical human wields the power over an incubus clan the way that she does,' I tell Paris.

'She's literally in a prison cell,' Paris chuckles, not taking my words seriously.

'With one of our own taking care of her,' I say, nodding.

'Theo's her doctor and you know he's got a soft spot for the humans.'

'It's not just that. Look at them,' I order.

I bring it up on my phone. They're still sitting on the bed, chatting like BFFs on a sleepover.

'When was the last time any of us had a conversation like that with a human?'

Paris looks at the phone and then at me dubiously, but I can see I've planted the seed.

'It won't matter after tomorrow anyway,' he says and he doesn't sound happy about it at all.

'So long as you realize that,' I say over my shoulder as I leave him alone to think about what I've said.

I want my love back in my corner and I'm not resting until I get him there.

Vic

MY CLAN IS MORE fractured than ever. I thought that if Sie's sanity returned, everything would be okay, but it looks like even Paris and Korban are hardly speaking to each other and it's because of Jane.

My eyes narrow as I look through the clothes that Paris brought for her, rolling my eyes at the sheer amount of them. Why did he buy so much stuff? There was never any way she was going to wear more than five outfits and he's got her thirty.

I scan them slowly, admitting that he does have good taste. She'd look great in all these things, but there's a specific appearance I'm trying to create tonight. I find what I want and, with a nasty grin I pull out the skimpiest dress I can find; low-cut, short, crimson, and bodycon. I'm going to make sure that Jane's reunion with Foley is as humiliating as possible for both her and daddy dearest. And then all of this will be over and we can go on with our lives.

My phone buzzes and I see a message from Maddox. He wants to know when I'm going to pick up the girls I asked to borrow. I send him a text back with one word.

'Tomorrow.'

I take the dress out of the closet, glancing at my watch. There's still an hour or so before we need to leave.

Fuck it, why not?

I go downstairs to the garage. Theo and Jane are still

lazing on the bed. He still hasn't fed from her. I don't get it. What's he waiting for? He's lost his chance now.

Theo sits up when he sees me, looking suspicious.

'You know what I'm here for,' I say to Jane.

She looks at me with her big, doe eyes, but, if anything, it makes me want to do this even more. I open the door and I wait. She gets off the bed, casting a glance back at Theo.

'Don't look at him,' I say. 'He can't help you.'

She comes with me quietly and I don't bother closing the cell, leaving Theo on the bed staring angrily at my back.

I take her up in the elevator.

'How's your ass?'

I smirk as her cheeks color and she looks down at the ground, not saying anything.

The doors open out into the second-floor hallway and I take her hand when she falters, leading her to my room. This time, I lock the door. Her eyes fly to it and then to me in alarm.

I don't take off my shoes. I don't unbutton my shirt. I don't care if I make her uneasy, but I do remove my suit jacket and lay it neatly over the chair in the corner.

When I turn back to her, I raise my eyebrows. She's looking incredibly uncomfortable, but she takes off her sweatshirt. I stare her down while she does it, wanting her to feel as awkward as possible before I show her that no matter what I do, I can always make her body respond to me without – *What does she call it?* – my supey mojo.

She's not the one with the power here. I am. Before we go, I want her to realize that.

Slowly, she eases down the sweatpants, pushing them off her heels with her feet. An accomplished seductress this woman is not but, somehow, watching her is hot as hell.

She stands in front of me in her little tank and underwear ... and her socks and I have to hide a grin because, fuck me, she does look adorable.

The scratches on her arms and legs are healing well and, in spite of how I should be reacting to an enemy, I'm glad of it. The thoughts I ought to be having about her try to intrude; that she's tricky and malicious, but I push them away. I've been impeded from feeding from this girl several times now. I'm going to enjoy this. I'm not going to feel bad about it, and, I look her up and down, I'm going to make sure she revels in it too; give her something to think about later when my plan is put into action.

I can't smell her yet, but if the hard nipples protruding from that tank top are anything to go by, she likes me watching her. Her eyes dart around though, not settling anywhere for too long. She's so nervous.

I love it.

I move towards her slowly like a predator, making her wait and I see the moment her fight or flight response kicks in. Her feet are shuffling around. She's stopping herself from bolting. I almost wish she would.

As if reading my mind, she suddenly makes a break for it, running across the room to the door and trying to unlock it.

I'm behind her in a second, pushing her into the hard wood and grinding against her.

'Now, now, Jane,' I whisper in her ear, 'you signed the contract, remember? What about poor Shar and her kids?'

Her breathing is hard as she looks back over her shoulder at me. She stops trying to get away, her hands resting on the doorframe.

'Very good,' I murmur, my hand coasting down her back to her ass where I grab a handful and squeeze. She rises on her tippy toes with a small squeal and I bunch up her underwear, pulling it up between her ass cheeks. I yank it hard as I spread her legs, making sure she can't escape me. I almost groan when the scent of her arousal hits me and I turn her around, practically tearing off her tank top. Her tits bounce into view and I lick one with my still-human tongue before I pick her up easily and carry her to the bed.

I put her on her back, but then I change my mind and flip her to her front, putting her on her knees, head down and ass in the air. I play with her underwear some more before I give her ass cheeks two playful smacks that make her body tighten with concern.

'Don't worry,' I croon, 'you haven't been a naughty girl, have you?'

She looks back at me with wide eyes and shakes her head. With a growl, I pull off her panties, the cotton ripping, and she gasps a little as my fingers part her ass so I can get a good look at both her holes.

'Good girl,' I say, noticing that her pussy is already wet for me and that she responds to my words.

I noticed that in the car before the crash too.

Baby girl's got a praise kink.

I grab her ass with one hand, my fingers digging into her. This time, I promise myself that I'll have a little more control. An idea comes to me and I remove my shirt and kick off my pants. I let my glamour down so that she can see my black skin and eyes. My horns. My tail. Her mouth opens, but she doesn't look afraid. She looks in awe.

'You're beautiful,' she murmurs and I shake my head at this weird little human.

I showed a girl once and I had to lull her immediately because she started to freak out, but this one ... I drag my claws gently down her spine and she shivers.

'Are you going to hurt me?' she wonders aloud.

'No,' I rasp.

Not directly anyway.

I shove the thought away and rise up on my knees to push the head of my demon cock into her pussy just a little. I think she's going to shy away, but she surprises me by pushing back onto it. It sinks it into her a little further and she closes her eyes, moaning softly.

I groan in response. 'You *are* a very naughty girl wrapped up in a *very* innocent package.'

She doesn't say anything and I roll my hips into her gently, easing out and pushing back in, the soft barbs of my cock make her tense and look over her shoulder to see what's making her feel like that.

I humor her, showing her my thick shaft. Ebony, spined, and practically pulsing with need to be inside her. Her eyes widen as she notices the spikes, and she looks a little bit afraid now.

'They'll feel good,' I promise, flicking them to show her how flexible they are. 'Not as hard as the rest of me.'

I smirk as I ease it in again and she lets out a low sound of pleasure. My long tongue flicks out and licks her asshole and she jumps, giving a high-pitched, shocked sound that I absolutely revel in.

I surge forward and begin to fuck her. I was going to take this part more slowly but I can't. My body drives her forward. I pull her back, my clawed fingers digging into her flesh, but not breaking the skin as I pound into her. The sounds of pleasure that she gifts me with make me even harder. My tail flicks around, coming to her lips. She stares at it for a moment and then opens for it.

With a moan of my own, I invade that pleasurable hole too and almost whimper as the sensitive tip of my tail is sucked on by that impish little mouth. I bet it would feel amazing in her tight little cunt, I think to myself. I can feel her pleasure building and the power of it surges into me as waves crash over her and she screams into the covers, the sound muffled by the smooth shaft of my tail stuffing her mouth full.

I wanted to luxuriate in this part, but there's not much time and I'm too aroused. I let loose in her, seeding her, my clawed fingers digging into her thighs. Everyone will be able to see the marks that I leave, and it excites me on a primal level that they'll all know she's mine. My tail leaves her and so does my cock, and I twist off her, falling onto the bed on my back.

Fuck, that was amazing. I wish I'd been able to do it sooner ... and more than once.

I glance at her. She hasn't moved but her eyes are moving over me, over my demon form.

She likes it.

I watch her in return and I notice the bruises that I've left on her. A moment ago, I was celebrating those marks as evidence of my possession of her and I'm not sure where my head was. Now, I can't help my dark smile. Whoever she works for is going to know who's she is tonight.

At my expression, hers shutters. Yes. She knows. *Bedroom Vic* is gone.

I get up and I go into the bathroom, turning on the shower and donning my human form. I was intending on just cleaning myself up, but then I have a better idea and I beckon her. She comes, but the guardedness is back in her eyes.

I draw her into the spray and I wash her gently, taking in her contours. She lets me soap her body before I hoist her up, her back to the cold tiles. I hold her as I lick her with my human tongue until she's quaking and wailing. I use it to take her to new heights before I lower her onto my cock again and fuck her more leisurely this time, feeding slowly and savoring every morsel that comes my way in my human body.

I'm surprised when her arms wrap around my neck and she gazes into my eyes. I put her under the spray, washing our bodies while we're still joined and it's not until the very end that I let her down.

I wash her intimately and she looks at the soap. I can almost see the idea as she gets it. She's getting bolder, I think. What would she be like if she stayed here with us, I wonder as she cups me, fondling me, and washing me. Her finger even delves very shallowly into my ass. Pushing her against the wet wall of the shower, I kiss her lips gently, relishing the taste of her.

She looks surprised, and I draw back.

'What is it?' I ask.

'I ... feel you,' she says with a gravitas that I don't understand.

Maybe it has to do with that neurodivergent brain of hers, but I don't ask her what she means. Instead, I turn off the water and leave the shower.

I pass her a towel without looking at her, suddenly afraid that I won't be able to do this.

'Come on. It's time to get ready.'

'For what?' she asks.

'You'll see.'

8

JANE

They've dressed me up again, even down to stupidly high heels they know I can barely walk in. To say I'm confused is an understatement, but as usual they're not telling me shit. I'm in a short, red dress that I definitely don't remember choosing when I went shopping with Paris. I suspect it was from the collection of horrible clothes he bought me before when he was trying to make me choose him and win Vic's game. I guess it was too much to hope for that all those outfits would be gone for good after I threw them out of Theo's room.

I look down, tracing the bruises that Vic left on my skin this evening. There's something weird going on. Well, a lot of things in my life are weird these days, but there's one specific thing that I'm worrying about right now.

After Sie and Korban fed from me, I thought I was just ... I don't even know ... *guessing* how they felt because I wanted to feel some kind of connection. I can never figure out how people are feeling at the best of times, so I figured I was imagining things.

But it happened again today with Vic. I *could* sense his

emotions in the shower. When he kissed me, I could feel that he liked it and me and I KNOW I wasn't making it up. But when I said something, Vic didn't seem to think it was important. Maybe it is just a side-effect of their supey mojo that no one bothered to tell me about. It wouldn't be the first time they hadn't told me the things.

The demon himself is right next to me and I glance at him, but he doesn't look back at me. I stare at the floor of the limo, at the four-inch heels that he tossed at me as we were leaving. I told him I couldn't wear them and he snapped at me to 'just fucking put them on or your friend Shar's house payment doesn't go through this month'.

I did what he said with shaking hands, my mind in shock at his icy demeanor. Then fell over when I tried to walk in them, so he carried me to the car while I silently raged at the humiliation. The guy who showed me his demon form, who fucked me to orgasm with his interestingly shaped demon dick is gone like he never existed.

Emotional whiplash!

They're all here. All five of the Iron I's. I look at each of their faces. Korban stares back, but he's the only one. None of the others will even meet my eyes and I'm feeling uneasy.

The last time I felt like this, they locked me in a freezing, pitch black cell.

I focus on Korban and wonder how this empath thing works. I reel back a little as it comes through like I turned on a facet full-blast and fury is spraying everywhere. He's angry. Really fucking angry and it makes me cringe away.

How do I turn this thing off?

I focus on Vic instead, but I don't get much. He's buttoned up on the inside as well as on the outside. So, I try Sie. His is harder. Where Vic has almost nothing, Sie is a Thanksgiving cornucopia of feels. There's more than one emotion coming off him. He's a Shrek. Lots of oniony layers.

Anticipation. Anger. Sorrow. Guilt.

He feels bad about something but is also looking forward to whatever we're doing.

'Is someone going to tell me what's going on?' I finally ask.

'Just wait' is all Vic says.

Theo's playing with something in his pocket. He does that a lot and I think maybe it's when he's trying to calm down. I fiddle with my hair and nails and put my fingers near my mouth to relax and unwind, so I can relate, but what's he worried about?

Sie is staring out the window. Paris' eyes are going back and forth between Korban and Vic like a kid whose parents are fighting.

We're parked in the dark under a broken streetlamp and all around us are warehouses not unlike the ones we walked through that night we escaped the cops at the strip club, but it doesn't have the same weird aura, so I don't think it's a bleedy-fae-world-area. It's just a late-night, dock-side spot. There are a couple of vans parked close by, but I haven't seen any other people at all since we got here and we haven't moved in at least an hour.

Vic's watch begins to beep and he stops the alarm.

'Showtime,' he murmurs.

They all turn their heads in the same direction and I follow their eyes. At first, I don't see what they're looking at but then I hear a squeaking sound and the wide, old-fashioned delivery door of one of the buildings on the corner opens a fraction.

A van with no headlights on drives quietly towards it and my eyes flick to Vic to find him watching me intently. I draw back, wondering if it's because I'm leaning on him a little to see what's happening over his shoulder.

'Are we meeting someone?' I ask.

None of them answer me and I go from worried to seriously starting to get a very bad vibe, which probably means that everything is already much worse than I think it is and we're potentially in real, actual danger here.

The van stops at the warehouse door and some guys get out. I can't see them all that well because of the low light, but I'm pretty sure they're human.

'Where is he?' Korban asks.

'Who?' I reply.

Vic answers Korban, ignoring me completely. 'The type of artifacts I put in that manifest are too valuable to trust with grunts. I know him. He'll be here personally for this.' His eyes find Sie. 'I know being so close to him is gonna be hard for you to take but lock it up. This is a long game and if you want him to get his due, we want him caught.'

I wonder what Vic means, but Sie seems to know what he's talking about, giving the Club President a single nod.

'Don't worry, Alex,' he grates out. 'I'm saving it all up for the right time.'

He looks straight at me. He's ... *worried* about me.

He turns to stare out at the street again and the sensation disappears.

'Tonight isn't the right time,' he murmurs.

The men in front of us begin loading boxes into the van almost silently and a black SUV turns onto the street from the other direction. It's lights are off and it goes slowly too, rolling to a stop just behind the van.

'The others are in place?' Vic asks quietly.

'Torun said they'd be here. Too late now if they're not,' Korban replies, glancing at me and then back outside.

Torun? Wasn't he one of the fae from the strip club?

I take a deep breath, hoping the fae *won't* be turning up because I want to be nowhere near this place if they do. I don't know who these guys in the warehouse are, but it looks like they're stealing from the supes ... or the fae.

They're sooooo fucked!

The door to the warehouse slides open the rest of the way all at once, the sound thunderous in the deserted street. There's a dim light inside and I can see the silhouette of a few more guys moving things around.

I let out a harsh breath. 'Will someone please tell me what's—'

I stop talking as a figure gets out of the SUV on the side that I can see and I squint. There's something familiar about him. I cant my head, trying to think. I'm sure I know that profile. I scramble over Vic to get closer to the window, straining my eyes to get a better look at the man who alighted from the car.

He directs the men. It looks like he's in charge as he points and they start loading the van with the boxes from inside the warehouse again. I can hear them talking in low voices to each other through the cracked window, but I can't make out what they're saying.

And then the man's face turns towards the light and my heart skips a beat.

Daddy?

I haven't seen him since I was a kid. That can't be him, can it? I second-guess myself. I'm bad with faces but I wouldn't forget my own father ... I'd be able to recognize him even though it's been well over a decade, right?

I clamber for the door. None of them stop me and I don't think to wonder why as I throw it open and leap out onto the wet street, making my way towards him.

'Dad!' I call, my echoing through the street.

He shifts to look at me.

I try to run towards him but only get half-way before I slip, sliding on the asphalt and scraping my knees.

Fucking heels!

I get up and make it the rest of the way, vaguely noticing that the men have stopped to stare, but I ignore them all in favor of the one in front of me.

It's him. It's my dad!

I throw myself at him, hugging him around his middle.

'Daddy!' I cry.

An arm comes up to wrap loosely around my waist and it's a few seconds before I notice he's not hugging me in return.

I draw away, looking at his face, wondering if I've made a mistake and it's not him at all. *That'd be embarrassing!* No, it's him. It's definitely him, but why isn't he hugging me back?

'Daddy?'

He doesn't say anything. Then, he looks over my shoulder at the car where the Iron I's are. I look as well. The window is open and I can see Vic and Korban just watching us from inside. When I look back at my dad, he's smiling, but it's not a happy smile, it's one that chills me.

'The fuck is this?' one of his men behind him asks.

My dad doesn't answer him. Instead he makes a point of looking me over, taking in the crimson, bodycon dress and the dumb shoes, his eyes lingering on my legs.

'So that's where you've been,' he mutters. 'You're a whore for the supes now.'

My brow furrows and it dawns on me what he's seeing. The short, low-cut dress, the bruises ... *the implications.*

He pushes me hard in the shoulder and I take a step

back to regain my balance, teetering on the heels and shaking my head.

'Daddy,' I whimper as reality comes crashing down and I see how stupid I am, realize what Vic – what the Iron I's – have done.

They knew my dad was going to be here. Vic dressed me like this. I look down at the fingermarks on my skin that everyone can see. He made sure that it would be glaringly obvious to my father what his little girl had done tonight ... and who she'd done it with.

I swallow hard and I try again. 'It's not like that,' I say, belatedly noticing that not only have almost all the men stopped what they were doing, but they're finding reasons to stand close enough to get a good look at me.

One of them chuckles. 'You're in the wrong part of town for a pick-up, baby.'

'He said she's a supe whore.'

'She's calling him daddy.'

'You can call me daddy, sweetheart,' another calls out and a few of the guys laugh.

My dad's ignoring the comments. He hasn't taken his eyes off Vic who's still in the car. Then he winks at the Iron I President.

'Be seeing you, demon,' he calls.

He turns away from me.

'This is a set-up,' he says. 'The supes'll be here any second. Time to go, boys.'

I grab his arm. 'Wait!'

He turns around and backhands me across the face casually, like he does this all the time. I fall to the ground with a cry, tears coming to my eyes as I look up at him. He leans in.

'The apple really doesn't fall far from the tree,' he whispers and even I can see the anger and the disgust in his face.

When he turns towards his men, he shrugs and laughs their comments off.

'What can I say,' he says, 'these girls can smell money a mile off.'

Cue more laughter as my dad gets back in the SUV.

'Get out of here, whore,' one of the guys close by says, kicking a dirty puddle at me while I'm on the ground.

The rain falls harder and the emotions swirling inside are a jumbled mess. I'm drowning in them. I don't look back at the Iron I's. This was their plan. My cheek hurts where my dad hit me and I don't know what to do.

As the cars book it out of there, the decision is taken out of my hands as all hell breaks loose around me. I'm given a second's notice because there's an unmistakable charge in the air and every human knows what that means. Magick. Fae magick. And *that means* you better fucking run!

But I'm frozen in abject fear for a millisecond, a thousand thoughts going through my head all at once. Thoughts like, *I'm a human in the open and they're about to start throwing magick around... OMFG I'm so gonna die. My dad doesn't love me. I'm wearing shoes I can't run in. I'd love a hot chocolate right now, I'm freezing. I need to get out of here. Ugh, I hate the rain! Why did Vic and the others do this to me? Fuck, I'm cold.*

I push everything back and I get my shit together, rising unsteadily to my feet. The shoes make me slip in the wet street as I attempt to run for cover. I manage to get around the corner before my ankle goes over and I fall with a wail, something popping and making my stomach flip.

Dragging myself up, I try to move. There's a blast of magick behind me followed by an explosion. I can hear men screaming, yelling. I can see fire through the dirty ware-house windows.

I shuffle down the street, the pain in my ankle making my stomach revolt. I can feel the magick behind me and everything in me is screaming that I need to get the fuck out of here.

I see an alleyway and get down it so at least I'm out of sight. I unbuckle the shoes and kick them off, throwing up on the ground next to me while I'm at it. I get ready to run – or at least hobble – as fast as I can.

But there's a part of me that's wondering why I'm both-ering, that's just now realizing how much I had pinned on the hope that I'd see my dad again one day, that he wasn't dead and he'd come for me and he'd be like Daddy Warbucks and we'd ride off into the sunset together or something.

But the way he looked at me ... I push the mental image away as I feel like hurling again. There's no time to sit in the street if I actually do want to survive – and I find that I do if only to spite the Iron I's who brought me here ... hoping for my death, I guess.

How did Vic know who my father was? How did he know he'd be here tonight? Why did he make certain that my dad would see his daughter in the worse possible light? There are so many questions and I need the answers, but even if I ask the Iron I's, I doubt they'll tell me anything. They're probably long gone anyway now that they've ripped apart whatever there was left of my old life.

The fire is spreading and the smoke is getting to me. I leave the alley and limp across the street to where there's less light and I can hide myself better.

A car screeches to a halt in front of me and the door opens.

'Get in,' Theo orders.

I shake my head. I don't want to go with them. I stand in the open, almost unable to comprehend what's happening. Why do they want me to get in the car? So they can torture me some more? It's Vic who gets out, lunging towards me and grabbing me. I struggle wildly, scratching, biting, kicking. I want to make him hurt the way he's hurt me.

I'm thrown inside, landing hard on the floor of the limo. The car begins to move fast, and I stay down, winded, as Korban barks orders to the driver.

I lay in a ball on the scratchy car-carpet, trying to keep in the tears as I look at the Iron I's. My bottom lip trembles and I stare at Vic accusingly. I find I can't actually speak any words. Too much just happened and I'm reeling in every possible way. I hide my face in arms.

The car goes for a while and no one says anything at first, but then, the one who finally does speak is Paris, of course.

'I don't understand what happened back there,' Paris murmurs. 'Is this another trick?'

None of the others answer him.

I feel their eyes on me and I make sure mine are dry when I raise my head up to look at them. I put my shoulders back and don't let them see what they've done to me. I still can't say anything.

We get to the house and the garage door opens. The car parks inside and we get out. I ignore Theo's proffered hand, getting out by myself and wobbling to the back room. I go to the cell. It's still open from earlier when Vic took me upstairs to enact his nasty little plan.

I go inside it and shut the door. It locks behind me. I don't touch any of the things that Theo brought down.

Instead, I sit on the floor and stare at the wall, trying to figure things out.

They come into the room, peering through the bars in silence. I don't get anything off Vic or the others like I did in the car, but I have a feeling that it's me. I mean I can't even deal with my own emotions right now, so theirs would probably send me into a tailspin.

Theo tries to talk to me and I ignore him. Luckily, none of them try to enter the cell because to be honest, I would choose violence.

One by one, they leave slowly until Vic's there by himself.

'What was that back there?' he asks.

I flick my eyes to him and open my mouth. It takes a minute, but I'm finally able to force out the words. 'You have all the answers,' I say. 'You probably already know.'

He stands there for a little while longer and then he leaves. He doesn't turn off the light this time.

I stay on the floor for a few minutes, but I start to get cold. I use the bars to hoist myself up to standing. I know they're probably watching me on the camera, but I don't care. Swallowing my pride, I get on the mattress. I'm a pragmatic gal and there's no point in cutting off my nose to spite my face.

Hidden under the covers, I let my tears flow. I always thought my dad loved me. I have memories of cuddles and him helping me with my homework, of cooking me dinner and showing me how to deal with bullies.

But the things he said to me ... Why was he even there tonight? Why was he stealing? He was a history professor. Why would he take anything from the supes? I've heard a couple things the guys have said to each other about missing shipments, but I don't understand any of this.

I lay back, putting on the headphones that Paris got me. My phone is dead, but at least I can't hear that drip. Closing my eyes, I try to come up with a plan. I need answers and I'm pretty sure the Iron I's have all of them.

Sie

THE SILENCE IS PALPABLE. We're all sitting in the living room except Jane, who's locked herself in the cell downstairs.

As I look around the room, all of us seem lost in our own heads, trying to process what just happened.

'Did Torun's people get Foley at least?' Paris asks.

Vic shakes his head. 'The fucker got away.'

I slam down my mug at Vic's words, my calming chamomile tea sloshing over the table.

Vic looks at me apologetically. 'I know how much you want him, Sie.'

No, you don't.

'This was the first time he's been out in the open in a place where we could get to him and the fae let him get away? This is bullshit! You should have let me get out of the car and go after him myself. If I had, *he'd* be in our cell right now instead of *his daughter*!' I rage, wishing with everything in me that Jane had been nowhere near that shitshow tonight.

The only positive thing that may possibly have come out of what happened is that I now know for certain that Jane is a human. Whatever I thought I saw or felt with her at the strip club before must have just been a coincidence. No supe would ever have been able to endure what she did in that street and not let *something* of their other side show no matter how disciplined they were. It's just not possible.

But the rest of tonight was a calamity wrapped in a catastrophe, and for what? For Foley to escape and Jane to be, perhaps irrevocably, hurt for no reason other than Vic's ego.

My eyes flash at my best friend.

'You made me choose revenge over her!' I accuse Vic and I don't know if I can forgive him for it.

But maybe the person I actually won't be able to forgive is myself.

'I didn't make you do shit!' Vic thunders in return. 'You wanted revenge and you decided that sacrificing Jane was worth it if you could get to Foley. I'm not denying I've made mistakes with her, but don't you dare try to lay that shit at my door, Sie!'

'He wasn't scared of us,' Kor mutters, interrupting what is likely to become an all-out brawl between us very soon. 'That human needs to be taught a lesson on how dangerous the Iron I's can be.'

'Well,' Theo says, standing up and going to pour himself yet another drink, 'at least Jane learned it, huh? And, hey! Bonus! We got to humiliate her, got to watch her own father and her own kind look at her like she was a piece of shit. And then, the best part *I thought*; we did nothing as he beat her in the street. Great job, everyone.'

He raises the cup in salute to Vic. Then he takes a gulp, swears under his breath, and knocks it all back, hurling the vessel at the wall when he's done.

'I mean, *what the fuck just happened*?' he asks loudly over the glass shattering, the bourbon and his anger clearly loosening his tongue because he's not usually the one who stands up to the MC President.

Vic regards him with an angry glint in his eye.

'What do you want me to say, Theo? Do you want me to tell you it didn't go to plan? Because that's a lie. I dressed her up and I humiliated Foley with his own corrupted daughter. I made sure there was no way he couldn't know that the enemy he despises has tasted what's between her thighs. And don't act like you didn't know what was going to happen tonight.'

'Shit,' Paris mutters, standing up and walking to the window. 'This is so fucked up.'

I agree.

'This is a war, boy!' Vic thunders. 'Go shopping with her, play your little games with her, but at the end of the day remember *what we watched her do* on that tape, remember that she is not what she seems to be, remember that she can *and did* hurt us!'

Now Vic stands and I feel the power surging through his tight control.

'I'm this Club's President because I can make the hard choices. Did I want to do that to her? No. Did I want to piss off Foley? Yeah, I did and I don't regret it. That asshole and his followers are a dangerous problem that needs to be gone.'

'Well, maybe next time we actually take Foley out instead of destroying his daughter,' Theo says.

I stand and put my hand on Theo's shoulder, trying to calm things down because this in-fighting is getting us nowhere. We have a hurt human girl in a cold garage and we need to deal with her first.

'If you keep drinking,' I say, finally speaking up, 'you won't be able to treat her tonight.'

Theo puts his head in his hands.

'Fuck,' he mutters, 'this is a shit show. We should have told her to leave the bar the moment she came in.'

Vic's face is impassive but I can see that he agrees.

'What are we going to do about Jane?' Paris asks, echoing my thoughts. 'We can't just keep her in the garage.'

'Neither can we trust her,' Korban says. 'I say we leave her where she is.'

Vic shakes his head. 'The cell was only supposed to be a temporary measure. We all thought she'd be gone after tonight, but the temperature is dropping. It'll be too cold for her down there long-term.'

'But if we let her back up here—' Kor starts.

'If we let her back up here, we all do our part,' Vic interrupts. 'She's not to be left alone and don't give her phone back.' He glances at Theo. 'Sober up and then take her up to the clinic to make sure she's okay. Once I hear from Torun, we'll figure out our next move.'

The others leave, but Vic motions for me to stay. Once everyone's gone, he turns to me.

'I'm sorry we didn't get Foley, but that aside, what are your thoughts on Jane?' he asks.

'I think,' I say with a long breath out, 'that things aren't exactly as they seem.'

'What do you mean?' Vic asks.

'Her father didn't react like a parent who cares for his child.' I shake my head. 'Even taking into account his hatred for us, the way he looked at her ...' *made my blood boil.* 'It was like she was nothing to him. He was also not very surprised to see her whereas she hasn't seen him since he disappeared when she was a child. I'd put money on that.'

'You don't think it's an act?'

I don't stifle my laugh. 'That girl couldn't act if her life depended on it. Watch her properly. She's as open as a book if you look at the right moment and she doesn't lie if she can help it. She's almost compelled to tell the truth, all of the information she has. If she's an agent of the Order, then I'm a fae lord.'

'You *have* been watching her closely. Why this obsession with her?'

'Because my gut has been telling me there's more to her, more to this. Why did Foley leave his daughter to be raised by strangers? Why does he hate the supes with such passion? No one even knows when he joined the Order or why. He was a teacher fifteen year ago. And how does he constantly seem to be a step ahead of us, of the supe authorities, of the fae? They should have caught him tonight. Why didn't they?'

Vic looks grave.

'So, what? All this was a coincidence? The bomb, the car accident, the shooting, our damaged camera files? How do you explain the Order being there tonight if Jane didn't feed the information to them about the fake shipment?'

I sit down heavily in one of the chairs. 'We've been focused on Jane because she was the most obvious choice, but let's say for argument's sake that it isn't her. Who could it be? Who else had access to the house? I keep thinking that there would be no point in destroying the video files unless there was something to hide. We need the rest of the footage. Maybe someone else went into your office. In truth, it could be any number of people. There were humans all over the place setting up for the party after the fight and then all the guests at the party itself. Maybe someone stole the information long before you left it out for Jane to see.'

Vic nods, thankfully accepting my council and I realize I've missed being his right-hand-man.

'You've raised some good points,' he says. 'Maybe you're right. Maybe Jane was just a convenient target who was in the wrong place at the wrong time. We need the rest of the videos cleaned up. I'll get Paris on it.'

I go to leave, but I turn back, knowing I need to say something to my best friend.

'Jane is strong but even she won't be able to take much more from us,' I warn.

'What are you saying?' Vic asks.

'Maybe she's suffered enough. It's obvious that we aren't going to kill her. It might be best to cut her loose.'

I see in Vic's face that that's the last thing he wants to do. She's under his skin just as much as she is mine. Even Kor is getting the Jane bug. He just doesn't see it yet.

I leave before I say anything else, going up to my room and firing up my laptop. I bring up the feed to the cell. Jane is laying on the bed under the covers, so I can't see her.

'I'm sorry,' I say quietly, knowing I need to make things right with her somehow, but having no idea how to even start.

There's nothing to see, and I know Theo will bring her up soon, so I minimize the window and settle in to do some more research on the Order and on Foley.

We need to get that fucker. *I* need to get him. Maybe then I can finally put the past behind me.

9

THEO

I sober myself up with a cold shower and a snack before I go down to see Jane. I'm furious at Vic for what he did tonight, but I'm more pissed off with myself for not trying to stop him. As soon as I saw her stagger out in that little red dress, I understood what his plan was. The humans aren't like supes. We all know that. We see how their females are scorned if they revel in sex the way that many of us do.

I spent the entire car ride trying not to stare at the bruises on her thighs that Vic had clearly put there on purpose. She seemed to be completely oblivious about what was going to happen even though she was supposed to have seen the paperwork and must know where we were going. And then her and her dad ... that had gone so much worse than I'd imagined and, if Vic's face was anything to go by, he'd agree with that though he won't admit it.

When I finally pluck up the courage to go downstairs, she's in the bed under the covers. I put the key in the lock and turn it, the sound reverberating through the garage. I cringe at the echo.

She sits up in the bed. When she sees me, she looks away and flops back down, but she takes off the headphones which gives me a sliver of hope.

'What do you want?' she asks, her tone devoid of emotion.

'I'm here to take you back upstairs.'

'Finally going to actually feed from me?' she prods. 'Don't forget to give me a bath first. I know how you like to pretend to be my savior before you hand me off to Vic. Or is it Korban this time? I guess it depends on which one of the Iron I's hates me the most, huh?'

And because it's been a fucking night and I'm pissed off with pretty much everyone, her goading tips me over the edge.

'Careful,' I growl low, stalking forward.

'Or what? You'll threaten me with Shar and her kids? You're a big, powerful demon, Theo,' she scoffs. 'Congrats.'

She's right. I'm being a dick. I pull it together and sigh as I sit on the bed. 'Maybe you're right about me.'

She looks up and I get the sense I've surprised her.

'I'm sorry about what happened. The truth is, I can't save you from Vic. However much I want to, I can't go against him except when he lets me. It's clan magick and it's strong. I can promise you that I'll protect you as well as I can from everyone and everything else.'

'Why would you promise something like that to me?' she asks, looking more perturbed than grateful.

'Because I care about you.'

She wrinkles her face up and draws her head back, clearly thinking I'm lying, but if she doesn't believe me, I promise myself that I'll show her.

'Can I see your ankle?'

She rolls her eyes. 'Fine, but only because it really hurts

and I'm afraid it's broken and I wouldn't want it to heal wrong and cause me a lifetime of pain.'

She doesn't notice my amused expression of course.

She moves her leg out from under the cover. It's swollen and purple on one side. I touch it and she hisses in pain.

I turn it this way and that.

'It's just a sprain,' I say.

'Just? It hurts like a bitch.'

'It'll be better in a couple of weeks.'

She shrugs. 'Okay well as long as it's not broken, I guess, but where will I be in a couple of weeks?'

'Not down here,' I say. 'Come on.'

'What about your mattress?' she asks.

'I'll burn it. I got a new one delivered already.'

I pick her up and swing her gently into my arms, making a mental note to come and get her stuff later. I carry her into the elevator.

She doesn't rest her head on my shoulder. Instead, she just watches me. As the doors close, she lurches forward and kisses me hard. I stagger back, pulling my mouth away because this isn't her.

'What are you doing?' I ask.

'My job. I'm a supe whore. That's what my dad called me. I might as well act like it even if I am so bad at it, you probably laugh about me with each other when I'm not around.'

'It's not like that,' I say with clenched teeth.

'Of course it is. It always is. Humans. Supes. Fae. All the same in my book. What I want to know is why you bother with all this seduction crap. Why not just feed from me like Vic and Sie and Korban? Why pretend you're something else? Something better? You're fucking liar, Theo. *You like me,*' she mocks and gives a brittle laughs.

'Bullshit. Did Vic send you down to make sure I wasn't about to ... How did you put it the other day when I was in your tub? ... Do something stupid? Well, you don't need to worry about me trying to off myself. I'm stronger than you assholes think.'

'I'm so sorry, Jane. I didn't know what Vic was going to do.'

'Yes, you did. As soon as you saw me you must have known his plan. You ignored my questions. You let Vic bring me without one word of argument. You let me get out of the car without even attempting to stop me.' Tears come to her eyes. 'I saw my dad for the first time since he disappeared when I was a kid. I didn't even know if he was alive, Theo.' She grips onto me hard like she needs a lifeline to say these words out loud. 'You used me to humiliate him. Did you hear the things he said to me?'

'I heard,' I whisper. 'I'm never going let anything like that happened to you again, Jane.'

She closes her eyes and rests her head on my shoulder. 'I only had one dad. There's no one else anyway.'

'I'm going to check you out in the clinic,' I say, shame burning through me.

She doesn't say anything more and the elevator doors open. I take her to my exam room and put her on the table. She watches me as I grab the bandages and wrap her foot up gently.

'I'll get you some ice packs for the first couple days,' I say. 'After that, we'll apply heat.'

She nods, looking despondent, indifferent.

'Hey,' I say, cupping her cheek and turning her face towards me. 'Please tell me what I can do to fix this, Jane.'

'There's nothing,' she mutters. 'You all keep showing me what you are. Maybe this time I'll remember the lesson. I just,' she heaves a sigh. 'I just keep forgetting that I'm alone when all of you are around me.'

'You're not alone, Jane.'

Her eyes narrow and she gives me 'a do-you-think-I'm-fucking-stupid' look.

'Of course I'm alone,' she says. 'I have been since they killed Angie. Everyone I get close to I have to leave.'

She points at me suddenly. 'You know what you can do? You can stop using your supey mojo on me. You and the other guys need to quit making me want you all the time. It's mean.'

I frown at her. She still doesn't know that our incubus powers don't work on her. If Vic hasn't told her, it's for a reason. Knowing him, it's probably a power play, but the truth is the least I owe her after all this. I try to ignore the fact that if she thinks we've been using it on her then she's been wanting us 'all the time' without it.

'Sweetheart,' I say slowly, 'our supey mojo doesn't work on you. It never has.'

She freezes, her mouth opening and closing. She starts to speak and then stops. She looks like her mind is blown.

'But that doesn't make sense,' she argues finally, sitting up straighter in confusion. 'What about all the times that I've wanted you and the others to ...'

Her cheeks color and she goes quiet.

'All you, baby,' I say with a small smile.

Her eyes widen. 'That's not possible.'

'Why isn't it?' I ask. 'Is it so hard to believe that you'd be attracted to us?' I grin. 'I mean, we're pretty hot, Jane.'

'N-no,' she splutters. 'It's because I'm not like that.'

'What do you mean?' I ask.

'I mean,' she takes a deep breath, 'I can count the number of men I've ever felt attracted to on one hand.'

My eyes narrow. 'But that's only fi ...just the Iron I's?'

She nods hesitantly.

'You never wanted anyone before us?'

She shakes her head. 'I thought it was because of ...' she taps her temple. 'I thought I couldn't let go enough to feel like that or maybe my brain didn't know how to handle it or something.'

She shivers.

'Are you cold?'

She's watching me strangely.

'No,' she says. 'I know this isn't the right time, but can you lock the door?'

'Why?'

'I want to feel better and I don't want to be alone.'

'I won't leave you alone,' I say.

'It's not enough.'

'What are you asking for, Jane?'

But I think I know and I'm not a good enough man to say no to her tonight.

'Do you want me to take you to my room?'

'No,' she says, looking around my clinic. 'Do it here.'

Jane

I DON'T KNOW what I'm thinking of. I'm mad at Theo, aren't I? But, right now ... being in here.

I am angry and hurt by the Iron I's and my dad, but it's been pushed to the edges of my mind. Being alone feels like the worst thing ever right now, but there's something more. I want Theo just as I did before in this room. It's not only about comfort; it's a deep need that must be satisfied. No different than breathing.

Theo hesitates and I resist the urge to clutch onto him for dear life. What if he doesn't do what I'm asking? What will I do then? I legit feel like I might die.

'Sit up, Miss Mercy,' he says in *the voice* and I almost sob with relief.

I do as he says and he eases the straps of the red dress off my shoulders. I stare into his eyes and he into mine, but he's looking for something.

Fear. Hesitation.

He won't find either.

He eases the fabric down, freeing my breasts. His eyes flicked down just for a second.

'Stand up, please,' he says, all business.

I get to my feet carefully and he peels the dress down my torso. It falls to the floor.

'Get on the table.'

I lie down on the soft leather and relax, staring up at the white ceiling.

'I'm going to tie your hands, Miss Mercy.'

My eyes fly to his and my heart begins to pound.

'B-but,' I stutter, my body tensing all over again.

'Don't worry,' he says, hovering over me and giving me a light kiss on the lips. 'You'll be able to get out of it if you need to, okay?'

I nod uncertainly, wondering if I should trust him. I don't think he's a bad person ... or the worst demon. In fact, if the conversations we had in the cell are anything to go by, we actually have quite a few things in common.

I thought maybe we were friends. But then tonight happened and I realized that any relationships I've formed here, however unintentionally, are hollow.

He sees the shadow in my eyes and cups my face.

'Say stop and we'll stop,' he says in his normal voice.

I nod.

'Hands above your head, Miss Mercy.'

I stretch my arms out and he locks my wrists into place. It's cold. Metallic. I take a steadying breath and then another, pulling slightly. They rattle a little, but don't give.

'Relax,' he tuts. 'The button's here.' He puts my finger on it. 'Press it.'

I do and both the clasps unlock, freeing me instantly.

'Okay,' I nod again and he locks me up.

His hands caress my arms to my shoulders, down my sides and my thighs to my legs. He straps them down and then does something to the table. It comes apart right up the middle to where my ass meets the seat, spreading my legs and then he moves the table pieces up and in, raising my legs and bending my knees, giving him an unobscured view of my core.

'Remember, you can ask me to stop at any time. Now, tell me, Miss Mercy,' he drones, 'have you ever been to a gynecologist?'

'No.'

'I'm surprised at you, Miss Mercy. Sexual health is very important.'

I tense when I realize I can't move my legs back together.

He clicks his tongue. 'Do I need to restrain you further?'

How could he possibly restrain me further?

But I shake my head.

'Then let me finish my examination,' he says, snapping on a pair of white surgical gloves that make my eyes widen.

What have I let myself in for?

He pushes my legs wider than they were before and I

give a squeak as he parts my labia gently, giving my pussy a thorough visual inspection.

My muscles clench under his perusal and I bite back a moan. I would never have thought I'd find this so hot in a million years. I'm one kinky mofo. Who knew?

He leaves for a few seconds, going around the curtain and coming back with a tray of implements.

'What are all those for?' I asked faintly, staring at contraptions I've never seen before.

'Well, you'd know if you'd ever visited the GYN, Miss Mercy. Why haven't you ever been?'

I shift under his gaze, getting the impression that he's annoyed that I've been neglecting my body.

'I didn't really go to the doctor. It's expensive and I never had insurance.'

Then, I frown at him. Why am I explaining? It's not my fault medical costs are out of control and my finances didn't lend me to unnecessary expenses.

'I'm a human waitress, demon. I chose to have a roof over my head and food in my belly over invasive doctor visits.'

'Touché, human.'

He leans over me, the bulge in his pants pressing against my pussy and I fight the urge to squirm against him, instinctually seeking friction.

'We'll discuss how you're going to put your health first going forward after this exam, but you're long overdue for one of these, Miss Mercy. I'm going to have to be *very* meticulous.'

He steps back and picks up a metal contraption that has me wanting to re-*re*think this entire thing, and it's on the tip of my tongue to tell him to stop.

But I don't.

'Do you know what a speculum is?' Theo asks as he coats the metal shaft in lubricant.

I swallow hard. 'I think so.'

'Good. I'm going to use it open you, so I can see your cervix.'

'Do you need to see that?'

He nods. 'Definitely. Especially if no one's ever looked before. It's important to have regular checkups.'

Before I know it, he's easing the cold metal inside me and I gasped a little as he widens it.

'Very good,' he says. 'We'll take it nice and slow ... this time.'

He pushes my legs a little wider as he bends down and shines a light inside me.

'Looks healthy, Miss Mercy,' he says a minute later.

I open my mouth to ask how he can tell when there's the unmistakable sound of his clinic door opening. I gasp and I hear him swear.

'Just a second,' he calls, taking the gloves off and leaving the speculum inside me.

I shake my head.

'Sorry, Miss Mercy, I'll be right back.'

Theo darts around where the curtain meets the wall and I hear Paris' voice.

'You don't have her on your table, do you? Let me see!'

'Absolutely not. You know my rules and why didn't you knock?'

'Aww! C'mon, Theo. You let me watch on the cameras when you ate her out in your bedroom.'

I feel my cheeks heat. I'm so confused. I finger the button that will free me. On the one hand, I'm terrified that Theo's going to let Paris come in to see me like this. On the other, I want him to.

'That was not in my clinic. Out!'

The door closes and Theo comes back through the curtain looking rueful. 'He's gone. Sorry. Everything okay?'

I give a tiny nod, sighing with relief – I think – and he's putting on a pair of clean gloves and stepping back between my legs in an instant. Twisting the speculum a little, he pulls it out and then pushes it back in, making me groan, wanting so much more than he's letting me have.

He eases it all the way out and puts it back on the tray, eyeing my chest.

'I suppose you've never done a breast exam either,' he says.

I shake my head and he tuts again. 'All women should know how to examine their breasts for hardened lumps.'

'Yes, Doctor,' I say with a grin.

'Have you ever had a catheter inside you?' he asks.

My eyes bulge as I shake my head. 'Are you into that?' I whisper, wondering how that can possibly be a sexual thing, but he only shrugs, not letting me know.

He pulls my labia apart, touching me with his fingers, poking and prodding. He pushes against my clit and I shift on the table. I can see by his smile, he knows exactly what he's doing.

'I'm going to give you an internal exam now,' he says.

'What do you have to do for that?' I ask.

'No more speculums, don't worry,' he smiles, taking two of his fingers and holding them up. He doesn't wait for my reaction, just slips them inside of me. I gasp as he does *something*.

'That's your G-spot,' he murmurs, doing the same motion and making me whimper. He pulls them out abruptly.

'Almost forgot,' he says, picking something up that I can't

see from the tray. 'Just need to make sure your temperature is okay.'

My mouth opens wide as something thin is pushed into my ass.

He winks at me and inserts his fingers into my pussy again. I gasp at the sensation. It's not a *fullness* exactly, but I can feel what's in the back and I can feel his fingers as well. He starts to pump them in and out gently, and I begin to writhe on the table as his expert fingers make my pleasure mount.

He leans down and gets very close, his fingers still working in me, and he takes my clit in his mouth, sucking gently.

I moan loudly at the feeling of his lips around me. I don't know what he's doing, but I've never felt anything like this before. It's so different than when he did this in his room that day while Paris was watching the camera feed.

I feel him chuckle against me.

'I thought you might enjoy this,' he says as a wave of pleasure hits me and my helpless body shudders. 'It pays to know a woman's anatomy intimately.'

I arch off the table with a cry, pulling at my bonds as his fingers work me harder and his tongue flicks my clit fast. I feel that need in me diminishing, being satisfied by what he's doing to me.

Finally, my body collapses back down. He rises from between my spread thighs with his fingers in his mouth. He sucks them clean as I watch and then he pushes the button on the cuffs that I'd completely forgotten about.

My arms come free and he puts the table back together, unbuckling the straps.

'I think that's enough for now,' he says.

I sit up feeling a little lightheaded and a little self-conscious. Why did he stop?

'Is everything okay?' I ask.

He shakes his head. 'Yes, it is,' he replies. 'I'm sorry. It's just I shouldn't be doing this now. Not after what's happened today. I don't want to take advantage of you.'

'You're not taking advantage,' I huff, a little annoyed with his White Knight Syndrome, or whatever it's called.

'That's what you would say if I was taking advantage. You might not even know it.'

'That's ridiculous.' I roll my eyes. 'I'm an adult. I know my own mind.'

I get off the table as a nasty thought crosses my mind.

'This isn't because I'm autistic, is it?'

I cross my arms over my chest as I pin him with a stare, remembering the time a well-meaning teacher in my new middle school saw me kissing a boy my age and made such a stink about it that, by the end of the drama, everyone in the school knew my diagnosis and the boy wouldn't even look at me. I still recall that teacher's words to me while we were waiting for Angie to pick me up, telling me that I must tell a 'caregiver' if anyone ever touched me on my chest or between my legs, as if I was a much younger child than the other girls in my grade who had boyfriends and everything. Ugh! The whole thing still makes me cringe.

'Don't you dare treat me like an on-call girl when it suits you and then infantilize me the next moment.'

Theo puts his hands up. 'I'm not. It has nothing to do with that. I promise you it doesn't.'

He sighs and envelopes me in a hug that I'm not expecting. 'I want to keep going. I really, really want to, but I'd rather know that you're okay.'

'All right,' I say, not really believing him.

He takes a syringe off the tray and I draw back, remembering what he did last time.

'No more drugging me.'

'Relax. This is just a painkiller for the ankle. It won't knock you out.'

I eye him suspiciously, but he could have done worse while I was on his table and he didn't. He's clawed back a little trust. I let him stick me in the arm.

He puts a little, round Band-Aid over the needle prick and hands me some sweats from a chair in the corner. I put them on, being careful of the ankle, but it's already feeling a lot better.

The rest of me is feeling better too. Maybe I really am as strong as I told Theo I was earlier. But I don't understand why the Iron I's took me to my dad to humiliate him. Maybe demons are just casually cruel like that for kicks.

But they didn't seem like they were happy when they brought me home. They'd been expecting something else to happen. What my dad did wasn't part of their plan.

The more I'm mulling it over, the more I think there's a bunch of stuff going on that I don't know. Vic knew who my dad was, probably from the file he had on me. But it was more than that. My dad seemed to know the Iron I's and they seemed to know him like they'd met before. I think back to what was said in the car. Vic told Sie not to do anything, so Sie specifically has a vendetta against my father, something that's personal. But what could my dad have done to him?

I need to find out what's going on. I wonder what the odds are of the Iron I's telling me dick. Theo's my best bet at this point. He's the one who let me know their power doesn't work on me, which is another crazy revelation. All the times

I thought they were *making* me want them and it wasn't them at all. It was me.

'While we're still in the clinic, do you mind if I ask if you've ever been on any medication for the autism?'

I jump at Theo's words because I was so busy thinking that I'd almost forgotten he was here.

'Trying to medicate me, Doc?'

He takes a step back, using his hands in mock supplication. 'I'd never presume.'

I snort. 'I was on something for a few months a couple of years ago, but I didn't like it.'

'Why not?' he asks.

'Well, it made my thoughts ... funny. Almost *manic*. Also, it messed with my body.'

'How?'

'Made me nauseous sometimes. Also ...'

'Go on,' he encourages.

'... I couldn't come,' I murmur, looking away.

'Ah. That's a common side effect for those kinds of drugs.'

'Yeah, well it might be a common side effect, but no one bothered to let me know.' I roll my eyes. 'Anyway, I do *that* to release tension and I couldn't, so it made me even more frustrated than just dealing with regular, everyday life. It wasn't worth it.'

He nods. 'Okay. No meds. Come on. Let's get something to eat.'

He takes my hand and leads me slowly into the hallway.

'Cereals?' I ask hopefully as I limp along just behind him.

He looks back with a frown.

'No, not cereals. Not fries, not burgers.'

I narrow my eyes. 'Don't try to keep me from them. You'll

never find the boxes without me. I've hidden them in a place you'll never, ever look.'

'Don't worry. You can keep them.'

I smirk. 'I know I can! Like I said, you won't find them, demon.'

He shakes his head, chuckling a little. 'You can help me make something healthy.'

I wrinkled my nose. 'That doesn't sound nice. Can't we just get a pizza?'

'No, Miss Mercy,' he says. 'As your physician, it's important for me to ensure that you're eating properly and getting the nutrients your body needs.'

'Well, that may be, Doctor Wright,' I reply as we go down in the elevator, 'but my mental health requires double cheese and pepperoni.'

He laughs, and I smile even though I'm feeling a little bit of trepidation as we get to the bottom and the doors open. We go into the kitchen and I see in the living room off to the side that the others are in there just hanging out. I guess they use this room like they did the games room in the other house. It's kind of nice that they spend time together.

I can't help the next unhelpful thought: That I wish I was able to relax with them.

Why do I want to be around them so badly? Why am I drawn to them when they treat me like shit?

With a sigh, I turn my attention back to Theo who moves around the kitchen, grabbing ingredients out of the fridge and putting a pan on the stove.

'Go sit down,' he says, gesturing to the other room. 'I got this.'

I glance into the living room. 'I'd rather stay in here,' I whisper as I sit at the breakfast bar and watch him throw some chicken breasts in a pot and cover them with a bunch of other stuff I can't even name.

I never learned to cook, mostly because I've never had a real kitchen. Sarge and other cooks over the years showed me a few basic things like how to boil an egg, but that's the limit of my cooking know-how. I get jobs as a waitress so I can eat the food where I'm working.

I hear the TV in the other room and, pulling up my big girl panties, I stand up and tiptoe over. I look through the door to see what they're doing. Vic is sitting in the corner, going through paperwork with his laptop open and his glasses on. Fuck, he's hot when he looks like a nerd. Too bad he's the most gigantic asshole ever.

Paris and Korban are sitting on the couch together watching *Great British Bake-off*, Kor's arm draped around Paris' shoulders in a casual show of affection that'd almost be endearing if he wasn't a demon who hated my guts.

Sie is lounging in the corner. I think he's reading at first, but when I actually look at him properly, I see he's surreptitiously watching me. He's just pretending to read. I stare at him for a minute. He hasn't spoken to me since that night at the club and I wondered if I'd done something wrong. But then last night happened and he didn't do anything to help me either.

I don't know how I feel about these demons anymore. I want to say it doesn't matter. I'm under contract. As long as they don't kill me, I'm pretty sure they can do whatever the hell they want with me and I should just be grateful that Shar and her kids aren't dead and that I'm not either. But this is what I do. I push things away and pretend they don't hurt so I can keep moving forward. I don't dwell because if I did, I wouldn't be able to get through my days. But I can't help but wonder where all these feels I don't let myself have go. Is there some part of me that's decaying and black and rotting because I never actually deal with the bad things?

The truth is, I was doing this for Shar, but after tonight, there's a new purpose now too. I want to know who my dad actually is and why he left me. I want to know why the Iron I's contracted me in the first place and why they've hurt me like this for what seems like no reason.

I glance back at Vic and I see that he's watching me as well.

'Turn off the TV,' he says to the others.

'But it's the semi-final.'

Vic gives Paris a look and Paris shuts the TV off without another word.

'We need to talk,' Vic says to me.

'About locking me up in the dark, dressing me up to embarrass a father I hadn't seen in years, or putting me in a position to be killed by the fae?' I ask.

'Come and sit down.'

I shake my head, walking backwards towards the kitchen.

'I'm not going to hurt you.'

'I don't believe you,' I whisper and I see something move across his face.

His fist tightens at his side. That means he's angry. I pull away instinctively before I pick up whatever emotions are coming from him. I don't want to feel the connection between us. This demon is the most dangerous of them all to me. I understand that now.

Step aside, Korban.

Vic stands up and I take another step back.

'Can you talk later?' Theo asks from the kitchen. 'It's almost dinnertime and she hasn't eaten in hours.'

'I'll make it fast,' Vic says, holding something out to me in his other hand.

I put my own out hesitantly and he drops a small pill into my palm.

'What is this?'

'I told you, we need to talk.'

'So what's the pill for?' I glance over my shoulder accusingly at Theo. 'You said no meds.'

'This isn't me,' he replies.

'For if you lie,' Vic says. 'It'll cause you pain if you do.'

'I don't understand. Why would I lie? What would I lie *about*?' I ask.

Korban scoffs from the couch. 'You've been lying since you got here.'

Vic swings his head to look at him. 'Enough.'

'Take it or I'll make you take it,' he tells me.

I feel the force of his power on me and I wince, turning my head away. I thought it didn't work on me – maybe it's just the sexy stuff that doesn't.

Great.

I throw the pill at him.

'You can't make me do everything you want just because I signed a piece of fucking paper,' I hiss.

I turn my back on him and go back into the kitchen, regretting my foray into their turf. Theo puts two plates out on the side with what looks like some kind of chicken stew, rice and broccoli on them. His hand takes mine and squeezes it.

'Are you okay?' he whispers. 'I'm sorry. I didn't know he was going to try that.'

I shrug, not wanting Vic to ruin dinner; the first dinner anyone's cooked for just me since Angie.

'I just want some questions answered,' Vic says from

behind me and I jump a little as I turn around and he's just behind me.

Creepy fucker.

'You could just ask me,' I say stiffly.

He nods.

'After dinner,' he says, going back into the living room. I hear *Bakeoff* back on a minute later.

Theo and I eat together in the dining room. The room itself is formal and I can't take my eyes off the chandelier hanging over the mahogany table. There's a glass of white wine in front of me that he says pairs nicely with the chicken and I humor him, but to me wine is wine.

I try to eat my dinner with some manners. I do know some. I've seen TV shows. I sit up straight, and I use my knife and fork and I take small bites.

'It's really good,' I say between mouthfuls because talking with a mouthful is apparently uncouth.

Theo keeps the conversation flowing, telling me about medical school and about his family who live in upstate New York.

I don't notice when I start feeling woozy, but Theo looks concerned from the other side of the table.

'Jane? Sweetheart, are you okay?'

'I feel funny,' I murmur, gripping onto the edge of the table.

I see Vic in my periphery.

'You asshole,' I say as the room spins. 'You slipped it in my dinner.'

Vic catches me in his arms before I fall on the floor. 'Sorry, Jane, but we need answers and we don't trust you.'

'Fucking ditto,' I whisper, my eyes closing.

10

VIC

Her grip on my shirt loosens as the drug begins to take effect. I straighten and turn towards the door in time for Theo to hit me hard in the jaw.

'You fucking asshole!' he yells, echoing Jane's sentiments.

I grit my teeth, not wanting to retaliate with violence nor with my power while I'm holding Jane between us.

'I'm sorry if I ruined your little dinner party,' I sneer, 'but we need answers to questions. We need the truth.'

'That's not why I'm ...' He turns away, running his hands through his hair, his hand flitting down to his pocket, but he clenches his fist and doesn't start playing with the stethoscope I know is always in there.

'You can't keep playing these games with her.' He shakes his head. 'You can't continue to treat her like this.'

'Treat her like what?'

'The cell, the humiliations, acting like you care about her one minute and then giving her the cold shoulder the next. She needs stability. She needs to know where she stands. She needs some semblance of a routine. I know you,

Vic. You read up about her neurodivergence. You know what you're doing. Don't act like you don't realize that you're using her autism against her, trying to break her even now.'

I stare at him, more than a little shocked. I locked her in the cell because I knew it would affect her senses, but that's all. Does Theo think I've done more than that? Is that what they all think? *Shit, have I been doing that*? It's possible. I'm a product of my father, after all. It's what he would do.

'You know exactly what I'm talking about,' Theo continues. 'You're going to hurt her in ways she can't come back from. You might have already. You can't just do whatever you want to her and expect no repercussions. It doesn't matter that you're the President of the Iron I's. It doesn't matter who your family is. Even you don't have the power to keep her from being irrevocably damaged by your actions.'

I make myself smirk and roll my eyes. 'You're being dramatic. What repercussions could there possibly be? She's ours. No one in our world cares about one human who's signed her life away regardless of what the media wants everyone to think. The fae certainly don't. They do this shit all the time. Where do you think the drug came from?'

'I care! Paris cares! And I think you care too.' Theo throws his hands up in the air. 'But you're intentionally misunderstanding what I'm saying. You know what I fucking mean. And what exactly did you give her anyway?'

I leave Theo to his self-righteous anger and take Jane into the living room, intending to put her in a chair in front of us so we can question her properly.

'Just a little faerie flower to loosen her up.'

'Faerie flower?! Are you fucking crazy? How did you even get that shit?' Theo rails from behind me.

'With great difficulty. Don't worry, the sprite I bought it

from said it's fine for a human in this dose. She's just going to feel high with a side helping of truth.'

'Fuck. I'm not going to be a part of this.' Theo turns and stomps out of the room.

I look down and find Jane staring at me with wide eyes. Her breathing is slow and she's looking past me. I look up too, but there's nothing above my head.

'How are you feeling, baby girl?' I ask gently.

'Weird,' she says. 'You gave me something and I know I'm supposed to be really mad at you, but,' she blinks and her eyes become unfocussed and she looks afraid. 'It's not forever, right? I'll go back to normal, won't I?'

There are tears in her eyes and I silently curse myself for what I've done *again*. Maybe Theo's right about everything.

'It's only for a little while, sweetheart,' I promise, trying to soothe her. 'It won't make you like this for very long.'

I try to put her down, but her grip on my clothes turns vise-like.

I push away the feeling that this was one of the biggest mistakes I've ever made. I had to do this. I'm the leader. It's up to me. Did I want to? Of course not. But I make the decisions my clan can't.

I don't let her go. Instead, I sit on the couch. I see Theo return quietly, hovering by the door to the kitchen to keep an eye on her just like I knew he would because he's a doctor first.

Kor is across from me, sitting forward in the chair and looking expectant. He wants to begin.

'Are you sure she's going to be okay on that stuff?' Paris asks, sounding concerned.

I cast him a look. 'Some of the human addicts take it all the time,' I say. 'She'll be fine.'

Sie wanders closer, his face bleak. 'How long will she be like this?'

'The sprite said it'll metabolize relatively quickly. We should have about an hour though.'

Theo steps closer. 'Should?'

Sie sighs, leaning over and moving the hair that's come out of her ponytail from her face. It's a gesture that's so tender that I'm taken aback. Sie hasn't been himself for so long that I'd forgotten he had a teddy bear side.

I try to ignore it, to focus on what I'm doing right now.

'All humans are a little different. He wasn't sure.' I say, glancing at Theo.

'Wasn't sure?' he spits.

'Look, I got it from a reputable vendor, but it is an illegal drug,' I snap.

'I can't fucking believe this,' Theo mutters. 'Her crimes don't matter. This is so far past cruel and unusual punishment.'

'Good thing the laws of the humans don't apply to us then,' Korban says. 'Get on with it. Time's a wasting.'

'Jane, can you hear me?'

'Yeah,' she says on an outward breath.

'You're going to answer some questions for us.' I shift her so she's sitting more upright. 'You have to tell the truth, okay?'

'What happens if she doesn't?' Paris asks.

'The drug will ignite her nerve endings,' Theo mutters angrily from the door.

Paris looks over his shoulder. 'What does that mean?'

Theo's eyes fall on me and then to Jane. He's furious and I deserve his wrath. He doesn't answer Paris' question.

'Fae Intelligence use this on their human captives for a

reason,' I mutter as my own eyes fall to Jane. 'Don't lie, sweetheart.'

'What's your name?' Korban asks, impatient to begin the interrogation.

Her hand comes up and fiddles with where my beard meets my hairline.

'Jane,' she says, not looking at Korban. 'Jane Mercy.'

'Who are you working for, Jane?'

'Nobody.'

Korban catches my eye.

'Who are the Order, Jane?' I ask.

Her brow creases as her fingers ease into my hair.

'Focus, Jane. Who are the Order?'

'They're supe-haters.'

'That's right. Do you work for them, Jane?'

She shakes her head. 'Nope.'

'Then why did you burn our Clubhouse?' Korban asks, standing up and looking over her.

Her eyes shift to him, but she doesn't cower.

'I didn't. Why would I do that?'

Korban's eyes narrow. 'So you don't work for the Order, but are they your friends?' he asks, making sure he's covering all the bases.

'I don't know anyone in the Order,' she murmurs, closing her eyes.

I tense, expecting her to feel pain at the lie, but nothing happens.

Korban locks eyes with me. 'The drug's not working.'

'Unless she doesn't know it's a lie,' Paris says. 'If she really hasn't seen her dad since he left, she wouldn't know he's part of them.'

My forehead creases. Could it all have been a coincidence?

'When was the last time you saw your father, Jane?' I ask.

'Last night.' Her face falls and she shuts her eyes.

'And before that?'

'He took me to get some lunch.'

I look down at her, ignoring Korban's triumphant expression.

'How old were you, sweetheart?'

'Ten. We had ice cream after.'

'Do you have any other friends we should know about?'

'Only Shar,' she murmurs. 'Sarge is dead and I always go no-contact once I move on, so no one gets killed.'

She opens her eyes and stares at the ceiling with a giggle at something we can't see.

'I tried pot once,' she says. 'I didn't like it. I don't like this either.'

She grabs onto me hard, panicking again. 'What if I don't go back to normal? What if I stay like this?'

'You're not gonna stay like this,' I say calmly. 'It's not going to last much longer. Now, what's your dad's name?'

'Donald Foley,' she murmurs.

She looks sad. 'I don't remember him being such an asshole when I was a kid. I can't believe he said those things to me. Who does that?'

'Jane, who sent you to us?'

'Sharlene from the diner. I told you that before.'

'I know you did. Just a couple more questions, okay, baby? Where did you get the orc stone?'

She frowns. 'I think I told you that too. It was my mom's. I didn't know what it was until last year. A woman stopped me in the street and told me to cover it because some supes might kill me for it, and a fae definitely would. She was a witch and she had purple hair and a jeweled cane. There was a yellow cat following her and she was trying to make him leave her alone but he—'

'Enough.'

Korban snatches her from my arms, holding her off the ground in front of him. 'Who was in on it? Who attacked us?'

'I don't know.'

'I want names!'

'Regina. Mark. Sandy. Roy. Tim. Kelly.'

'Trust you to be a smart ass even when you're high,' Korban growls.

He's clearly taken aback when she suddenly laughs.

'What if you guys' demon forms were pink?' She dissolves into a fit of giggles. 'That'd be hilarious. You'd all just be like super adorable monsters!'

Her hand comes up and caresses his face and I leap up from the couch, expecting him to lose it and hurt her, but he doesn't.

He looks from her to me, and I almost laugh at his bewildered expression. Korban isn't used to humans not being afraid of him.

Then he smirks. 'One last question, Jane. How much do you want a repeat of the other night with Paris and me?'

Her eyes clear for a moment as she stares up at him.

'I don't,' she says.

Then her back bows in his arms and she shrieks, high-pitched and agonizingly.

Korban looks surprised, changing his hold to cradle her instead of giving her to me when I reach out for her.

'Tell the truth!' I tell her as she continues to writhe, crying out in agony. 'Tell it and the pain will stop.'

'ALOT,' she screams, collapsing into him as the pain evaporates.

She whimpers, hiding her face in his chest.

'Why did you ask her that?' Paris asks Korban, looking angry.

'Wanted to make sure it was working.'

'Bullshit,' Paris says. He leaves the room and Korban stares after him, his face unreadable.

'It wasn't her,' Theo says. 'All of this punishment we meted out to her and it wasn't even her.'

'We need to figure this out,' Korban says, still staring at the door Paris disappeared through and holding Jane.

'Yeah, we do,' I say. 'Somebody take her.'

Theo comes forward, but it's Sie who gets to Kor first. He gathers Jane into his arms and goes and sits in a chair in the corner with her.

'This doesn't make sense,' Korban says. 'You're sure the drug worked.'

'You saw for yourself that it did. She only lied the once. We've been looking in the wrong place, punishing the wrong human.'

I glance at Jane, snuggling into Sie's large chest and I look away, even more ashamed. It's not something I often feel, but its warranted now.

'Your suspicions were right,' I say to Sie. 'Someone else went into my study and got that info. It's plain to see that it wasn't Jane.'

I take out my phone and message Paris to ask how far his program has got with cleaning up the video files from the Clubhouse before the explosion.

Theo paces around the room.

'A lot of things are plain. Like the fact that she hadn't seen her dad since she was a kid and you made whatever that was the other night the first time she'd seen him in over a decade,' Theo says, twisting the knife in my gut.

'I had no way of knowing,' I say, but my defense wouldn't stand up to a paper plane.

Theo sits, watching Sie comfort her, murmuring soft words. Her eyes are closed and it looks like she's succumbed to sleep. Hopefully she'll be back to normal when she wakes up.

She's going to be so pissed at me and I deserve it.

'So what, it was a coincidence that she turned up with that orc stone?' Paris asks, coming back into the room suddenly.

'There are no coincidences,' Korban mutters.

'Then maybe all this happened for a reason. Maybe it was instigated,' Paris says. 'Who's to say the fae aren't somehow in on this? They don't do direct assault. This has their stink all over it.'

'We need to find out who else looked at that fake paperwork.'

'I'll find them,' Paris promises. 'But it'll take time. What's left of those video files is like a digital mire.'

I pour myself another Scotch. 'I need to think.'

I leave them, going down into the garage to the gym door, but instead I find myself in the entrance to the cell. It's empty again. I guess Theo cleared out all Jane's stuff. I stare at the space for a long while, thinking about all the reasons this human should hate me. All the reasons *I* should hate *her* are rapidly disappearing and there's a part of me that's terrified. If I have no reason to keep her at arm's length, I won't be able to. Except for her fury when she wakes up, of course.

A part of me is actually looking forward to it. I want her to punish me. I need her to. I want her fury to consume me to make this right. Then, I'll apologize. There will definitely be groveling involved, maybe even some magickally binding promises made. I will make this up to her properly.

But what if she can't forgive me? Us?

I shake my head at my thoughts. When did the President of the Iron I's care about anyone's *feelings*?

But I do care about hers. I care about *her*, I realize and it's not something I can distance myself from. She deserves me on my knees in front of her, begging her forgiveness and she'll get it if that's what she wants. That and more. But will it be enough after everything? I want her to smile at me the way she does at Theo. I want her to talk to me. I heave a sigh and turn to leave. I find Sie behind me.

'Where's Jane?' I ask.

'Theo's with her. We need to talk,' Sie says.

'What about?'

'Her.'

My phone rings. 'It's Maddox. I need to take this. We'll talk later,' I say. 'For now, just make sure she stays in the house.' I leave the garage, taking the call on the way upstairs.

'I thought you were going to pick up those on-call girls,' he says.

'Change of plan. We've decided to keep ours.'

'Interesting. Would you consider a trade?'

That's more interesting.

'No,' I say without missing a beat. 'She's ours.'

'A pity,' Maddox mutters. 'Oh well, I'm sure I'll get over it. Anyway I heard about the authorities showing up at Ada's the other night. There's some other information that's recently fallen into my lap too and I think we need to have a conversation in person. I'm in Metro for a few days. Come to *The Dark Lounge*. Bring your human if you like.'

'After what happened with her at *The Circle* last time, no fucking way.'

'Callaghan has been dealt with. Permanently. He won't be bothering anyone again.'

I'm surprised, but I don't let on. Why would Maddox get rid of Callaghan, his best fighter, for Jane? A part of me whispers that Jane could be Maddox's but she already told us she's not working for anyone.

I decide we *will* go to his club in Metro and I'll ask him directly then. I want to see his face when we talk and when he sees Jane again. There's something here that isn't adding up.

'We'll come. I'll text you when.'

'Good.'

The line goes dead as I enter the living room. Korban is sitting on the couch looking a little lost.

'Everything okay?'

'Nothing's okay,' he sneers.

That's a fucking understatement.

'Where's Jane?'

'The human is upstairs with Paris. He's trying to calm her.'

'What the hell happened now?' I ask, ignoring the urge to go and find her myself.

He shrugs. 'I don't care.'

I pause and really look at my enforcer, in that moment realizing that he does care. A lot. More than he's admitting even to himself.

So that's all of us now. We each have a soft spot for Jane. We like her far more than we should, far more than we cared for any of the others. When did we stop seeing her as merely a means of our survival? When did she become more?

Maybe that's why I took her betrayal so personally.

Except that she didn't betray us at all.

I take the steps two at a time. I'm going to see Jane and I'm not leaving until I've apologized properly.

Jane

Paris is holding me tightly, but his pretense of giving a shit isn't really helping.

Why did they do that? Why did Vic do that?

What information do they think I have?

I'm shaking a little and my eyes keep watering. Whatever fae garbage Vic slipped me is starting to wear off and my brain functions are feeling a little more 'normal' again, but I'm jittery and I feel sick.

'I'll be right back,' Paris murmurs and lets me go, easing me gently onto his bed. I lay there staring at the window, wondering how it came to this. I want Shar to be okay. I want her kids to be okay. I want to find out about my dad. But I don't know how much longer I can do this.

Earlier I was so cocky, thought I was so strong but holy fucking shit. It's literally one thing after another with these psychos. How much more can these demon assholes do to me before I break? Are they actually trying to kill me?

And why am I surprised at the levels they'll sink to *again*? This is what demons do. This is every morality tale, it's in every human story about the supes and fae. I thought it was just racist nonsense, but maybe it's all true.

'Jane.'

I swallow hard and look up at the voice even though I already know it's Vic.

'What?' I ask despondently.

'I want to apologize.'

'Oh, really? THANKS! I'm so glad you're sorry for pumping me full of drugs the fae use to torture humans,' I scoff, so far past giving a flying fuck about what he's going to do if I piss him off.

He moves forward and I sit up because if I'm going to die, I'm not doing it laying down like a little bitch.

But he stays at a respectful distance.

'I'm sorry, Jane. I handled that badly. We thought ... I thought ...'

'Your apology is too little, too late,' I murmur. 'I mean what was all that about? Those questions?'

I wasn't even going to ask, but curiosity has got the better of me.

Fuck!

'We thought you were behind the fire in the house.'

'Yeah, I got that from the interrogation. So that's what you've thought since the car accident? Since we came to Metro?' I wrap my arms around myself. 'That's why you've been so ...'

'There's footage of you in my study at the Clubhouse. You looked at some paperwork on my desk.'

I let out a frustrated sound, wondering why I'm even trying to defend myself, but I am because I actually do care what he thinks of me ... like an idiot.

'I went in there to turn off the fucking light you'd left on. I was helping to save the polar bears, asshole!'

'Well, the papers detailed a shipment; the one from the other night.'

'That's why you took me to the warehouses.'

'Yes.'

'Well, I guess you didn't find what you thought and you

know why? Because I didn't read your papers. All I saw was that report you had on me, the one that told you everything about me, the one that told you about Angie and my brain … and my dad, I guess. That's all I saw. I turned off the light, and I left the room and Paris found me in the hallway.'

'Jane …' he comes closer, 'we *did* find what we thought.'

Huh?

I draw back. 'I don't understand. What did you expect there to be?'

'The Order.'

'But … my dad was there.'

I'm so confused.

'There was a picture of you and your dad in the file. I knew who he was the second I saw it. Once I knew you were Don Foley's daughter, it pretty much sealed your fate.'

I shake my head, getting up off the bed. 'I don't understand. How do you know my dad?'

'Jane, your dad basically *is* the Order. He's second-in-command of the whole fucking organization.'

My legs feel weak, but I don't sit back down.

'That's ridiculous.'

'Is it? You said yourself, you hadn't seen your dad since you were a kid. How would you know what he's been up to in all that time?'

'So you thought I was … What? Like an Order agent sent here by my dad?'

'You have to understand. This is a war, Jane. Just because the news isn't covering it, doesn't mean it's not happening. The Order are getting more and more powerful every day. They're destroying entire packs of shifters, covens of witches, clans of supes like us. The attack on us was systematic. We had a mole and you—'

'I checked all the boxes,' I murmur. 'So you decided to get even.'

'That's not—'

'Do you think that being autistic means I'm stupid? That's why you locked me up in the garage in the cold and the damp in the dark with the noises. Why you *spanked* me in the elevator. It's why you dressed me in those clothes, marked me, and,' I let out a pained sound, 'took me to my dad *at his place of work*. You wanted to humiliate him ... and me.'

He opens his mouth to speak, but he wisely shuts it again.

I step closer to him so we're toe to toe and I look up at him.

'And then you drugged me with *that stuff* that the fae use on humans to torture them. I thought you hated them as much as the humans do, but you know what, *Alex*? From where I'm standing, you look exactly the fucking same.'

With that, I slap him hard across his face and I stare him down as I feel the power of his anger pushing at me.

I hear a noise at the door. Paris is standing there with a drink in his hand. For me, I guess. He's looking back and forth between us awkwardly. I guess I've done something really bad in the human-to-demon relations book. Maybe an on-call girl isn't supposed to hit one of her demon masters.

'Fuck your apology,' I say to Vic because if these are my last words I'm going out like motherfucking Chuck Norris. 'I don't want it. There's nothing you can say that will fix this, but don't worry, I'm just the human whore who feeds you. We're a dime a dozen.'

I leave him standing there and blink tears away, gritting

my teeth because I'm not going to cry in front of these assholes.

'I deserve your anger,' he says quietly, not moving from where he was. 'I did all those things and I regret almost all of them, but, Jane, I didn't spank you to get even with you. I did it because I knew you'd like it.'

I walk out of the room, and I go to Theo's because he's the one I know the best and he's brought all my stuff here. Yeah, this stuff they've bought me is *mine*. I'll accept everything they give me without a fuss. I deserve all the things for the crap they've been putting me through and I'm going to collect. I grab my headphones and lay in the bed. I close my eyes and drift into a very unsettled sleep.

WHEN I WAKE UP, it's late morning of the next day. I take a shower in Theo's bathroom and then I get dressed in some jeans and a hoodie and grab my phone that's appeared in a charger on the bedside table while I was asleep. I don't want to see the Iron I's, not any of them, so I grab my cell and my headphones and I walk down the stairs. My sneakers don't make a sound and I've already memorized where the creaks are in the floor.

That's just New Place 101. I've worked out I can climb along Theo's roof to the next house if I need to pretty easily too.

I hear murmuring in the living room and I dart past the archway, getting to the front door. I open it, wondering if some magickal spell is going to let them know that I'm leaving, but as I step over the threshold cringing, nothing happens. I close the door silently behind me and, for the first time in weeks, I'm away from them.

I walk down the street slowly, enjoying being outside in

what's quickly turning into winter. I'm not trying to escape, I just need some time to process what's been happening without them whispering in my ear that they're sorry, that they won't do it again. I'm literally in the definition of an abusive relationship with five demons. I love Shar and her kids, but it's getting to the point where I don't think it's worth it anymore. Maybe my questions about my dad don't matter either.

I think I should take these demons for everything they're worth, fly down to Hawaii and Shar and me and her kids can just disappear. It's a pipe dream, but it makes me feel a little better.

I keep going for a couple of blocks and see a coffee shop on the corner. It looks like a cozy, independent place with autumn leaves in the windows and those gourds they sell at this time of year that no one ever seems to know if you can eat or not.

The bell on the door jingles pleasantly as I go in, and I order a cappuccino, sitting in a corner with it. I put on my headphones and zone out for a while, just drinking my coffee and mulling things over while I browse the socials on my phone.

I'm jarred back to the here and now when I see someone in black moving towards me slowly. I look up and my eyes widen. It's two cops, supe cops, and they've got guns pointed right at me. I raised my hands up, but I can't hear what the closest one's saying. I slowly take my earphones down.

'I said get on the fucking floor!'

I do as I'm told, my heart pounding my chest. Did Vic and the others call the cops on me? Is this their newest torture plan? Send the human girl to supe jail?

My arms are wrenched behind me, while a knee in the middle of my back keeps me immobile in a move that's over

the top for a little human like me. I stifle a cry as my arms
are secured behind me.

I can't get out of this like I could on Theo's table.

I'm breathing fast, trying to pretend that I can move my
arms. I clasp my fingers together to pretend that *I'm* doing
this, that I can just undo it if I want because I know what
happens if the human loses her shit while in custody. Even
though I'm cuffed and clearly not a danger, I'll get the shit
kicked out of me, a spell put on me, or they'll just
shoot me.

The cops lead me out of the café while everyone rubber-
necks, and one of them shoves me in the back of their patrol
car. They get in and the car starts moving.

'Am I under arrest?'

One of them eyes me in the mirror. 'We don't need to
arrest a human to detain them.'

I swallow hard. Did I piss off Vic too much? Is this how
he's going to get rid of me?

'Can you tell me why I'm being detained then?'

He glances at his partner.

'Humans,' he mutters and his partner chuckles.

They don't answer my question.

We pull into the station a few minutes later. They take
me out of the car and lead me up the clean, marble steps
into the building. There are supe cops everywhere and I try
very, VERY hard not to freak the fuck out.

A shifter walks past me, staring me up and down with a
look on his face that even I know screams, 'I'm going to
fucking kill you if I get a chance, human!'. His hands are
behind his back like mine and I realize he's a perp, not a cop.
It doesn't make me feel better.

I'm sat on the end of a row of hard, plastic chairs that are
bolted to the floor.

'Wait here for processing,' the cop who brought me in says and he leaves me there.

Another cop pushes a bald, tattooed pixie into the chair next to mine. He glances over at me.

'What the fuck did you do, little human?' he asks.

I glance up at him. 'I have no fucking idea.'

He leans back, like he's trying to get a better look at me. 'Well, good luck. You're gonna need it.'

Another supe with a detective badge on his lapel approaches me. He's thin, tall. He looks like he's got fae in his ancestry. The pointy ears are a dead giveaway.

'Jane Mercy?' he asks.

I look up and nod.

'Come with me.' He leads me to a desk. 'I'll be processing you this afternoon.'

'Can you tell me why I'm here please?'

'Yep.' He scans his screen. 'Looks like there was a warrant out on you from Welford.'

I close my eyes and grimace. Of course. Those two cops from the diner told me not to leave. At least it wasn't Vic, I guess.

'How did they know where I was?' I ask.

He glances at me like I'm the dumbest criminal ever. 'We have tracker spells strategically placed through the city to locate those on the wanted lists. As soon as you walked into that coffee shop, the nearest patrol car was notified.'

'Looks like the detectives who questioned you in Welford will be conducting your interview. I imagine they'll have some questions for you on why you left town.'

'The cops who questioned me before are detectives?'

'Yep. Detectives Lewski and Sanchez.'

I must look confused.

'It's not unusual for some of us to go into the field

dressed as regular officers,' he elaborates. 'Okay, that's you processed.'

He waves another officer over and I'm taken down in a rickety elevator into the depths of the precinct. Dark cells line the corridor.

'Stay away from the bars,' the officer mutters low like he hopes I don't hear him.

I'm kept in front of him as we walk. The lights overhead are flickering and I'm trying not to lose control but this is supe jail. This place isn't for humans.

I ignore the whistles and cat calls, staring straight ahead and keeping my focus in front of me. Some of the cells are so dark that I can't even see what's inside. I probably don't want to know.

We get to the end and there's one dingy cell by itself. Inside there are two guys. I look up at the cop, fear rising.

He snaps his fingers and the cuffs keeping my wrists together come loose. I breathe a sigh of relief and unclench my fingers, which have long since gone numb. I shake them out and rub them.

'You're not going to put me in there with them ...' I say disbelievingly.

'Only got one human cell right now,' he answers with a shrug. 'Flooding.'

'But—'

He doesn't wait, just pushes me inside and locks the door.

I swallow hard. I remember from a movie once that when you go to jail, you have to kick someone's ass the first day or become someone's bitch. It was a comedy, but I figure it still applies and I look around for something to use to 'kick someone's ass'. But there's literally fucking nothing except the clothes on my back.

I might be able to strangle somebody with my hoodie Jackie-Chan-style, but I don't really want to take it off and give these guys an unencumbered view of my body. I might end up with worse problems.

I stand at the side. One of the guys looks at me through stringy hair. He doesn't move, just leans back and watches the ceiling like he's reading a book up there, his eyes swinging from side to side. The other one stares. He doesn't take his eyes off me.

I clench my fists, getting ready to die swinging even though my chances are not good. This dude is shifter huge even though he's human. But he doesn't move. He just sits there and stares. I go to the corner of the cell and I slide down to the floor, not going near either of the other two humans.

I shouldn't have left the house. My bad.

I'm keeping my eye on the men as the minutes tick by. I hardly blink, not wanting to give them even a millisecond to surprise me, but I still scream when the bigger one jumps forward, leaping towards me. I cringe back and kick out with my foot, but he grabs something next to me. It's spiky and sharp and looks like some kind of bug leg.

It was slowly coming through the fucking bars towards me!

I scramble back, watching this dude pull the limb and then break it in half, using the bars for leverage.

Something in the dark cell next to us that I thought was just part of the corridor lets out a high-pitched sound that makes my ears hurt.

'Stay in the middle of the cell,' the big guy rasps at me, going back to his seat and sitting down hard.

What the fuck was that?

I'm shaking so hard that it's all I can do to sit on the floor as I was told. He's gone back to staring at me.

'Thank you,' I say.

He doesn't answer.

I'm going to die down here and the guys aren't even going to know where I was taken. I know it's ironic as shit, but I kinda wish they were here. They're massive dicks, but I know they'd protect me. Not because they care, but, I mean, I'm like their only food source so they have to keep me safe.

It feels like hours before I hear the door open at the end of the wing, but realistically it might only have been about forty minutes. The cop who brought me down opens the cell and beckons me out. He re-cuffs me and takes me back upstairs and to an interview room. The two detectives I remember from before, Sanchez and Lewski, are already in there sitting at the table.

'Take a seat.'

I sit in front of them and they both stare at me.

'We told you not to leave Welford, Miss Mercy. Can you tell us where you've been for the past weeks?'

I don't lie. 'I went to the Iron Incubi.'

They glance at each other.

'Why would you do that?' Lewski asks, his eyes looking over me.

I know how this goes. I know what the supes think of us and it looks like he has his suspicions about the poor AF human girl, so I feed them.

I shrug. 'Chuck disappeared and the diner was closed. I needed to make money and they needed an on-call girl.'

'Just like that?' Sanchez asks, her eyes boring holes into me.

'Just like that,' I say. 'Sometimes things just work out.'

Lewski sits forward. 'I saw you the other night in Ada's bar. They take you there?'

Oh, shit, these cops were in the strip club?!

I bluff like my life depends on it because I'm pretty sure it does, sticking to a version of the truth so they don't know I'm not telling them everything.

'Yep. They wanted me to learn some moves,' I say with what I hope is a flirty smile. 'You know, to please them.'

'Bullshit,' Lewski hisses. 'You better start telling us the truth, human.'

'I am telling the truth,' I say.

Lewski stands up, leaning over the desk and I cower a little in spite of myself. Shit, he's huge even for a shifter.

'Then where are they? If you're theirs, why are you in jail? You know what I think, Jane? I think you're full of shit. You're part of the Order. I think you killed the *supe-lovers* who worked at the diner and Dreyson, your Iron Incubi boyfriend, too. The Iron I's don't let their people get arrested.'

'I wasn't arrested. Just detained,' I answer, using the patrol officer's words.

Lewski glances at his partner. 'We got a wise-ass here. Maybe we go old school and get the phonebook out.'

Sanchez makes a point of looking up at the camera over the door. 'No can do. The cams are working again.' She looks at me. 'Last chance before things are set in motion that can't be undone, Jane.'

I look between them.

'I'm telling the truth,' I say. 'Give me one of those fae pills and I'll prove it.'

They both laugh and I'm taken aback.

'You think we're going to let you get high?'

Lewski turns to his Sanchez. 'I think we got an addict on our hands. She might get violent. Maybe she goes in Gen Pop while she detoxes.'

'You can't do that,' I say, my blood freezing in my veins.

If they put me in the regular cells, I won't be coming back out again.

'You're in our world now, supe-hater,' Sanchez whispers. 'We can do whatever the fuck we want to you.'

The door to the interview room bangs open.

'We're in the middle of a fucking interrogation,' Lewski bellows.

'No, that can't be what's going on in here,' a voice growls. 'Because I *know* you two detectives aren't dumb enough to be talking to a member of the Iron I's without her lawyers present.'

Paris strolls through the door and I close my eyes, thanking whatever gods exist that he's found me. He looks around arrogantly, dominant and in control of the situation.

Fuck, that's hot.

I mean, I'm scared out of my freaking mind, but it's still hot.

'This human is a suspect,' Sanchez tries.

'I certainly hope not, Detective,' a suit from behind Paris says, taking a step forward, 'because if she is, your actions here will mean your case is going to fall apart ... if it even gets to court, which I doubt it will once I speak to the prosecutor at the Governor's party tonight.'

I can tell a lawyer when I see one and there are three behind Paris. They look expensive as fuck.

'What the hell is going on in here?'

Another supe enters the room. He's older and dressed in a grey suit with the emblem of the mages on it.

'Mr. Deloitte, to what do we owe the pleasure?' he asks, shaking Paris' hand.

'Chief,' Lewski says, 'we were just—'

Lewski goes silent at a look from his boss.

'Chief Artic. Good to see you. I'm afraid two of your

detectives were going a little cowboy on Miss Mercy here. She's a member of the Iron I's. Her lawyer hadn't even been called. Clearly an oversight. Luckily, I was able to find out where she was being held before these two upstanding detectives made a mistake that cost them their badges.'

The chief looks me over as if just noticing me sitting at the table with his detectives. 'Please accept the Metro PD's apologies for the mix-up, Miss Mercy,' he says to me.

'Not at all,' I grind out because this seems to me to be one of those situations where everyone pretends to be polite even when they don't want to be.

'Cut her loose,' Artic orders, 'and you two,' he points at the detectives. 'My office. Now.'

I stand up shakily and Paris takes my hand.

'Let's get out of here.'

I nod and we leave the building, an officer handing me the few items they took off me in the café including my earphones on the way out. Paris takes everything for me and I'm grateful because my hands are shaking so hard I doubt I'd be able to hold them.

Outside, at the bottom of the steps, the Iron I's car is waiting on the street and I'm pretty sure I've never been so happy to see anything in my life before, except for Paris in that interview room.

I turn to him with a cry, throwing my arms around him.

'Not here, Jane,' he murmurs, his game face still on.

I draw back and get into the car.

As soon as it begins to move, I lose it, sobbing into my hands.

Paris gathers me into his arms.

'Shh, princess, it's over now. Tell me what happened,' he says, his hands rubbing my arms and back soothingly.

And this time he is making me feel better.

11

PARIS

'I wasn't r-running away,' she hiccups and I breathe a sigh of relief even though by getting her out of jail in a very public way I pretty much just ensured that Vic can't let her go even if that was the plan. Our enemies have become hers.

He could still tear up her contract if she asks, but I know him. He won't. He'll protect Jane the best way he can and that means she stays with the Iron I's because every supe in the city is going to know who she is now. It'll spread like wildfire. Even if we find those stalkers who she came to us about in the first place, it's not going to matter.

We'll still take care of them, of course. No one threatens the Iron I's and Jane is pretty much one of us now. I've been looking into everything she's said about them. There's not much to go on, but I haven't given up. There's always something to find, and it only takes one breadcrumb.

I lean back in the seat and close my eyes, trying to calm my heart that has been thumping in my chest since I realized she was gone.

I had no idea she wasn't in the house when my phone

pinged her location. I was frantic, figuring she was trying to give us the slip again, but not understanding why she'd turned up at the Metro PD Headquarters of all places because a human would never voluntarily go there.

'I just wanted out of the h-house for a few minutes. I went to the coffee shop down the street. I was just sitting there when two supe cops showed up with their guns out. They cuffed me and put me in the back of their squad car. Then they took me to the station.'

She looks up at me and a shudder runs through her. 'They p-put me in the cells.'

What?

My jaw clenches and it takes everything in me not to punch the window out next to me. Those fuckers put our girl in the cells next to the worst supernatural criminals in Metro. If even one of them had got hold of her ...

I take out my phone and start texting the others. Heads are going to roll for this. Vic will make sure of that and he'll pretend it's to save face, but the truth is, no one touches Jane. She's ours.

'In the cells?' I prompt, wanting her to continue because I have a feeling after seeing those two detectives in the inter- view room that her story is going to get worse.

She nods.

'Tell me exactly what happened,' I murmur gently, successfully keeping the edge out of my tone because I don't want her to clam up.

'They took me in an elevator to the basement levels, down a corridor lined with cells that were mostly dark. At the end there was one with two humans inside.

'Females?' I ask

'No.'

'Go on,' I say, trying harder to keep my voice calm.

'One of them was huge, like a lumberjack and the other one was small, with stringy hair, and neither of them moved. The bigger one was staring at me the whole time and the other one pretty much ignored me. I sat down in the corner of the cell away from them. I didn't realize that there was another cell next to ours because the light in the corridor was out.'

'Fuck,' I mutter. 'What happened?'

'Something came through the bars to snatch me. I didn't see it. The big guy ... he moved so fast. He grabbed it.' She shudders. 'I've never seen a supe like that. It was like a spider leg or something. Anyway, the big guy hurt it and I moved to the middle of the floor. I didn't see it again. That guy saved me.'

She cuddles closer to me. 'I was down there for a while. I don't know how long exactly. Then the cop came back, and he took me up to the interview room.'

'And what happened in the interview room?' I ask, so tense that I feel like I'm going to explode. Odds are she won't notice that I'm angry, but I don't want to upset her anymore. She's been through enough because of us.

'I got into the room and it was the same two cops from the diner who asked me questions when Dreyson was killed. They acted like they were beat cops in the diner, but they're detectives. They asked me why I hadn't stayed in Welford like they told me to. I said that I had signed a contract with the Iron I's for money.'

She breaks off and swallows hard. I grab her a water from the minifridge and she gulps it down.

'They didn't believe me,' she continues. 'They said I was part of the Order. A supe-hater. They said I had killed Drey and the others. They said something about a phonebook.'

She shrugs. 'I don't know why they needed a phonebook. Do they even still make those?'

I let out a breath, but I don't tell her what the cops here used to use those for back in the day.

Fuckers.

'Anyway, they couldn't do whatever they were thinking because the camera was working, so they were going to ...' She closes her eyes and lets out a hard breath. 'They told me they were going to put me in Gen Pop until I told them the truth.'

The color leaches out of my face at her words. I have no doubt those two would have done it. Worse crimes happen behind closed doors when humans are in their custody every day. I know that for a fact and I can't say I've ever given police corruption much thought. But if I hadn't gotten to her in time ...

I'm not just going to make sure their badges are taken for this. By the time I'm finished with Lewski and Sanchez, they're going to wish they'd never met Jane.

'I just wanted to get out for a little while. Clear my head,' she whispers.

'It's okay,' I say. 'You're okay now and we'll make sure they don't come at you again.' I pull her tightly against me. 'But maybe don't go anywhere without us, huh?'

She clutches at me suddenly, her fingers digging into my arm.

'Thank you for getting me out of there. I thought they were going to let me die.' She lets out of sob. 'There are so many stories of humans that go in and never come out. I thought I was going be one of them.'

'It's over,' I say, hating how upset she is and vowing I'm going to get even with those fuckers for her in every way I can.

'How did you find me?' she asks in a small voice.

'As soon as you walked through the doors of the precinct, my phone was pinged.'

I don't tell her I how scared I was when I saw that notification.

'The cops have their spells and we have ours,' I elaborate. 'It makes sense for the Iron I's to keep tabs on who they arrest in case we need to intervene.'

'You guys really are the Kings of the World,' she mutters.

'We are what we are,' I say with a tight smile, 'and after today, everyone is going to know not to mess with Jane Mercy.'

She draws back, her eyes searching my face. 'That sounds like a big deal.'

I tell her the truth. 'It is. By getting the lawyers involved, I just announced to the supe world that you're one of us.'

She shakes her head. 'But ... I don't understand. You guys don't ... you aren't ... all the things you've done ...'

'No one messes with the Iron I's,' I say instead.

She nods, accepting my response, but still looks lost and upset.

I take her hands in mine and she lets me.

'I'm sorry for my part in everything,' I say. 'I'm sorry that we hurt you. I'm sorry that we put you in that cell.' I look away, hating myself when I think about it. 'The house, Vic and Sie's injuries ... We thought you were the bad guy, Jane and ... I should have known better. I should have done more.'

I don't want to see Jane hurt anymore. I didn't enjoy watching her suffer and I wasn't the only one. I want to make her happy and the realization is an odd one.

I squeeze her fingers a little. 'But I promise you that all

of us will protect you. If you're ever able to trust us again, we won't betray it.'

She stares at me in that way she does, not giving anything away.

'Are you okay?' I ask, cupping her cheek.

'I don't know,' she says, but she leans into me a little. 'Everything's been kind of shitty.'

'Since you met us?'

'No, well, yeah, but before that too, if I'm honest. I've been trying to make it through my life ever since my dad ... left me, I guess. Foster wasn't great. I was difficult and they didn't know I was autistic yet. I mean it wouldn't have mattered. They wouldn't have known the first thing about how to deal with a girl like me anyway. I was moved around a lot.' She chuckles. 'Some of my foster parents were real dicks too.'

I make a mental note to get their names. In for a penny, in for a pound. I'll take every single fucker who's wronged her down. I'll delete their digital presences, bank accounts, entire identities. They'll wake up one day and find they've been erased.

'And then you went to the one who was going to adopt you?'

She smiles. 'Yeah. Angie was great. She tried really hard to help me even though I was an ungrateful, asshole teenager. She did help me. And then,' she heaves a sigh, 'I got a letter telling me to run away. I ignored it and when I got home from school three days later, Angie was dead. I found her on the kitchen floor. Her eyes were cut out.'

'Fuck, I'm sorry, sweetheart. What did you do then?'

'What the note told me. I ran away. I was on the streets for a while and then I got a job as a waitress at a truck stop. The owner was nice. She let me stay in her spare room.

Then, about six months later, I got another letter. I didn't want anyone else to die because of me, so I left.'

'And that happened for ten years? You never made any friends you could keep? Never had anything permanent?'

She shrugs and I pull her close, silently declaring that she'll have that with us now.

'You never knew who was doing it?'

'Never, but they always found me sooner or later and they'd make me move on.'

I frown. 'How do you know it was more than one?'

'What do you mean?' she asks.

'Well, you never saw them, so how did you know it wasn't just one person?'

'Oh, it was the handwriting. It used to be mostly notes at the beginning and the handwriting was always different.'

I hold her against me and she lets me.

'We'll figure it out,' I tell her.

She smirks at me. 'What do you care? You already got the stone, and me to sign up to be a buffet. Why bother?'

'I just care,' I reply.

She still doesn't understand what I did back at the Metro PD, what it means for all of us.

We pull up to the house.

'Is everyone in there?' she asks, fidgeting.

'No, Vic had a meeting. Kor is training for his fight with Mad Dog in a few days. Theo is at the clinic, and Sie ... I actually have no idea where Sie is. That's why I came for you without the others. If they'd known, they would have been there too.'

Breaking down the door of that room to get to you.

'I doubt that,' she mutters, but doesn't give me a chance to say anything as she gets out of the car, goes up the steps, and enters the house.

'Why did you lie?' I ask as I follow her into the kitchen. 'When Kor asked you if you wanted another night with us?'

'Uhhh.' She looks embarrassed. 'Because I didn't want you to know.'

She says it like it's obvious and I frown because it's not.

'Why?'

She sighs. 'Because Theo told me that your power doesn't work on me.'

'So?' I ask, not understanding what she's getting at.

She looks down. 'So, if I wanted it then ... then that was me.'

I shake my head in confusion.

'So maybe my dad was right. I actually am a supe whore.'

'No, princess, that's ...'

I don't even know what to say to her. She's clearly struggling with this and I'm angry with Vic and her asshole father all over again.

'Human society isn't the same as yours,' she says, looking up at me. 'Your other on-call girls signed for the high, for the money at the end, maybe even to help someone else like I did. But they knew that things wouldn't be the same for them if people found out where they'd been when they went home after their time was done. And they wanted to be with you because they got addicted to your power. It's not like that for me. I enjoy like ... *demon sex* or something. I mean, shit, I'm a deviant.'

'You're not a deviant,' I say, unable to help my chuckle.

She scowls at me. 'Whatever. Why do you guys care if I want to again, or not, anyway? It's going to happen no matter what. It's my job, right?'

I look at her for a moment. She's beautiful and smart

and funny. I want to tell her something real, something I've never even explicitly told Korban.

'I've never been with a human without the lull before,' I say. 'The others have, but I was always afraid to even try.'

She's silent for a minute before she speaks.

'What were you afraid of?' she asks, tilting her head.

I shrug. 'Of them not wanting me back,' I whisper.

She looks up with surprise. 'Bullshit,' she says. 'You could double as an underwear model. There's no way that humans wouldn't be interested.'

'It doesn't feel like that,' I say.

I look away. I'm giving her too much she could use against me. 'Well, it doesn't matter. Even if a human is interested, I'm not allowed to do anything.'

'Except with me,' she says quietly.

'Except with you,' I echo.

She licks her lips slowly and I wonder if it's accidental or if she's attempting a seduction. Either way, it's hot as hell. I step closer and she doesn't move.

'I know you've been through a lot,' I mutter. 'I don't need to feed. If this isn't okay, you can tell—'

She puts her hand over my mouth. 'It *is* okay.'

I pick her up and I put her on the kitchen counter. It's just at the right height for what I have planned.

I pull down her jeans and underwear in one swift move, leaving her ass bare on the cold kitchen counter.

I pull them the rest of the way off, over her sneakers and she clearly doesn't like her shoes still on because she kicks them off as well.

I open her legs wide and crowd between them.

'I've been wanting this,' I murmur. 'Just you and me.'

She doesn't say anything, but she kisses me and my arms caress up her back to unclasp her bra under her sweatshirt.

She lets out a breath as my hands flit around and knead her tits gently. I unzip my pants. My dick is ready for her and I don't hesitate, impaling her on it hard.

Fuck, she's exquisite. Her body feels like it was made for mine.

The sounds she makes as I drive into her is music to my ears. I've been wanting to make her scream only for me. I want her to call out my name louder than she has for the others and I'm going to make sure she does.

I pick her up and slam her back down again. She's biting her lip. She squeals again. She likes it like this.

'More,' she says and I grin, setting a punishing pace.

Hard. Fast. Thrusting into her like my life depends on it – which, for once, it doesn't. I'm not even very hungry but I want her more than I've ever wanted anyone. She's on par with Kor.

I pick her up, moving her to the wall and holding her up against it, giving me the stability I need to drive into her harder, deeper. I pull off her shirt and cast it aside. Her bra's next. She's completely naked and I'm still fully clothed, and something about that drives me wild. She's small and vulnerable. Maybe Vic's onto something with those power games he likes to play.

My thumb presses against her clit, rubbing it gently back and forth, completely at odds to how I'm ravaging her pussy with my cock and I'm rewarded when she bucks against me with a cry.

'PARIS!' she screams like she knows my mind.

Her body shakes against me, and I can feel the muscles inside her contracting, shuddering. But still, I don't stop. I'm not even near ready. I lift her up, hug her spent body close and take us to the elevator, jabbing at the buttons.

On the second floor, I stagger into my room, not even bothering with the door, and throwing her on the bed. I turn her over, grab her ponytail and pull her back towards me, pushing my dick into her again. I keep her where I want her with my fingers intwined in her hair. Her back is arched and she notices the mirror behind the bed with wide eyes. I give her a hedonistic grin. She hasn't even seen the one on the ceiling yet.

She watches herself, and what I'm doing to her. She's staring into my eyes. I slap her ass and her hands come up to play with her nipples, twisting them hard, pinching them.

At the last moment I flip her over, throwing her on her back and putting her legs on my shoulders. I come with a bellow, and she follows, screaming my name again as she throws her head back.

Then she does something that no other human – or supe for that matter – has ever done to me before. I'm still coming as she parts her legs wider and, as they fall off my shoulders to the bed, she lurches up and bites me, drawing blood on my chest.

It's so fucking hot that it draws out my climax, my whole body going rigid as the sensations of her envelop me. This human ... I've never felt anything like this before. I collapse on top of her, enjoying the way her small body wriggles until I realize she probably can't breathe under me.

I roll off her, panting.

'You bit me,' I exclaim, looking down and seeing a trickle of blood.

'I'm so sorry,' she says, staring at it with what I'm slowly learning from her myriad of *extremely* subtle facial expressions, is horror. 'It just seemed like something I needed to do.'

She tries to get up, but I pull her back down.

'Stay,' I say, but it's more of a question than a demand.

I get up and close the door. I lay back down on the bed and turn to face her.

'What are you thinking?' I ask, wanting to feel closer to her on a different level.

She wrinkles her nose at me.

'I was thinking I'd love vanilla cupcakes.'

I collapse back with a laugh. 'I'll get you some.'

She gives me a grin and shrugs and I know that we have a long way to go before she trusts me, but I think we've taken a significant step with the fact that I saved her from the cops.

I vow in that moment that I'm never going to give her cause to not trust me again. If Theo can be her rock, then I'm going to join him and we'll make a *freaking granite* island of safety for her.

'Paris,' she murmurs next to me.

'Yes, princess?'

'Why didn't you guys tell me I'd know what you were feeling after you fed from me? It seems like something that should have at least been mentioned. It really freaked me out the first time. I thought I was going crazy.'

I open my eyes to look at her. 'Jane, what are you talking about?'

'You know, the empath thingy.' Her brow furrows. 'When you guys feed from me, afterwards I can feel what you feel. I can do it with Sie, Korban, Vic and now you. It was hard at first, but it's a lot easier now.'

I swallow hard. She's not joking.

'Do you know what I'm feeling now?' I ask.

She stares at me like she's looking into my soul. 'Uh, you were feeling pretty happy and content and *satisfied*, but now you're getting more worried and tense the longer I talk.' She draws back. 'You don't know what I'm talking about, do you?'

'No,' I say, but I'm afraid I know exactly what she's talking about and I don't know what I'm supposed to do.

This is impossible.

My eyes flick up to the camera and I take my phone out, deleting the file from the past few minutes.

She waits, watching what I'm doing with a slightly puzzled look on her face.

After I've made sure no one stumbles upon what she just said, I turn to face her, gripping her shoulder and making sure I have her complete focus.

'Don't tell anyone,' I whisper.

Kor

I'M STILL STANDING at the door though Paris and Jane have already left the kitchen. I'm staring at the space where I watched Paris pounding Jane into the countertop, where she was screaming his name.

I'd be lying if I said I wasn't a little jealous, but it's not because Paris is mine.

I lean against the doorjamb, trying to figure out where my head is at.

Jane isn't what I thought. I've been reeling since last night. She's not the bad guy. I've been blaming an innocent woman. Paris was right. I was biased because of what she is. I keep thinking of her in my arms when she answered my questions last night. I can't get it out of my mind; especially that last one. Paris was pissed that I asked her if she enjoyed her night with us, but whether it was because of the pain she was in or because he's salty about something else, I don't know.

I check my phone. It's still on the text that he sent to us all earlier when he found Jane in the Metro PD and my stomach drops again just like it did the first time I read it, even though she's here safe with us now.

Those fucking cops are going to regret threatening what's ours.

I glance at the elevator. No doubt Paris is still going strong upstairs and although I'm tempted to join him, I know that would be a mistake. Paris wants some time alone with Jane. I understand that and, hey, I'm secure enough in our relationship to give him that even though I can't have the same with her. I'll need him there with me, but I *will* be having my own fun with Jane soon.

I go down to the gym, avoiding even looking at the door to the cell.

I hit the pads for a while. My next fight is tomorrow and Mad Dog is a decent opponent. Even better than Callaghan was. Won't be fighting that asshole again though. Vic told me Maddox got rid of him after that night in *The Circle Club*.

Not sure why that British prick lied to Vic. I know he saw me and the human prospects snatch Callaghan after *The Circle Club* and throw him in the trunk of that car. I mean, no one's going to find what little there was left of him after I was done, but Maddox must know what I did to his best fighter, why that sorry piece of shit hasn't been around lately.

If I were Maddox, I wouldn't be able to let that disrespect stand. I've been waiting for him or his clan to show up to give me my dues, but the other incubi clan leader is a strange one. He hasn't come for me, and by all rights he could. I took out one of his guys. There will be a price to pay for that. Maddox isn't one to let things like that slide even if he was going to off Callaghan himself, which I suspect he was. I saw his face when he found Jane being mauled by that fucker. I've never seen the bastard so furious. He usually keeps his emotions under very tight control. Stiff upper lip and all that. But he let it loose that night. Yeah, he was going to take Callaghan out all right, I just made sure it was me who got him first.

Maybe Maddox is glad I did his dirty work for him. In my opinion, it was a long time coming. Callaghan was a good fighter, but not much else besides *maybe* a liability. I'm interested to see who Maddox comes up with to take his place.

I HEAD UPSTAIRS in the elevator after a few hours to take a shower. It's dark and as I wander through the corridor towards my room, I see a hulking shadow standing at Theo's door.

So Sie's still skulking around her.

'What the fuck is going on with you?' I hiss at him.

He doesn't look at me. 'Nothing. Killing time is all.'

'You're standing outside her room in the dark, bro. Even for us that's creepy.'

'Your fight is with Mad Dog tomorrow, right?' he asks, changing the subject.

I sigh. 'Yeah. Why?'

'Vic has a meeting with Maddox after in *The Lounge*. He says we're taking Jane.'

'Why?' I frown in the shadows, not liking it and not only because he might be intending outing me for torturing Callaghan to death.

'*The Lounge* isn't a place for humans and with all the shit going on with the Order, we should be getting out of Metro while we plan our next move, not partying. There were three more bombings yesterday and four prominent supes have disappeared in the past two days. They're ramping up again. Even the humans who aren't with them know this city is a powder keg until this is over one way or another.'

Sie's shadow shrugs. 'Someone will get 'em.'

'Even the fae can't figure out how they keep escaping,' I scoff. 'This is going to get worse before it gets better.'

Sie looks through the door again at Jane sleeping in the bed. 'Well, they have enough stolen fae artifacts to give them an edge. Maybe they have help. Supes.'

'Who the fuck from our world would do anything for those racist fuckers?' I hiss.

'Time'll tell,' Sie mutters, taking a step down the corridor.

'Wait.'

He looks back at me.

'What is it with her?'

'I don't know.' He stares at me for a long moment. 'Do you?'

He asks it like he knows about my extracurricular activities, but how could he?

When I don't answer, he goes into his room and closes the door quietly.

I peer inside Jane's room as I go past to my own. I take a quick shower and throw on some clothes. Then, I grab the thing I saw the other day while I was doing recon on the Demon Dogs and I return to her, silently stealing into where she's sleeping.

I'm like Santa!

She's on her back, one of her hands next to her head, fingers curled. I hang the thing I brought by the window so she sees it in the morning and then I stand by the bed. I'm as bad as Sie is I think as I brush her hair from her face, remembering the last time I was watching her sleep at the Clubhouse when I unzipped her jacket and saw what those humans had done to her.

What would she say if she knew that I'd made sure that none of those boys could ever hurt her again either? I grin. She might thank me but I doubt it because she's not like that. She pretends she's hard and not as innocent as she looks, but I'm pretty sure she's the first human I've ever met that I wasn't afraid to turn my back on.

I still can't believe what the true answer to my question was the other night. If it wasn't for that faerie flower Vic slipped her, I'd never have believed she wants a repeat of Paris and me.

I thought I hated her. Fuck, I wanted to, but I'm starting to realize that that was never the case. I felt betrayed and hurt and I jumped to conclusions. I became her enemy when she was never mine and, after everything, I know it would be best to let her go on with her life.

But Paris has made sure that's impossible. Jane's the Iron I's weak link and everyone knows it now. She needs to stay close where we can protect her.

Besides, we never did deal with those stalkers of hers and now that she's been in the open at the precinct, and we've publicly claimed her as a member of our clan, it's only a matter of time before whoever it is makes an appearance. Personally, I can't wait for the day they show themselves. I'll have them down in that cell squealing like pigs for what they've done.

The depth of my protectiveness over Jane no longer surprises me. I've been feeling it since the beginning, on that very first day when she came into the bar to stare us down with that oblivious courage of hers.

But it does scare me.

I sit on the bed carefully as I watch her sleeping. My fingers caress down her face very lightly, hardly touching. Watching her and Paris earlier has left me wanting and I'll go find him in a little while, but, for the first time *since the first time*, I want a human and not to feed from.

I indulge myself for a minute, my fingers following the contours of her neck down to her to her collarbone that I can just see over the blanket.

She moves in her sleep, writhing a little before whimpering a word.

'Kor.'

Did she just say my name?

My eyes fly to hers, but they're not open. She's still asleep. Is she dreaming about me? I watch with bated breath as her hand goes down her body under the covers and to the place between her legs.

I practically leap off the bed, fleeing the room before I do something. I lean against the wall in the corridor and put my face in my hands, panting. Fuck, I want to go back in there. I want to wake her up with my face buried between her legs.

But, instead, I go to my room, having to force each step until I'm through my door. I close it, lock it, and hurl the key across the room.

I thought I'd be able to resist her, but the truth is I want her *without Paris* and that is dangerous.

I don't want to hurt Jane. I don't want to kill her.

I need her to stay away from me when Paris isn't around or that's what's going to happen.

12

JANE

It's crowded. The atmosphere is frenzied and energized. There's lust, but not for sex; for violence. I can tell it's loud too; with the kind of sounds that would have me making for the nearest exit with my fingers in my ears. I can see people screaming, shaking their fists, taking bets with each other, laughing and jostling to see the fight. But, I can't hear any of it.

'Are you okay?' Paris asks from next to me.

I receive his voice clearly through the earphones that he got me. He's modified them so that he and the other Iron I's can talk to me, but nothing else comes through at all. I can't hear anything beyond their voices. I move one of ear pads slightly and the roar, the screams, make me cringe, my heartbeat ratcheting up a notch. I put it back quickly. I grasp Paris' hand and he looks surprised for a second, but then he returns my grip.

'Are you okay?' Paris asks again, and I'm getting anxiety off him that's at odds with the smile on his face.

He's nervous about something, but I'm not sure what. I lock it down though. He told me not to tell anyone about the empath thingy and I took that to heart. He was afraid of something and that rubbed off on me.

I nod. 'Yeah, where's Korban now?'

I watch him push his earpiece in further so he can hear me through it. There's too much noise here for me not to have to scream to be heard without it. He looks at his watch.

'He'll be getting ready for the fight downstairs. He's up next.'

We walk slowly through throngs of people, Paris close by all the time. I'm kind of excited. I've never been to a fight before. There are people here for the entertainment of it. They're acting like they're having a great time, but there are others who just watch from the fringes like they have a lot more than fun riding on the outcomes.

'Do you ever worry about him at these things?' I ask Paris.

He looks back at me with a cheeky grin. 'A little, but you'll see what an amazing fighter he is. He doesn't get his ass handed to him often.'

'Where do we watch from?'

He points up at a room above us with what looks like thick Plexiglas all around it for viewing.

'That's what passes for a VIP section at these things,' he says. 'Do you want to go up there?'

I nod, hoping it'll be a little less nuts away from these crowds, and he leads me up the stairs to the top of the ring that's surrounded by old, wooden bleachers and TV cameras.

We enter a large room with screens and a bar. The bouncer takes one look at Paris and doesn't even bother to approach us.

Guess everyone knows the Iron I's in this seedy underbelly.

Paris puts my arm on his and escorts me through the

room. With his black suit and my new inky, chiffon outfit, we probably look like some kind of freaking power couple. The flowing dress I'm wearing is modest and chic with a thin belt at the waist. Even my hair is up in an elegant French twist that Paris did for me when I appeared downstairs with my usual ponytail earlier, looking frustrated because I clearly have no business even *having* hair and the pretty dress was making me want to do something different.

I sit down at a table with six chairs and a small reservation card for the Iron I's in the middle of it. Blatantly, I watch the demon who's been given the job as my bodyguard-chaperone for the duration of our time here. I thought Paris was just some dumb, frat boy asshole who happened to be an incubus that first night when I met him at the bar. Even afterwards, I figured he just fucked around, living life like it was one big game, but I'm beginning to see that there's a lot more to Paris Deloitte than what he shows everybody.

A cocktail appears in front of me and I look at it like it might bite me.

'I didn't order this.'

'It's okay,' Paris says, putting a hand on my shoulder lightly as he sits next to me. 'I did.'

I gaze at the big screen in front of us, watching the two supes in the ring beating the absolute shit out of each other. As far as I can tell, there are no rules here. Anything goes. Guess that's the supes though. They don't do stuff by halves.

'There are a lot more humans here than I thought there'd be,' I observe as I scan the bleachers.

I'm the only human in the VIP area though. I noticed that as soon as we came in. There are mostly shifters here and a group of vampires in the corner, even a fae at the bar. But no one like me.

Paris' lips turn up at the corners and he shrugs. 'They like to watch the supes pummel the shit out of each other.'

'What can I say? We have few pleasures.'

He chuckles. 'Hey, it's a little quieter up here. Do you want to take the headphones off?'

I pull one away from my head and find that I actually can't hear anything from the outside. It's just a dull roar from the TV screen showing the fight, the clink of glasses, and general murmur of conversation. I take them down and leave them around my neck, having a sip of the drink in front of me. It's fruity and strong.

'This is nice,' I murmur.

'I thought you'd like it.'

I look up at him and give him a small smile. He's been different with me the past few days. He doesn't seem to just do things without thinking to get in my good books like he was before. It's like he's actually trying to understand me and make me happy.

Despite the warning bells, I like it. It's like a blanket around me even though that voice is telling me that this is definitely a trick and he's going to turn on me again just like they all did before.

I look down at the table and, thankfully, he's turned to look at the screen again. One of the supes is on the ground and he's not getting up.

'Fight's over,' he mutters. 'Kor will be up there in a minute.'

'Where are the others?' I ask.

'Theo will be down there near the ring. He's the official doctor for tonight.'

He points at the TV and I see Theo climbing under the ropes to take a look at the shifter who's writhing around on the ground.

'Vic is usually mingling. He likes to get that part of the Club business done all at once, doing the President thing—'

'Kissing babies and shit?'

Paris laughs loudly. 'Yeah, and shit.'

He takes a gulp of his beer. 'Sie is with him now that he's the Pres' right-hand man again.'

'Again?' I ask.

'Don't worry about it.'

I let out a loud sigh and prop my head up with my fist under my chin and my elbow on the table.

He shakes his head and rolls his eyes a little. 'Okay, fine. Sie has been a little bit … not himself for the past couple of years. Some dark stuff happened to him and when he came out of it, he wasn't the same. That happens to us sometimes. We incubi go a little nuts and we don't usually get better when that happens.'

'A little nuts?'

'Yeah.' He taps his head.

I wrinkle my nose. 'Actually crazy or me crazy?'

He frowns. 'The kind where we have to take you out back and put a slug through your head like Ol' Yeller,' he says absently.

He sits forward in his chair, angling himself towards me. 'You aren't crazy, princess.'

'No?'

He takes puts his hand over mine on the table. 'No.'

I heave a breath, wondering why I'm getting choked up right now.

'What about that other thing?' My eyes seek his, boring into them.

With Paris, this is the last thing that happened before the dad incident that we haven't talked about, the only thing left that I keep thinking about. It's a loose end and it needs to be tied up.

'What other thing?' he asks warily, and I realize he thinks I'm talking about the thing he told me not to talk about.

But I'm not.

'I heard you that time ... even though you muttered it under your breath,' I whisper. 'When you went to get my shoes from upstairs in the Clubhouse and you called me a reta—'

He puts his finger over my lips, his expression darkening. 'I'm sorry about that. I was an ignorant prick, a dumbass who didn't even know what he was saying, and I'm sorry, Jane. I will never hurt you like that again.'

I give him a nod, kind of shocked that he just apologized like that, that he seems to actually care that he hurt my feelings ... that he understands I *have* feelings even though I don't show much of what goes on in my head ... or my heart.

Before said heart can thaw anymore, the bell dings and I turn my eyes to the TV. The fight has started and I stare as Korban and a guy named *Mad Dog* face off against each other. The other dude is covered in tattoos even more than Kor is. He's got a crew cut and muscles bulging like a 90's G.I. Joe doll. He's scary as shit.

'Is Korban going to be okay?' I mutter.

Paris gives a small laugh, but his hand tightens almost imperceptibly over mine and I feel his worry, so I squeeze it back.

'You said yourself, he's a great fighter.'

'I know.' Paris gives me a quick smile before his eyes go back to the screen.

We watch Mad Dog tear into Kor, but he hardly ever manages to land a punch. I stare, watching the way that

Korban moves. He's so fluid that it almost looks like he's dancing. I don't know much about fighting, but even I know that he's amazing. He's methodical and practiced, but as graceful as the girls were on those poles in the strip club the other night.

Then, Mad Dog gets in a lucky strike and Kor staggers back. Fingers tense over mine, and I move our clasped hands off the table to my lap, letting him know that it's okay. No one has to even see that he's anxious.

'Come here,' he murmurs, pulling me gently over to him.

He sits me on his lap, my legs to one side so I'm facing the TV. I can still see everything, but I can rest my head against his chest, so I do. He puts his arms around me. I know this is just as much about his comfort as it is about mine, but I'm able to relax into him in a way that I have never been able to with anyone outside the Iron I's.

That must mean something, but damned if I know what.

'Are you okay?' he asks.

'Why do you keep asking me that?'

He watches me for a minute. 'Just making sure.'

'Does this have to do with what I said—'

His lips crash against mine and, after a token sound of shock, I melt against him like starlet from a movie in the '40s. I can't even help it, nor the moan that he elicits from me as his tongue dances with mine.

Wait, is this kiss to shut me up?

I hear someone make a derisive noise next to our table and I break away from Paris to look up, forgetting what I was saying to Paris for the moment.

There's a fae male standing beside our table staring down his nose at us.

'I'd heard your clan had publicly claimed a human, but I didn't think you'd actually *bring it out.*'

I tense up. Humans don't mix with fae EVER if we can possibly help it. I go to slide away from Paris, but he tightens his grip on me, so I can't leave.

'What are you doing here, Walter?' he asks.

Walter?

'Here to see your president.' The fae gestures to me. 'Are you going to feed from the human here, *out in the open*?' he asks with a salacious smile on his face that makes my skin crawl. 'You incubi are so single minded in your need for sustenance.'

'Vic's around somewhere,' Paris mutters.

He takes a drink, his eyes moving over me and back to the screen. Even I can tell that's a cue for the fae to leave.

'Well, be a good little fuckboy and run along and let the real demons know I'm here. Or are you too busy playing with your toy?'

I look up at the guy sharply. I've never heard anyone talk to one of the Iron I's like that. I glance at Paris, a little worried, but he doesn't look riled. He feels it though and I frown. Why is he letting this fae talk to him like he's a piece of garbage. People used to do it all the time in the diner and I used to let it go because I wanted to get paid, but Paris doesn't work for this guy. He's letting himself be treated badly for no reason that I can see.

Anger rises up in me fast, a lot more than I used to feel when people spoke to me like *I* was scum. I could let it roll off my back, but this isn't me.

I'm suddenly sitting up as straight as I can in Paris' tight hold and craning my neck to look into the smug face of this fae fuck.

'Paris *is* too busy actually. Why don't you go find them yourself, *fuckboy*?'

Paris is surprised but amused and I see the corners of his mouth turning upwards.

'Listen, you little human bitch,' Walter hisses, bending down to get in my face.

I don't cower because I refuse to be that human and his finger comes up to point at me.

He opens his mouth, probably to obliterate me with magick, but he doesn't get to say whatever spell he was going to conjure up because he's pulled back violently by Sie. Vic is next to him.

'Walt,' Vic claps the fae on the back hard enough for him to wince. 'I thought I told you we'd see you when the fight was over. I'd thank you to leave our human alone. We're here to watch Kor. I'll talk to you after.'

'But I—'

'You heard him,' Sie says, thrusting the fae away from our table hard enough that he's halfway to the bar by the time his body stops moving.

My eyes widen. Yeah I said what I said and I expected a punishment, but you can't just *manhandle* a fae. But no one says anything. No one does anything. The fae legions I was afraid were going to melt out of the walls to destroy us don't appear. The bar clientele sitting at the tables close by just chuckle and go back to their conversations while Walter picks himself up, straightens his clothes, and leaves quietly.

'Fucking lower fae asshole,' Vic mutters as he sits down next to us.

'Are you okay?' he asks me.

I frown at the same question.

Why do they keep asking?

I just nod though. This is the first time he's really spoken to me since I refused to accept his apology.

'What was all that about?' Sie asks.

Paris is grinning. 'I don't think our girl liked me being spoken down to, did you, princess?'

'I guess I didn't,' I say, trying to work out why he looks so pleased and wondering at his choice of words.

Our girl?

I mean, I am their girl, I guess. I *am* contracted to the Club.

'I don't think I've ever heard a human speak to a fae like that before, not even a lower one with no magick like him.'

Some of them don't have magick?

That's news to me.

I shrug. 'I didn't know there were lower ones.'

Sie frowns, putting a hand up to silence Paris when he starts to speak. 'So you said that to him even thinking he was a High Lord who could kill you as easily as breathing and probably would have?'

'Uhhhh. So there are different types of fae?'

'You're fearless, princess.' Paris' smile gets wider and he sounds different, like the dumb frat boy I thought he was when I first met him.

Holy shit! It's an act!

Why would he pretend to be something he's not?

'She's not fearless, she's stupid,' Sie mutters, turning to Vic. 'If we're going to continue taking her to places like this, she needs educating properly. She's ignorant of too much in our world.'

Vic looks from him to me. 'Agreed. You can see to it.'

Sie takes a step back. 'I didn't mean ... Paris or Theo would be better.'

Vic shakes his head. 'They have other things they're

doing for me. Besides, you know more about supe lore than the others.'

Sie sits down at the other side of the table, staring at me. I stare back. What's his problem? I'm excited to learn about supes. I've always found everything about them interesting.

I'm a supeaphile!

Maybe I won't say that out loud.

He frowns. He's annoyed that he has to spend time with me, so I frown back.

Paris, though, turns my head towards him and gives me a lingering kiss that makes my fingers grab at his lapels and forget that Sie doesn't want to spent time with me.

I have to stifle another moan as his lips finally leave mine. I want so much more.

'I like you being protective,' he says, 'and I thank you for it, but don't ever put yourself in harm's way for me, princess. I'm not what you think.'

'I know,' I say breathlessly. 'I think I just figured you out, Paris.'

Vic clears his throat and I turn to see both he and Sie staring at us.

'This isn't the time,' Paris says, his eyes locked onto mine as he puts me back in my seat much to my disappointment.

We watch the rest of the fight, all the things niggling at me about Paris, Sie and Vic making my brain feel messy. I focus on Korban. Mad Dog is fast, but Kor gives as good as he gets and by the end, although I don't like all the noise, there's something about the exciting atmosphere that pulls me in.

They're evenly matched and I'm just wondering if there's such a thing as a tie-breaker in fighting when Korban gets a strike through that's so hard that Mad Dog's face flies to the side and I'm sure I see a couple of teeth hurled across the ring. He sways on his feet for a second before he falls back, landing with a thud. The crowd goes wild outside and I can hear them screaming Kor's name even from in here.

The guys stand as soon as it's done. I guess they don't spend any more time here than they have to. We turn to leave when Vic stops in his tracks in the middle of the room.

'I didn't know you'd be here today,' he says to a man standing in front of him.

His emotions hit me like a gust of icy wind. He's sooooo not happy about this guy being here that I cringe. Paris pulls me in close to him.

The man is older than Vic with black hair that's just greying around the temples. Broad shoulders are encased in a black, tailored suit (that I only know is tailored because Paris explained to me the difference between that and 'off the rack'). He looks like he spends a fair amount of time keeping up his silver fox physique and takes a lot of care to look immaculate. If I didn't know better, I'd say he was a vamp, but he's not.

He's an incubus.

For some reason, I find myself getting scared and I half-hide, pressing myself into Paris' side behind Sie.

'You've been avoiding my calls,' he replies to Vic.

He and Vic shake hands in a very formal way that screams, 'We hate each other!' and I cast a look at the others, wishing I knew who this man was.

'Not at all,' Vic says. 'I've just been busy.'

The older incubus gives Vic a tight smile. 'So I keep hearing. How's the house?'

'Being rebuilt.'

'Lose much?'

'Nothing that can't be replaced.'

'Good.' The incubus says, surveying us, his eyes lingering on me for an extra second. 'We need to talk, Alex.'

'We have a meeting at *The Lounge* now.'

'Hmm. Can't be late or you'll miss your window. I'll follow. Give me chance to look at Maddox's operation and get to know your ... *newest member*.'

Is he talking about me? If he is, his tone is unsettling AF.

Vic nods. 'See you in a little while then.'

The incubus steps aside and we file past him somewhat awkwardly. I feel his eyes on me as I go past him and all the way to the door. I don't look back, just put my headphones on and stay as close to the others as I can.

'Who was that guy?' I ask as we make our way down to the ring through the crowds of screaming Korban fans.

The three of them exchange a look.

'Leonel Makenzie,' Vic murmurs over the audio feed. 'My father.'

My eyes widen.

I just met (sorta) Vic's dad?

I glance back and find the incubus staring down at us ... or is it just at me?

Stop it, Jane. You aren't the center of the damned universe.

I hurry down the steps with the others to the front near the ring as Korban climbs out through the ropes and hops to the ground.

Two supe females run from the bleachers at him and I tense when one puts her hand on his bare chest.

I get an insane urge to stop her, to tell her that he doesn't like being touched, and I have to look away for a second to stop myself. What is going on with me tonight? First Paris and now *Korban*? He fucking hates me. Why would I even care about saving *him* from a little discomfort?

I look back in time to see a couple of bouncers walking

his way, but he's smiling at the two girls, signing their shirts. One of them gets closer to him, up onto her tip toes and whispers something in his ear, her fingers grazing down his peck. He chuckles at her words. He looks like a completely different guy.

A pang of something painful hits me right in the chest and I shrug it off. He's nothing to me, I tell myself. But then his eyes meet mine and he pulls her face up for a deep kiss.

I turn away, letting out a breath, not sure what I'm actually upset about. But turning inward and rapidly wanting to get the hell out of here.

No one's speaking, but Vic takes my elbow and leads me out through the back of the bleachers to a couple of rooms with banks of lockers and the fighters who are up next. I can feel his power coming off him like steam off a wet road in the sun. He's pissed. What have I done now?

We go through a door that leads out to the parking lot. In the fresh air, I breathe a sigh of relief as I take down my headphones. It's dark and it's been raining, the glow of streetlights making the asphalt shine underfoot.

The others are behind us, including Korban, and I take special care not to look in his direction. Paris hands me the silver wrap that he told me would go with the dress better than my old jacket, which I wanted to wear for the pockets, and I throw it over my shoulders as the wind picks up.

We all pile into the car except for Korban. No one says anything, but I brace myself for a Vic lecture on whatever I did to make him mad. He doesn't say anything though.

I frown and let out an annoyed sound, deciding to just be direct because I don't want the worry of it hanging over me all night.

'If you don't explicitly tell me what I did to annoy you in

there, I'm probably not going to be able to figure it out by myself. You know that right?'

'What are you talking about?' Vic asks.

'You're mad. I can tell.'

He lets out a sigh. 'I'm not angry with you, Jane.'

I look at him with blatant suspicion. 'You're not?'

He shakes his head and I sit back in the seat between Theo and Sie, rubbing my head.

'You okay?' Theo asks.

I frown. 'I'm FINE. Please stop asking.'

I wince as I look at him.

'Sorry,' I say, not attempting to try to explain that my brain is in a jumble.

It'll take time to unknot all my thoughts and interpret any feelings that are mixed up in there. Honestly, I'm tired just thinking about unraveling it.

'Nothing to apologize for, Jane,' Theo says, giving my arm a slight squeeze.

'Where's Korban?' I ask, and that voice in my head tells me he's probably gone to spend some time with his fangirl incubus-style.

I winkle my nose at the thought that they can likely fuck any supes they want, it's just humans they aren't allowed to sow their supey seeds in all willy-nilly. But if that's true, why bother with feeding from humans at all? Maybe I should start a list of things I want to ask Sie.

'He'll be along in a bit,' Theo tells me. 'He likes to take a drive after a fight.'

Paris lets out a derisive sound that I don't understand.

Theo ignores him. 'He'll meet us at *The Lounge*.'

'What's that, a club?'

Theo glances at Vic who's staring out the window into the rain.

Great, more stuff I'm not allowed to know.

But Vic surprises me by honing in on Sie. 'Make sure she knows everything she needs to about where we're going for her own safety.'

Sie lets out a long breath, but I'm already turning towards him, getting excited to know the things.

I stare at him expectantly and he lets out a weary breath.

'Fine,' he grates out then tapers off.

He scratches his beard, hesitating before he starts again.

'Okay, so there are three rules you must not break. 'Don't take *anything* you're offered. Don't wander off. Don't talk to strangers.'

I nod, thinking about scenarios that may or may not happen.

'What if I get something myself, like if no one gives it to me?' I ask.

'That's okay.'

'What if I do wander off?'

'Don't.'

'What if I can't help it? What if it's some supey mojo that makes me.'

'Then you'll be lost in the fae realms.'

My mouth falls open. 'I thought we were just going to a club!'

'We are,' Paris says to me. 'It used to be a fae club so it's close to places they like to hang out in; magickal places that aren't for humans. Maddox owns it now and it's mostly supes that go. It's not much different to *The Circle* where we went before.'

'Sounds different,' I mutter. 'What if I start talking to someone I think I know, but they're *actually a stranger* and I don't realize at first because the fae tricked me?'

Sie groans, putting his head in his hands and Theo sniggers.

'What? They do that. They're crafty!'

'Just don't talk to anyone except us and stay with us at all times,' Sie grinds out through his teeth.

'Okily dokily,' I say, sounding waitress chipper, but I'm kind of nervous now.

The Iron I's don't have the best track record where my, and in fact other humans', safety is concerned. They suck at keeping us alive to be honest. I'm basically a kid's goldfish or any houseplant I've ever owned.

'Maybe you guys could drop me off first?' I ask.

Vic shakes his head. 'The city knows who you are after your little trip to the Metro PD, baby girl. You're safer with us.'

Debatable.

~

Sie

WE PULL up to a crumbling brick wall around a vacant lot. I glance at Jane, I can tell she's wondering where the entrance is.

'Remember,' I say, 'this used to be a fae club. You know how they are. It's not a door the way that you would see a door. They love all that shit.'

I watch her while she's not looking at me. I do that a lot. At first it was because I was trying to work out if she was human or not, but now it's a habit. I like to make sure she's okay. She usually seems it, but it's hard to tell with her. I think she buries a lot and we certainly haven't made her already hard life any easier since she met us.

I frown. She does seem fine, but I don't buy it. Despite her lack of reaction at the fight, I could tell she was upset when Korban kissed that shifter girl in front of her. She ran out of there like a hell hound was on her heels. I wanted to comfort her like I did before.

My fingers twitch in my lap as I remember how I held her while she was tripping and scared. It's been a long time since anyone sought me for comfort, but the way she snuggled into my chest, the trust in her eyes that I didn't deserve, was enough to make me remember what that closeness is like. I didn't realize I missed it, how alone I've been.

Vic opens the car door.

Jane looks a little confused and very anxious. I want to put her mind at ease, but it's best that she goes in scared. Scared *and careful*!

'Stay with me,' I remind her.

She nods and we get out of the car, standing in front of the wall as a group with Jane in the middle of us.

I check my watch. 'Should be open now.'

Vic steps forward through the solid wall and we all follow. I hear Jane gasp as he disappears into the invisible doorway before her and she pulls back at the last second. I put my large hand in the small of her back and propel her forward with me.

'Hesitating at a portal is a great way to be lost in the ether,' I murmur in her ear and she grips onto me tightly as we go though, screwing up her eyes.

We come out the other side a second later, transported to Maddox's *Dark Lounge*. Jane opens one eye, cowering next to me like we're about to be consumed by a ball of fire or something.

She surveys what's in front of her and, clearly deciding

everything's fine, she lets go of me and straightens, but she stays very close and I'm glad. I like that she's near me. Safe.

We're in an Art Deco foyer with accented homages to the old world in the form of murals dating back thousands of years depicting the supes and humans warring with each other.

Cute.

Maddox's delightful sense of humor isn't far off the fae's.

The man himself comes out of an anteroom with two of his clan; the twin brothers Jayce and Krase. Jane stays just behind me, peering around me. After her many infuriating questions on the way here, I half-wonder if she's going to try to try to escape me just to see if she can, but Theo sent me a text in the car reminding me that she sometimes needs extra information.

She's looking around in awe, but regarding Maddox and the other two warily. After what happened in *The Circle Club*, I don't blame her and I survey the three of them through narrow eyes though Maddox and Vic greet each other relatively warmly as incubi clan leaders usually do even if they are technically rivals.

Maddox leads us to a massive, old-fashioned wrought iron elevator. He grabs the door handle to slide open the door and I spin to Jane, remembering her forgotten headphones lying on the seat in the car. I immediately put my hands over her ears to save her senses from the echoing roar. She startles as my skin makes contact with hers, but she figures me out pretty quick and looks up at me with surprise.

'Thanks,' she whispers.

I nod and turn away. It's not a big deal. Vic told me to keep her safe. I'm just doing my job.

We all pile into the oversized cage. The thundering door

is hauled shut and slams hard, but Jane's waiting for it and she's ready covering her ears.

The box begins to move down slowly.

'Where are we doing this?' Vic asks Maddox.

Maddox casts his eyes upwards and shakes his head.

'Give it a minute,' he mutters.

I follow Maddox's eyes up, but all I can see is the empty shaft above us. No one talks. Even Jayce and Krase, who are known to take almost nothing seriously, are looking uncharacteristically solemn.

What is this? I thought we were just here to talk logistics for keeping the Order away from our enterprises, but they're acting very clandestine. I share a look with Vic. He's wondering the same thing.

Jane's hand brushes mine and I move so that I'm just shy of being pressed against her, pretending that it's because the elevator is crowded.

I keep second guessing myself, but I'm ninety-nine-point nine percent sure she is human after all. I was being paranoid before ... I mean I was on the wrong side of crazy less than a month ago. Can I really trust myself completely?

We get to the bottom of the shaft and there's a distinct smell of chlorine.

'Can we talk yet?' Vic asks.

Maddox glances back as he leads us down a wide, stone corridor. His expression has lifted. It's almost playful once more.

'Should be fine now,' he says.

'Good. My father cornered me at the fight. He wants to talk to me and said he'll meet me here. If you could keep him distracted for a while, it would be appreciated.'

Maddox gives a small chuckle and checks his watch. 'Well he might not make the window. The portal is closing in a few minutes. I thought you were going to miss it to be honest.'

I roll my eyes. Fucking fae bullshit. 'How long are we going to be stuck here this time?'

'A few hours at most,' Maddox replies pleasantly, 'but we'll know for certain once the doorways close and the timings can be calculated properly. You'll receive an automated text with the exact time it'll reopen.'

Vic looks long-sufferingly at the other clan leader. 'There had better be a damn good reason you wanted to meet here, Maddox. We weren't intending on getting stuck here all night.'

Maddox shrugs. 'It's one of the prices of dealing in fae pastimes and pleasures, I'm afraid. But at least if your father does make it through before the portal closes, he'll be kept busy for as long as you wish; a hundred years if you feel like it.'

Vic snorts. 'You'll find he knows most of the fae's little tricks. I doubt we'll get more than an hour before he tracks us down.'

'We'll see,' Maddox says, leading us further down the long hallway.

At the end is a lounging area with some couches and a reception desk in the corner.

'I chose this location because we're deep underground,' he says. 'The baths themselves don't open until tomorrow and the walls down here are the original stone. They're several feet thick. There's no way anyone can be listening in.'

'Who do you think would be?' Vic asks.

Maddox doesn't answer the question. Instead, he opens a door and gestures.

Beyond him is a large, steaming pool. Sconces line the

walls, giving out a warm glow. The floors are unfinished grey marble and there are modern lounge chairs jutting out from the walls.

'Is this like a spa?' Jane asks me.

'In human terms, yes, exactly.' Maddox answers her and she draws back, staring at him with a blank expression. 'I heard about your stint in the lock-up. Hope it didn't have any lasting effects.' His eyes try to look into hers and she shies away from the contact. 'Still, it ended with your induction into the Iron I's, so silver lining, eh? Would you like Jayce here to show you around *The Lounge* while we talk business?' he asks her.

He's acting friendly, but she doesn't even look at Jayce. She doesn't buy his charm.

Smart girl.

'No.'

Her demeanor has gone arctic and it makes me realize how much she must trust the Iron I's even if she doesn't want to, how much she's changed with us since she met us.

'She stays with us,' Vic says.

Maddox nods like he expected as much, but Jayce looks disappointed and I make a mental note to keep my eye on him where Jane is concerned. He looks well-fed, but he wouldn't be the first Incubus to forget himself and steal another clan's human to snack on. It's rare, but it happens and Jayce is still quite young.

'Changing rooms are through there and there,' he says, pointing at a door on one side of the lounge and one on the other. 'Everything is provided.'

He and his clan-mates go through the door on the right.

Jane surveys it and then the one on the left, giving me a questioning look.

'I'll take a look around first,' I say.

I go into the other changing room. I pass a bank of dryers, lockers, showers and I make sure there's no one there. I feel for any magick residue that would indicate a conjure, but it's clean.

'It's okay,' I call to Jane who's waiting by the entrance. 'Get changed. I'll stay here and one of us will be waiting for you poolside. Remember the rules, okay?'

She nods and I go back to the door, waiting for her to let me know she's ready.

It's not long before she calls to me that she's going through into the baths and I hot-foot it into the other changing room, shucking my clothes and throwing on some trunks I find on the bench. I walk out into the heat of the thermals, finding that everyone's in the hot pool already. Jane's in the water between Paris and Theo and my body unclenches.

She's right there. Everything's fine.

When I'm close enough, my breath hitches and I have to cough to hide my reaction to the black and gold bikini she's wearing that I can just make out beneath the water.

This isn't the time, I remind myself as I make my way over to them all and slide into the pool where everyone's chatting just as Maddox zeroes in on Paris and points to his chest.

'What's that?'

Paris looks down at the mark, his cheeks reddening. 'Oh, uh, just got bit ... by a cat I was playing with.'

I stare at the small circle of teeth marks and frown, all at once remembering what Jane tried to do that night when I caught her in the gym. She tried to bite me, but this doesn't make any sense. There's been nothing since the strip club to indicate that Jane is anything other than human, right?

Maybe she just gets *bitey* when she has sex. I'm being paranoid again.

'Must have been one angry feline,' Krase laughs, but Maddox doesn't look convinced.

His eyes stare at the mark, at Paris, and then he glances at Jane as if trying to figure something out about her.

She doesn't notice.

'Why are we here?' Vic asks Maddox, obviously getting impatient.

'Straight to the point. Very well,' Maddox sighs. 'Do you know how many clubs I own?'

Vic nods. 'Twelve.'

'More like twenty.'

My eyes narrow. I thought I knew everything there was to know about Maddox and his clan just as they know practically everything about us. We like to keep our friends close.

'You own some that we don't know about?'

Maddox looks a little uncomfortable. 'Yes, purchased through shell companies. No one can see they're mine.'

'Why would you bother going to the trouble,' I ask. 'Everyone knows that's where most of your assets are.'

'Because they're fae clubs,' Vic answers me. He looks at Maddox. 'Right?'

Maddox nods. 'Very high-end. The fae lords don't let supes like us anywhere near them, but there are ways to get around their laws ... and their magickal systems too. I'm a silent partner and the money trail doesn't go to me directly. It's a risk and we're fucked if they wise up, but it's worth it to keep tabs on those slippery bastards.'

'So we're here because you heard something,' I murmur.

'One of my employees. A lower fae girl who's since disappeared.'

'What did she see?' Vic asks.

'She saw a member of the high council, one of The Ten.' Maddox takes a final look around, as if he's afraid the fae could somehow be here. 'He met with Don Foley,' he whispers.

'What? But Don Foley's ...' I cast a look at Jane.

She seems like she's not paying attention, but she heard what Maddox just said about her father. She had to have.

'It's surprising, but not shocking. It only confirms what we've been suspecting since they increased their activities. We assumed they had help, but I expected it to be some rogue shifters if I'm honest,' Vic says, not looking anywhere near as shaken as I feel. 'The Order has grown too fast and become too powerful to not have some serious backing and they've had help evading the authorities for some time now.'

'But why are The Ten bankrolling the Order against us?' Paris asks.

'Because it's what they do,' Maddox says, leaning back against the side of the pool with a discontented breath, 'when they decide our populations are getting dangerous to their interests and need thinning.'

'They start a war?' Theo asks, sounding incredulous.

Maddox nods. 'They have us and the humans kill each other for a while and then they broker a peace. They pick up the pieces, get a little richer, and emerge as the seemingly benevolent leaders we all need at such a dark time.'

'C'mon,' Theo scoffs. 'If they'd done that before we'd know.'

'How?' Maddox asks, turning his piercing eyes on Theo. 'Whoever's in power can make history whatever they want and the fae have been in power for a very long time. I have proof that they've done it a few times, old texts that survived their purges. The last example of this was over a thousand years ago. The Ten and the high lords have the longevity and the power to pull this shit off with the humans, us, and even most of the lower fae not having a clue.'

'This is insane,' Paris mutters.

Jane still hasn't said anything.

'There's more,' Maddox says.

I lock eyes with Vic and his are saying to get Don Foley's daughter the fuck away from Maddox right now, but it's likely too late. The other incubus leader deals in information and hers only took a couple of days for *us* to get. The odds of him and his clan not already knowing who Jane is are very slim.

'How much worse can it get?' Paris mutters.

Maddox lets out a mirthless laugh. 'I'll let you be the judge of that. We've been trying to find out who the leader of the Order actually is, but we're coming to realize that there is no Grand Wizard.'

'You mean it's...'

'Foley. He's the head of the Order. His superiors don't actually exist. My agents also found evidence of coded messages. A lot of them. They reference seven cities; not by name, but it's clear one of them is Metro and something big is coming.'

'What is it?' Vic asks.

'I need to get out,' Jane murmurs to me and I nod, keeping an eye on her as she swims to the steps and gets out of the pool slowly.

Maddox throws up his hands as he answers. 'More bombs? The beginning of all-out war between the humans and us? Who can say? But we need to be ready for anything.'

His, Jayce's, and Krase's eyes follow Jane's movements as she grabs a towel and wraps herself in it before sitting on one of the loungers. She's not looking at any of us, but every single pair of eyes is on her, including the other clan's and I wonder if we're going to have a different problem than the one Vic was envisioning with them.

A door opens and Korban saunters in fully-clothed with Maddox's two other clan-mates, Iron and Axel, behind him.

'Better late than never,' he drawls, his eyes moving from us in the pool to land on Jane.

She ignores him. He grabs a drink from a table and walks up to her. He tries to hand it to her. That's an olive branch if I've ever seen one from Kor.

But she shakes her head, not even looking at him.

'No thanks. I'll get one for myself,' she mutters and I realize she's taking the rules I gave her to heart while burning Korban at the same time.

Bet he wishes he hadn't kissed that shifter now.

I hide my grin.

13

JANE

I'm sitting on a *sun lounger* in an *underground* spa, trying to get my head around my dad being public enemy number one when Korban beckons me. I'm tempted to ignore him, but he's probably going to pick me up caveman style and forcibly put me wherever he wants me, so, with a huff, I rise and make my way over to him.

I make sure I have my towel wrapped around me because this bikini doesn't leave much to the imagination. It's not the Iron I's I'm worried about, it's the others. Maddox and his clan haven't taken their eyes off me since we got here. That combined with what happened at *The Circle Club* with them is making me very uncomfortable and fidgety. The feelings of worry I'm getting off Theo, Paris and Vic don't help either and I'm trying to tune them out, but it's hard.

I'm thinking that there's something different about me, that maybe I'm not like other humans, but for once it has nothing to do with my neurodiversity. I haven't had chance to ask Paris anything since he shut me down, but he was more than a little concerned by what I said. He was scared.

He literally barged into a building of supe cops to save me and my little revelation was terrifying? He knows something and I need to get him to tell me what it is.

'Where are we going?' I ask Korban.

As usual, he barely answers me, just opens the door to the changing room with a grunt.

'Rude,' I mutter, rolling my eyes as I go through the door to get my normal, comfy clothes back on.

But as I walk over the threshold, the room melts away.

I look around in alarm. I'm on a grassy hilltop. The sun is shining. I can feel it's rays on my skin. There are flowers everywhere.

My stomach drops.

Fuck!

I turn around. There's no door there, just more countryside.

Trying to keep my panic at bay, I turn in a slow circle, taking everything in. As far as I can see, there are rolling hills that look exactly the same as the one I'm standing on, small patches of forest, and I can hear water. But not the tinkling of the spa. It's more like roaring river water.

Fuck, fuck, fuck, fuck, fucking fuckity fuck!

Trust me to go through a door and end up in freaking Narnia!

At first, I don't see any sign of life at all besides the flora and fauna around me. Then, I notice a twist of fairytale smoke coming from a wooded glen. Casting my eyes up to the heavens, I grit my teeth and start walking. Maybe there'll be someone there who can help me ... *or put me in an oven, or turn me into a mushroom, or lock me into a fae-style, give-up-your-first-born bargain.*

I silence that voice.

Not helpful!

I make my way towards the smoke, using convenient steppingstones to get over a babbling brook with little, pink, sparkling fish darting around in it. I'm tempted to stop because they're so mesmerizing, but I'm pretty sure that stopping is going to get me killed or worse in here. I just have that feeling.

I wrack my brains for all the fae stories I've ever heard because – and I don't want to generalize or perpetuate harmful stereotypes – the fae are usually tricksters who want to steal human souls and shit.

Maybe they *want* me to stop to look at the pretties, so I keep going.

But then I start thinking: What if it's a double bluff? Maybe they *don't want* me to stop.

I make a small sound of distress. I can't even understand what motivates my own kind. I'm sure as hell not going to be able to figure the fae out. But I keep moving forward because I stick to my goals!

I get to the edge of the wood. The trees are twisted and gnarled. It looks uninviting and completely foreboding. But I just walked for a half hour and I'm not going all the way back to where I started from! I'm committed.

I shake my head.

'I'm too old for this shit,' I mutter to keep my bravado at high enough levels so I'm not too scared to take that first step into the trees.

I start moving, trying to keep going straight in the direction of the smoke I saw because I don't want to start floundering around in circles and get lost in here.

After a little while, I come upon a house amongst the trees. It's an old cabin with a crooked chimney and tiny windows that I can't see into. Taking a steadying breath, I go to the door and knock.

It creaks open, but there's no one there.

'Really!?' I say into the nothing.

I let out a long breath.

Am I really doing this?

I walk through the door.

But inside it's not a cottage. The interior is a large lounge with dim lighting. I survey the leather and mahogany, the deep reds of the décor.

'I've been waiting for you.'

I turn with an involuntary gasp and find a man behind me. I tilt my head. I've seen this guy before.

'You're Vic's dad,' I say.

'You know who I am.' He seems pleased. 'Good. That'll make this a little easier.'

He stalks closer and I back up, not liking his sudden proximity.

'What do you want?'

I know I can't trust him. He might be Vic's family, but he didn't seem very fatherly to me. I also get the feeling Lionel Makenzie doesn't like me. With the way he's acting, he's probably taken a leaf out of *my* dad's book to be honest.

'Come here,' he says. 'Don't bother trying to run, cherub. You're just delaying the inevitable.'

He adjusts himself in his expensive pants.

Ew.

OH!

Okay, maybe not like my dad.

'The inevitable what?' I ask, trying to buy myself a little time.

I'm still backing up and he's prowling across the room after me. I jostle a table at my back and steady it with my hand behind me. Something heavy rocks and my fingers close around it. The object is smooth and stone. I pick it up and lob it at him as I turn and dart to the side.

I get to the door I came through and open it. There's a brick wall behind it.

Fucking FAE!

I look over my shoulder. He's almost on me!

'What do you want me for?' I ask, leaping away from him and looking for another exit.

'I can't believe my stupid son hasn't figured it out yet,' he murmurs as he advances. 'I knew it as soon as I saw you.'

He grabs my towel and rips it away, looking his fill of my scantily clad body.

'Look, creeper, I belong to the Iron I's,' I say, my voice shaky.

'Come,' he says, holding out his hand. 'I just want to talk, my beauty.'

I don't move. What a crock. I'm not doing dick this guy wants me to do.

He grabs me by my wrist and pulls me towards the couch. I resist, so he picks me up and I let out a scream, struggling and bucking in his arms.

'Put me the fuck down!'

But, of course, there's no getting away easily. This guy is huge like Vic. Unlike Vic though, I'm nowhere near interested in the incubus in front of me. His silver fox vibes are not doing it for me. I'm literally repulsed and it makes me realize how much I'm *not* repulsed by Vic ... by the others too.

When he throws me down on the couch, the wind is knocked out of me. He kneels between my legs and I feel him trying to lull me with his power.

It doesn't work on me, asshole!

But I go lax, trying to look like Monique when she was in

Sie's room that time, and I see the triumph in his eyes as his fingers slip under the waistband of my bikini bottoms. While his attention is on what's between my thighs, I ease my leg up and I kick him hard between his.

He pulls back with a yell, grabbing his crotch, and I slip out from under him, running across the room to the other door I saw. I tear it open and freeze. It's pitch black in there; an abyss of nothing. I turn around. He's recovered and he's coming for me, making noises like an animal.

A rock and a hard place.

I let out a growl of frustration and I run into the darkness. There's a floor. It's not an abyss, after all. It feels cool and smooth beneath my bare feet and that makes it easy to keep going because if it was crunching like Fortune Cookies (if you know, you know), I would be leaping back through the doorway and taking my chances with sex-crazed Lionel.

I realize as I go that it's not as dark as it seemed to be either. I can see shadows and my steps create echoes. Wherever I am, this place is huge and cavernous, but it is a room.

A light flickers a few steps ahead and I make for it. It's cold in here and I'm pretty sure that if the lights were on, I'd be able to see my breath in the air. My skin is goose-bumpy and I wrap my arms around myself because I'm dressed in a *damn bikini.*

My first spa trip is not going well.

I get closer to the light and I see it's a lone candle on a pedestal. I glance around. As far as I can see, there's nothing else here.

And then I hear a whisper.

'Jane.'

I look in the direction the sound came from and I hear it again. That's Korban's voice. I'm sure of it. I walk towards it.

'Come in here quick.'

A hand reaches for me from behind a curtain I didn't see before and I'm pulled through into a pool hall.

I look around me. There are other people. Supes. Some shifters and vamps. No fae that I can see.

I grip onto Korban, not caring that this is *Korban* because I'm not liking this club at all.

'That was scary as fuck,' I mutter.

'It's okay, I found you,' he says.

He takes a cue off the nearby rack and offers me it.

I frown. Even for me this is kind of weird. 'You want to ... *play pool*?'

He nods. 'The portal back to your world doesn't open again for a few more hours. We have some time to kill.'

I gesture to myself. 'Dressed like this?'

He waves a hand. 'No one cares here.'

A quick survey of the place confirms it. No one's even looking at us. I nod. 'Okay. Where are the others?'

He shrugs. 'Probably still talking business.'

He racks up the balls and takes a shot. He gets none of them in and I smirk. I lean over and put the solid red in the left corner pocket. Pretending to be modest, I straighten without looking at him.

This is my game, bitch.

Korban shoots again, and again he misses. I take my turn. Solid yellow bounces off the side and into a pocket.

'You're very good,' he says.

'I know. Why did you kiss that girl?' I blurt out and then I put my hand over my mouth in horror.

I didn't want to say it like that. It just came out. He looks at me and that's when I realize what's bugging me about him and what we're doing. I can't feel any of his emotions, not even the anger that always clings to him. I'm getting nothing off of him at all.

I've been using this funny little power I have a lot more than I thought..

'I'm sorry about that,' he says. 'Truce?'

He holds a drink out to me and I glance at him as I take it, careful to keep my face blank. We already did this earlier. Korban tried to give me a drink in the spa and I told him it was against the rules. All at once, the words he said before we started playing come back to me, 'the portal back to *your* world', like he doesn't live there ...

I force a smile and bring the glass to my lips. He's watching me intently. He cares if I drink.

I pretend to take a sip and then I put it down on the edge of the pool table. When he turns away to take his shot, I wipe the residue off my lip, making sure I don't take in even a drop as my blood runs cold.

This isn't Korban.

You're not roofying me, mofo!

I glance around again, looking for someone to help me, but no one catches my eye. I take my turn, pocketing another ball, and fake Korban gives me a look. I think he's annoyed that I'm *completely destroying him* at this game.

As fake Korban takes his eyes off me to play his shot, I look around at the supes that are here playing pool and drinking around us. I frown. They're all still doing the same things that they were when we first came in. If I pay attention to them for more than a few seconds, it's like they're on a video loop.

When I turn my attention back to the pool table, fake Kor is watching me and I think he knows I know. He looks at the drink on the pool table next to me.

I pick it up and silently cheers him with the glass, pretending to take another drink, but his eyes narrow on me.

'Smart girl,' he sneers.

'Who the fuck are you?' I ask.

Before my eyes, he morphs back into Vic's dad.

What is it with this guy?

'I do love these games you like to play,' he says. 'If it makes you feel better about it, you can give me the runaround all you want. But know that you won't give me the slip. You will be mine.'

'Look,' I say, 'as long as I'm not gonna get in trouble with the Iron I's, we can do whatever you want.'

He looks surprised. 'Anything I want?'

I shrug. 'Of course. I love supes.'

I sidle closer and put my hand on his chest, trying my best to act the way I saw the other girls doing when they were around the Iron I's in the Clubhouse. You know, before I got the blame for it blowing up, burning it to the ground, and turning them into barbeque.

I try not to dry heave. Vic's dad stinks of old man cologne and has breath that smells like a dentist's. I lean up like I'm going to kiss him and I watch as he closes his eyes.

Ha! Everyone always does that.

I throw the drink in his face and leap back. He yells, wiping frantically at his skin and spitting on the floor.

'You bitch,' he hisses, lunging for me.

I yelp, panic, and hurl the glass at him, hitting him on the forehead. I run down the pool hall to the end where there's a bar. The waiter on the other side looks like a vamp and unlike all the customers in here, this guy looks *real*.

'How do I get out of here?' I yell.

He head-gestures to a red, neon sign that says 'EXIT' ... like I'm an idiot.

Hilarious.

I leave, scrambling up the stairs and I find myself back in

the spa. It's empty except for Theo who's walking around the pool with his back to me.

But, maybe it's not Theo. I turn around. The door I came through is closed and I'm filled with a sensation of impending doom. I need to get out of this freaky deaky club.

I move slowly towards the other end of the room, wishing I had a weapon of some kind because this is probably Vic's dad again and he definitely knows all my moves now. I mean, I only have like two, but in my defense they usually work on the unsuspecting attacker when I have chance to use them.

Theo turns and I cringe. Ugh, now I'm going to have to run again. I don't like Maddox's clubs, I decide. I don't understand how anyone could have a good time on a night out when their life is on the line the whole time. I'm giving his clubs zero stars on my Yelp review, that's for sure.

~

Theo

I DIDN'T GO with the others to look for Jane after she disappeared. Instead, I stayed in the spa area in case she found her way back. They'll locate her, but I'm still pacing around the pool, trying not to worry about her. As I turn, I notice her behind me and breathe a sigh of relief. She looks okay.

'Jane?'

She's backing away from me. She looks wary and she's out of breath like she's been running.

'Jane are you' – I stop because she keeps getting annoyed when we ask her if she's okay.

'How are you?' I say instead, wincing inwardly because I sound like a jackass.

'No way!' she practically yells, pointing at me. 'You're not going to trick me again, Vic's dad. And I'm not going down without a fight. You powerful supe types are all the same, thinking you can take whatever you want from us. Fuck you, dude!'

I haul myself out of the hot tub.

'Jane, what the hell are you talking about? It's me. Theo.'

Her eyes narrow. 'If you're really Theo, how many times have you fed from me?'

'None.' I look away, a little embarrassed. 'I've been waiting for the right time.'

'Lucky guess,' she scoffs. 'What was the dinner you made for me the other night when I was in the kitchen with you?'

I take a step towards her. 'Chicken Cacciatore.'

She opens her mouth and then hesitates. 'He never told me what it was called,' she mutters.

She shifts nervously from foot to foot.

'Okay, I don't know if that's true or not ... What did you give me to eat in the cell?'

'Fries and a burger,' I say.

She seems satisfied with my answer because she heaves a sigh and comes towards me.

'I don't like it here,' she says. 'Everything keeps changing. Those rules Sie gave me are not enough for this place. I'd need a whole manual to stay safe!'

'You mentioned Lionel Makenzie. What has he being doing, Jane?' I ask, wondering why Vic's father would waste his time bothering our human.

She sinks down onto one of the loungers close by but doesn't answer my question.

'You know, before I met you guys, pretty much no one looked at me twice. Now I have dudes trying to get all up on me all the damn time. What's that about? And Vic's *dad*? Gross!'

My eyes narrow. I thought she meant he'd been playing his games with her, passing the time while we're stuck in here. He's like that. He enjoys taunting diversions like the fae do.

'Lionel's been trying to *sleep with you*?'

Her eyes widen and she looks at me. 'That's what I've been saying! He tried to fuck me in a rich people living room and then, after I escaped, he pretended to be Korban. He's been chasing me around all different places in this dumb club.'

I wrap myself in a towel, sitting down next to her and trying not to let my eyes linger on her lack of clothes.

'I'm sorry, sweetheart. How did you get separated from Korban? I thought you guys both went through the door together.'

She sniffs. 'All I know is I went to change and I was suddenly on a hillside in the middle of nowhere. Nobody was there except me. I was trying to find you guys, and then I thought I had and I was playing pool with Korban and I realized it wasn't him. Vic's dad tried to make me drink something.'

She sighs, leaning into me and I forget about portals and magickal physics for the moment.

'I just want to not be here. It's trippy and nothing is what it seems. It's a mind fuck and I hate it.'

I put my arm around her and look at my watch.

'Come on,' I say. 'Let's go find the others. We still have a few hours before the window opens again, so we're stuck here until then, but I think you'll feel a lot safer with all of us around you.'

She stands up with me. 'Did none of you think it might be important to tell me any of these things? Why does Vic's dad even want me *for that*? Is it some weird incubus dad thing?'

'Definitely not,' I say. 'Vic is going to be pissed when he finds out. I don't know what Lionel is doing. He has his own ways of feeding and they should not ever extend to our ...' I hesitate because I don't think I'd call Jane an on-call girl anymore.

'Female,' I finish with a mutter.

There's no reason he would want Jane other than the reasons that *we* want her, but he did seem to be staring at her a quite a bit earlier at the fight. Could it be that he just thinks she's hot?

'I don't want to go through another door,' she says, pulling back as we approach the one to the male changing rooms.

'It's okay. We'll go through together and then, if we do end up somewhere else, we won't be separated.'

We turn sideways and go through the door into the men's changing room as one, but as we do, I realize it's not a changing room at all. It's just an empty parking garage.

I walk in and heave a sigh.

'I don't understand,' Jane says, 'Why do the rooms keep changing to different places?'

'All part of the fun,' I mutter.

'Doesn't seem all that fun,' she says, frowning at me and squinting at the shadows around us that I'll admit are making me want to cast my glamor aside so I can protect Jane properly just in case someone's lurking out there.

'Supes who come here love it,' I say instead, not wanting

her to be frightened. 'It's something that was reserved for the fae for a long time so it's an entertaining novelty. If you can figure out the rules, it's pretty easy to navigate.'

'What are the rules?' she asks, looking annoyed as she paces in front of the door that brought us here and I know it's grating on her that she doesn't understand them yet.

I shrug. 'It's not really something I can tell you. You just have to learn for yourself. Try thinking of a place you want to be and then open the door. It should be there.'

She looks at me like I'm crazy. 'No way.'

'Yeah, it should work,' I say. 'You just have to be thinking about it hard enough.'

She closes her eyes, her hand on the knob. She turns it and opens the door, walking through without waiting. I rush to go with her so she doesn't get lost again.

I find we're in my bedroom in the Clubhouse. The one that doesn't exist anymore because it was burned to the ground.

'It didn't work,' she says looking disappointed.

'Where did you want to go?'

'A coffee shop.'

'Maybe that's what you were thinking about, but you actually want to be here. It makes sense. This room is comfortable for you. You're used to it. You're feeling upset. This place would make you feel better.'

'I do miss this room,' she says quietly, 'the whole house actually.'

She sighs heavily, eyeing me. She's looking at me weird.

'Do you think I'm not me again?' I ask.

'No,' she says, 'I think you're you.'

She sits on the bed and looks at me, shuffling her feet around and looking awkward.

I frown at her. 'Then what's wrong?'

'Nothing's wrong,' she says, looking behind her at the bed and then at me.

Could she be wanting ...

'Jane,' I say, watching her closely, 'do you want to have sex?'

'Yes, please.'

I chuckle. 'I wanted to wait for the right time.'

'This is the right time,' she says, standing up and messing around with her bikini top.

My eyes fall to her to the globes of her breasts. They're jiggling as she's trying to untie the back and I step forward, stopping her before my mind gets clouded by my dick.

'Do you not want to?' she asks, tilting her head.

'I do. This just is a weird moment to pick.'

'Well, you said yourself we're going to be here for hours,' she says. 'Might as well pass the time.'

I frown again and she stares at me.

'I'm sorry,' she says. 'I'm not understanding something.'

'What are you not understanding?' I ask.

'I don't know, but I think I've upset you. I didn't do this right. I'm sorry. I'm not very good at seduction.'

'It's not that,' I say, taking her hands. 'It's just I ... I want our first time to be a little bit more than just passing some time.'

Her eyes widen. 'Oh! No, I didn't mean it like that. I just ... I want to and it'll make the minutes go faster, so two birds, one stone. That's all.'

Aside from the fact that she said *minutes* and not *hours*, I'm at a loss.

I let out a groan, putting my head in hands and shaking it. I feel like romance might be wasted on this girl.

But I step forward with a grin and caress her face, giving her a quick kiss on the nose.

'So you wanted to be in my room for this?' I ask.

She nods slowly. 'I think so. All the other times, I've been where *they* wanted. Maybe I want this to be special too,' she whispers. 'Plus, you keep stopping in your clinic so I thought maybe you didn't want to do it in there.'

I move closer to her slowly, not wanting to spook her, but she seems like she's all in. I kiss her lips gently and I feel her sigh. Her body relaxes against mine.

'Did you want to play doctor?' she murmurs and all of a sudden I'm aching to be inside of her. She may not think she knows how to do this, but she's doing a pretty good job from where I'm standing.

'Not this time,' I say. 'There'll be plenty of other days *and nights* to play in the clinic.'

She flashes me a grin and sits on the bed, shuffling backwards. I follow her, kissing her lips, down her neck to her breasts. I pull them out of the bikini, but I leave the bikini on and it holds her tits unnaturally high for me to worship. That's what I want to do with this girl. I want to worship her.

'I want to see the other you,' she murmurs and I look up at her from her chest.

'That's a very personal thing to ask,' I murmur as I kiss down her stomach.

She shifts under me.

'Too personal?' she asks.

'Not for you,' I reply and I mean it.

I let my glamour down. My skin turns midnight blue. I grow taller, thicker, more muscular.

She's surprised. She assumed I'd be smaller than the others. A common mistake.

I'm bigger.

Her mouth falls open as she takes in my horns, white against my dark hide. She stares at my face, into my eyes that are ice-blue. Her fingers flutter up to touch my hair and I let out a deep rumble of satisfaction.

My female definitely likes what she sees.

'Wow,' she breathes. 'You all look so different.'

'Demons,' I say by way of explanation. 'None of us look exactly alike.'

'Do you have a tail?'

I shake my head. 'No, but I do have these.'

I spread my wings and she gasps loudly, lurching up onto her elbows.

'Holy shit! Do they work?'

I grin at her. 'Do you mean can I move them? Yes.'

'No, I mean can you fly?'

My grin becomes an all-out smile. 'Yes, I can fly.'

'Right now?'

I push her back down to the bed. 'No, princess,' I growl low. 'Not right now.'

She shudders at the low timber of my tone and I can tell she likes the sound of it because her breathing stutters and the scent of her becomes more intoxicating.

I pull her towards me and lower my head, giving her mound a nip, scraping my now very sharp and much longer canines across her smooth skin. She quivers under me, but she's not afraid. She doesn't take her eyes off me until I give her a tentative lick up her slit and she shuts them with a moan, angling herself up for me. I smirk at her from my position between her thighs.

'I'm not going to do this now,' I say and her face falls in acute disappointment that makes me yearn to do whatever she wants just to banish that expression.

'Why not?'

She thinks I mean I'm done.

How wrong she is.

I spread her legs as wide as they'll go, looking my fill of her pretty, pink pussy. It's already glistening and wet, but I'm going to take my time.

I kiss my way back up her body to her lips languidly and I can already feel that she's getting impatient. She's used to this going much faster and that is a travesty that I'll have to remedy.

'What's wrong?' I ask as if I don't know.

She's panting and writhing under me, her hips moving, seeking me.

'I feel ... I want ...' she whimpers in frustration when she can't articulate her desires properly.

'I know,' I rasp into her ear, putting her out of her misery. 'Don't worry, sweetheart. I'll give you exactly what you need.'

I move back down slightly and I line myself up with her. My shaft is smooth unlike some supes but quite thick, so I know it's going to take some patience on my part. I ease in the tip and she relaxes with a moan. But before I realize what she's doing, she's locking her heels around my hips and pulling me inside her with surprising strength.

She squeals as I sink into her hot core. I can't stop her and I tense up, afraid I've hurt her. I try to pull out, but she won't let me move back even an inch. She doesn't stop until I'm fully seated and our bodies are locked together. The look in her eyes is wild and frenzied. She sits up and wraps her legs around my waist tightly, using me as leverage to pull herself up and impale herself again. She snaps forward, quick as a viper, and her K-9s pierce my hide. She bit me! I vaguely realize she must have bitten Paris too. I'm surprised somewhere in my head, but mostly I'm stuck on *fuck, that's hot.*

She seems to think so too. Her eyes roll back in her head and she lets out a long, sensuous moan.

'You in charge here?' I murmur and she grins.

'I think I am, Doctor Wright.'

'Then by all means ...' I flip us over, so that I'm on my back, my wings folded beneath me, and she's on top.

I give her a challenging look, which she misses, of course, but she begins to move anyway, undulating her hips, taking me in and out slowly, setting a pace that's relaxed. She's clearly savoring every moment.

I try to hold out as long as I can, but her hands are all over me, gliding down my pecs and across my abs. She leans forward and licks my nipple.

'Is that nice?' she asks and I give her a nod.

Her smile is self-satisfied. She's a happy girl when she thinks she's doing things well. I wonder if she likes to be praised.

'You're amazing,' I say and watch as she practically preens at my approval, moving her hips a little faster.

I grip her gently, filing that away for another time as I begin to meet her movements with well-timed thrusts of my own until we're gasping and quivering and very close to the finish line.

Power flows into me, through me, filling me up to the top and it's like nothing I've ever felt before. It's like the difference between a Big Mac and a lobster dinner. There's no comparison.

I catch her lips with mine as she screams and the sounds of both our climaxes are muffled, our bodies moving in erratic weakness. I'm still inside her as we sink into the bed. Her head is resting on my chest and she sighs with contentment.

I clutch her to me, glad I waited because this was the

single most amazing encounter I've ever had with anyone, supe or otherwise. Being with Jane was everything I never knew I wanted. We have a connection. It wasn't just sex. I care about this girl and she cares about me. I've never had that before. She's still on top of me, unmoving, and at first I think she's asleep, but when I look down at her, she's just staring at me with a look on her face that I don't understand, like I just unlocked the secrets of her universe.

'What is it?' I ask.

'All the feels,' she whispers on a breath.

'I knew you were different,' she says dreamily.

I shake my head. 'What do you mean?'

She seems to come back to herself all at once. 'Nothing.'

She flashes me a little smile and gets up, putting her breasts away all too soon and finding her bikini bottoms at the foot of the bed.

'How do we find the others?'

I blink. Guess we're done.

'Just think of them,' I say.

'Great,' she replies awkwardly, her eyes looking everywhere but at me.

'Hey.' I get up and go to her, restoring my glamor as I go in case it's suddenly my demon form that she doesn't like. 'What's up?'

'Nothing,' she says again, but she grips my hand meaningfully. 'Sorry, I don't mean to be weird.'

'You're not.'

She ignores my words as she glances at the door in the corner. 'Do you think that's still a bathroom?'

I go to it and open the door. 'Looks like it.'

'Okay,' she says, sounding too chipper and disappears inside.

'Hey, Jane, look, I'm sorry if I've done something to make you feel weird,' I call.

She doesn't say anything.

'Jane?'

Nothing.

I ease the door open and curse loudly when I see the small room beyond is empty.

Shit! I hate this fucking place.

14

JANE

I had to get out of that room. Theo's emotions were an onslaught. I had no idea he feels so much all the time. He was so easy to read. It was like a flowing river. I loved it because the emotions weren't mine. It was like watching a movie.

I don't think I could filter him out like I do the others even if I wanted to. I loved feeling everything he did when he was thinking of me. I had no idea that he truly cares about me and I loved it, but I hated it as well because it made me realize how much I care about him too.

'Stupid, stupid, stupid, Jane,' I mutter to myself and I don't even bother to mute that mean voice because I deserve it.

I'm an on-call girl. That's all. They're not *mine* and they never will be. I'm a human. They're supes. Most human kids grow up with warnings from adults. The supes might be pretty and glitzy and powerful, but they aren't for us.

What's worse is that I realized how much I care about the others too even after everything and I know how ridiculous it is, how pathetic it is. But I can't help it. Aside from the fact that they're literal demons, how can I care about men who have fucked up my life so bad? After all the cruel things they did, even Theo as much as I hate to admit it.

I care about him the most. Maybe I even love him, but I have no idea because I don't know what that even feels like.

I wash my hands and pull the door, not noticing until it's fully open that Theo's room has disappeared and in its place is a long, dark hallway.

'Fuck!' I hiss, slamming it closed again and thinking as hard as I possibly can about Theo and his bedroom. I throw open the door again and, sure enough, his room is there as he said it would be if I focused hard enough.

Only he's not in it.

I shut it again and squeeze my eyes together, thinking only about Theo as hard as I can. I crack the door and I find another room that I don't recognize. There are other supes in here and I watch them from the doorway for a minute. They aren't on a loop. Maybe that means they're not part of whatever magick this place is made of. I don't know if that's a good thing or a bad thing.

I look down at myself. I'm still dressed in a bikini and I don't want to invite unwanted attention. There's a robe on the back of the door. I grab it and put it on. At least that's something.

I walk out. It looks like a regular bar. There's quiet conversation and some very light music in the background that I can't really hear above the murmur of voices. I walk around, surveying the room as I go to see if anyone I know is here. But there's no one, not even any of the guys from Maddox's crew.

I make my way to the bar and try to get the barman's

attention. There's a mirror behind and I see Vic over my shoulder. He's right behind me. I twist around with relief, but he's not there.

What the fuck?

I turned back. I can still see him in the mirror. He raises a hand, telling me to wait where I am.

But what if it's not him? What if it's his weirdo dad again pretending to be Vic? Ugh that would be so nasty! I don't want to wait around for *him* to find me.

Vic (or fake Vic) looks ... concerned maybe, but without him being right there for me to actually feel him, I'm not sure.

Sie walks up to him, but a quick look behind me confirms this is all still happening in the reflection. He notices me in the mirror and looks next to him and then back at me. I can see he's as confused as I am.

He says something to Vic and I see their brief exchange but I can't hear what they're saying. Sie puts his hands up like Vic did.

'Wait there!' he mouths.

'Are you lost?' someone says from behind me, but I don't know the voice.

It's not Vic or Sie. I turn around, but there's no one there again. I pretend that I'm not afraid, but more than one supe turns their head in my direction proving that they can literally smell fear.

I am very much aware that I am the only human in a supe bar, in a supe realm. I have no protection here at all. I lock eyes with Vic and Sie.

'I said, are you lost?'

I twist again and I find a member of Maddox's clan. It's one of the two brothers who look the same. Sie told me their names are Jayce and Krase, but I don't know which one is which.

My first reaction is to feel relieved because at least I know who this person is, but have I just gone from the frying pan into the fire?

I look him over. He's tall and broad like they all are. He's looking at me strangely and I don't get a good vibe. But there's no one else who can help me here. Maybe he won't do anything bad to me. I mean, he knows I'm with the Iron I's and Vic is definitely a force to be reckoned with. Maybe the mere threat of him is enough to keep me safe.

'Yes,' I say, 'I *am* lost.'

He tuts. 'They shouldn't have left you so unprotected, little bird. This is our busiest night of the week and *everyone* is here looking for some fun.'

He takes my hand and, not letting me wriggle out of it, he leads me across the floor and through a door. On the other side of it is a gloomy room and my breath hitches. Where has he brought me? I can still feel his hand in mine but I can't see him clearly. And then he's gone as well and I'm alone.

I hear a light snap on. It sounds very much like the one from the cell in the garage, which immediately puts me on edge but the light that shines down from above is very far away and very dim.

I look around me and shriek, jumping back. But I realize it's my own reflection, contorted in a funhouse mirror.

'Hello?' I call, but there's no one there.

I walk forward down the corridor of mirrors, each one changing the way I look in a different way.

Someone laughs right behind me but when I look, there's no one there and I'm starting to see a trend.

I swallow hard. There's a reason I don't watch horror movies. Wasn't there one about mirrors where someone gets trapped on the other side of the glass and there's *things* living in there?

'Stop it,' I say out loud.

Stop freaking yourself out.

I keep walking and I see in one of the reflections that there's someone behind me again. It's a demon I don't recognize and he's walking in step with me. Another trick. I don't turn around. I watch as he puts his hand on my shoulder in the mirror and I ignore it with a roll of my eyes. But then I *feel the hand on me* and I shriek, whirling around and jumping away.

He disappears and I hear laughing.

'Stop it!' I scream, using my hands to cover my eyes, but the sounds of my words echo through the room, reverberating off the mirrors and becoming deafeningly loud.

I move my hands to my ears as I sink to the ground in distress. I call for all of the Iron I's. I don't even care if I'm a damsel in distress as long as they can take me away from this place. At this point, I think I might just pledge my undying love for them all regardless of what they've done in the past if they just help me.

The sounds fade and someone draws me to my feet. I open my eyes tentatively, hoping with everything in me that it's Vic or Sie. Hell, I'll even take Korban at this point, but it's the same guy from before.

'Why are you doing this?' I ask.

All he does is shrug.

Another one of them appears. This must be the twin, I think. He looks pretty much the same except for different clothes.

'Time to leave her alone, bro. The Iron I's won't be happy if you break their female's mind.'

The first one smirks. 'Who knew it would be so easy?'

My eyes narrow and I wipe tears from my cheeks. 'Hey, fuck you, man. You don't know me. I have medically documented sensory issues.'

He looks contrite for a millisecond before he grins like torturing me and scaring me was just a little fun.

'Are you going to help me find the Iron I's, or not?' I ask the new one.

They both look at each other and I have a feeling I'm not going to like the answer.

'Maddox asked me to come find you,' New One says.

'Is that a good thing or a bad thing?' I murmur as I look around at the 'fun' house I'm in.

'Depends on how you look at it,' he replies.

'Quit messing with the stupid human,' I say.

They look at each other again and something passes between them. I roll my eyes and turn away.

'I'm done with this.'

I go back up the hallway without them, but I can't find the door I came in. I look back. They're still standing where I left them.

'Are you going to help me, or not?'

They come to me.

'Sorry about Krase,' New One says, so I guess this is Jayce. 'He's got medically documented *psychotic* issues.' He looks at his brothers. 'You should go find Maddox. He said there was something weird going on.'

Krase nods. 'Be seeing you, baby.'

'I don't think so, *baby*.' I say to his back and I hear him laugh.

He just opens a door out of nowhere with a flourish, and both he and it disappear as he goes through.

Jayce steps too close to me and grabs my hand, doing the same thing and I find myself back in the supe bar, except with him this time.

But now the quiet conversation has ceased and in its place are crashes and screams. The mirror behind the bar is shattered. A group of young shifter girls run past us, clearly terrified.

'They're coming. Run!' someone yells and there's a sudden stampede as more supes follow the first ones.

I get caught in the wave of bodies and I'm thrown to the ground. I hear yelling and screaming around me and Jayce pulls me up, throwing me over his shoulder.

And that's when I see them coming out of the smoke. Red robes and grotesque silver masks. They're grabbing everyone they can get their hands on ... and they're killing them.

Easily.

They're stronger and faster than the supes here and there are so many of them.

'What is going on?' I yell.

Jayce barks out a curse but doesn't reply. Instead, he pulls me through another door into a small closet.

'Stay here if you know what's good for you. They won't give a shit who you are. They'll just gut you.'

He leaves me there before I can beg him to stay with me.

I can hear scuffling outside, muffled whimpers and more screams. Someone is giving orders and cruel laughter follows.

'You supes had this coming to you,' someone chuckles from just outside the door where I'm hiding.

'Bet you didn't think this was going to happen tonight, huh?'

I can't stay here. One of them is going to find me.

I crack the door and see stragglers running down the hall followed by more of the masked men. I gasp as one grabs a struggling shifter girl from the ground by her hair and slits her throat with a silver knife. I must make a sound because he drops her and looks me straight in the eye.

I shut the door and fumble for something to bar it with, but it's too late. He's already opening it. I push back and miraculously it closes, but then someone thuds into it hard and I'm forced backwards, my bare feet unable to gain purchase on the smooth floor.

The door opens and two of them push their way in.

'What do we have here? A supe-lover?'

I wonder errantly how he knows I'm human. He and his friend share a look and the door closes, trapping me inside with them.

I look from one to the other.

'Please,' I say. 'I don't even know how I got here.'

The first one pulls my robe apart and laughs when he sees my bikini. 'Bullshit.'

The other takes off his mask.

He's human.

He looks me up and down and steps forward, driving me up against the wall.

'I think you need a lesson on why you should stay with your own kind,' he says to me.

'How is assaulting me going to do that?' I ask, genuinely curious.

He draws back and shakes his head a little. 'We got a crazy one.'

'I like 'em like that. They have some fight.'

'Please,' I say, pressing myself into the wall as the one closest tries to kiss me.

'She's begging already!'

The other one chuckles.

No! This is bullshit and it's not going to happen to me again.

A hunger rears up inside me, something I quickly acknowledge as having always been there. I *pull* and I feel something come from them, much like I felt in that alleyway with those frat boys that time AND from all of the Iron I's when they've been feeding from me. I just didn't notice it before.

I drag in whatever it is and it tastes like *clouds of cotton candy* ... or when someone's vaping and it smells *really good*. Except that instead of being disappointed when I realize the thing is only a delicious fragrance, I'm *also eating the thing* because it's real. I can smell it *and taste it* and it's sooooo satisfying.

One of them falls to his knees.

'What the fuck are you doing to us?'

'I don't know,' I say, 'but I'm going to keep on doing it because fuck you assholes.'

I yank hard and the other guy falls too. It's only when they're both slumped over that I stop sucking them both dry like Slurpees through straws.

I don't actually care if I've killed them. At the end of the day, they're a couple of murdering rapists. I step over them and open the door carefully. The way outside is clear and I run – straight into Korban.

Relief almost makes me throw my arms around him, but this could be Makenzie Senior again and until I feel him I won't know.

'Where have you been?' he growls.

Well, it certainly sounds like him.

I sense annoyance and fear coming from him and I let out a breath, feeling a little lightheaded as I grip his forearm. I'm safe ... and he was worried about me. I don't have time to think about why that might be before he puts his arm around my shoulders in almost a protective gesture.

'Come on, princess,' he says, drawing me across the hallway and through what seems to be a *normal* door into a stairwell.

He closes it.

'There are more of them coming,' he says and I realize he's not talking to me, he's talking to someone *behind* me.

I turn around. Maddox is there.

'At least you found her before they did,' Maddox says, looking me over.

Not quite.

'What the hell is going on?' I ask.

'We don't know,' Maddox says, keeping an eye on the stairwell. 'But the club is under attack and they have weapons that kill supes.'

'Where are the others?' I ask, looking over the railing, hoping they're close by.

Maddox shrugs. 'They're big boys. They can take care of themselves, but the magick that keeps this engine running is starting to rip it apart. As soon as the portals open, we need to get out of here or we'll be lost in the mazes forever.'

'How the fuck did they even get here?' Korban growls from his place at the door.

Maddox shakes his head. 'It shouldn't be possible. Once the passages between worlds are closed, there's no way in or out until the portal door swings back around.'

'Could they have snuck in and have been lying in wait since the doorways were open?'

'No,' Maddox says. 'We would have known they were

here, but I'll tell you this for nothing, if they could find us here, then something else is going on too.'

'What do you mean?' I ask.

'Everyone knows this is the hottest supe club. Everyone who's anyone is … *was* here tonight. This is a coordinated attack on us.'

'They're human,' I mutter.

Maddox nods. 'The Order. There are more of them than we thought.'

'We can't just leave the others,' I insist.

'Don't worry, darling.'

Korban lets out a growl from the door and Maddox tuts.

'Just a term of endearment, Korban. I know she's yours.'

I look from one to the other, frowning. 'Not really the time for a pissing contest, guys.'

'When the doors are open, the others will go back to the house and so will we,' Korban says to me, not taking his eyes off the hallway. 'That's always the plan when we get separated.'

Maddox checks his watch. 'We have 2 minutes. Once the passages open, every door of the club will lead out for an hour … or until the entire place collapses.'

I stare at Korban's back. Yeah this is definitely him, but is that any better than Vic's dad really? Do I want to go somewhere with him alone considering how casually cruel he's been to me ever since we met?

The lights go out suddenly and I scream. Kor's arms are immediately around me, his hand over my lips.

'Shut her up,' Maddox hisses, 'or I will!'

Kor turns me around to face him in the black, keeping my mouth covered.

'Close your eyes,' he says. 'It's okay. I know you don't like the dark. Just a sec.'

A tiny light appears in his hand and, although it's small, it's something for me to focus on.

'Thirty seconds,' Maddox says.

There's a noise from below us.

'I heard a scream.'

'They're coming,' I whisper in panic.

'Twenty seconds.'

'There!' someone shouts.

Shit!

I hear the pounding of boots up the metal stairs. We're out of time!

'Ten seconds.'

Maddox has his hand on the closed door.

The men are getting closer.

'Up here! There's three of the fuckers.'

Just as two of the masked men come into view, Maddox throws open the door and leaps through. Korban picks me up, cradling me as shots ring out behind us.

We're out in the street.

Maddox slams the door shut and I see it disappear.

They won't come out in the same spot now,' he says.

He looks past Korban and me.

'Fuck,' he mutters.

Korban turns and his eyes widen slightly. I feel a burst of fear from him, but he dampens it a second later.

I can see a fire down the street, smell smoke and hear sirens in the distance. It's night and only some of the street-lights are on. I can hear wailing, muted crying as if someone's hurt close by.

'What the fuck is happening?' Korban says, not speaking to anyone in particular.

Maddox shakes his head. 'That wasn't just an attack on

my club. It was on Metro too. The Order just declared war on the supes. Come on. We can't stay in the open.'

He takes out his phone and swears. 'The network is down.'

'It's okay,' Kor says. 'Our place isn't far from here.'

We move into the shadows, travelling quickly and silently, Korban carrying me the whole way. For once, I can't feel anger from him. There's nothing at all. He's keeping everything down, like a well-trained, compartmentalized soldier.

We get to the house without incident and Korban deposits me on the couch.

I get up.

'I'm going to change,' I say, daring him to stop me because I'm tired and scared and worrying about the others and I don't need his shit right now. I'm also still dressed in a freaking bikini and it's freezing!

'Not by yourself,' he says and I stare him down, anger coursing through me.

'I'll come with you,' he says and I step back.

Oh.

He comes up the stairs with me, a gun he grabbed from somewhere in his hand. He checks Theo's room before he lets me in.

'They're not here, are they?' I say.

He shakes his head.

'What if they didn't get out in—' My voice catches.

'Why would you care?' he growls and I feel my lower lip wobble.

I sniff hard, not trusting my voice.

'They did,' he says, looking away.

I swallow hard. 'But how do you kn—'

'Just get some clothes on, princess,' he says, brooking no argument.

I make myself nod and go into the closet, grabbing some jeans, sneakers and a sweatshirt, putting a thick jacket on top.

When I come out dressed, Korban is still there and I can tell he approves of my practical outfit.

We go back downstairs in silence.

Maddox is in the living room, eyes glued to the news.

'There have been attacks all through the city, and not just this one. Squads of humans in red robes armed with spells and magickal weapons have been taking out any supe they see. They've bombed the police headquarters and the supe hospitals in Metro and other cities are reporting the same. The Order isn't just a group of supe-hates anymore. They're an army.'

'Fuck,' Kor says. 'They've been planning this for a long time.'

'Yeah. It sounds like most of the supes have fled the cities and are hiding where they can. We can't stay here. They're going house to house and executing anyone who can't prove they're fully human.'

For the first time Kor looks lost. 'Where can we go?'

'I have a place,' Maddox says. 'But you have to come with me now.'

'What about the others?' I say just as Korban asks, 'What about Jane?'

'Leave them a message. Bring Jane with you,' Maddox says, answering us both.

'What's the price of this help, Clan Leader?' Korban growls in distrust.

Maddox smirks. 'Consider this a freebee, Enforcer. Now, come on. It's too dangerous in Metro now.'

But Korban doesn't move, staring at me, thinking something I can't figure out because he's still got his emotions pushed down deep. 'Not for a human. We could cut her loose.'

What does he mean? My heart leaps in my chest. Is he going to leave me here?

Maddox stops and turns around. 'She's not human, Korban.'

'What?' He stares at Maddox. 'What the fuck are you talking about, you British bastard? Of course she is. Look at her!'

'You really don't know?' Maddox's eyes find mine. 'You don't know either, do you, darling.'

He steps closer, shaking his head in disbelief.

'I suspected it that night at the club when you knew we were trying to lull you ... and when it didn't work.'

'Suspected what?' Kor growls.

Maddox gives me a small smile that doesn't reach his eyes, ignoring Korban altogether.

'Fate was cruel when she put you in the path of the Iron I's before my clan,' he murmurs, reaching out to caress my face, but stopping before he actually touches me.

He draws back slowly as if retreating is painful.

'You're a succubus, Jane.'

You're a wizard, Harry.

The fuck?

'That's impossible,' Korban and I say in unison.

But what if this was what Paris was talking about?

'I thought it was too, but here you are.' He turns to Korban. 'I think we can both agree that as the last of our females, she must be protected at all costs.'

Korban nods almost imperceptibly, looking dazed.

'Then we have to go.'

He takes something out of his pocket and puts in on the door to the kitchen. He presses a button and opens the door and, like in his club, it now leads somewhere else.

I look at Korban, feeling newly betrayed because he wanted to leave me here alone. I don't trust Maddox either, and I want to find the others, but Korban picks me up.

Then he falters with a groan, falling to one knee and I look at my hand that was just on his back because it feels wet.

Blood.

The gunfire when we were leaving.

'Why didn't you tell us you'd been shot?' I shriek.

'I'll be fine,' he grunts through clenched teeth as he gets to his feet with me still in his arms and doesn't say anything more as he staggers towards the open door that Maddox has disappeared through. But he pauses at the threshold and looks at me warily.

I know Maddox has it wrong. I'm not a succubus. I can't be. But I don't want him to leave me here either, so I keep my mouth shut.

'We'll find the others,' he says as he takes me through the portal and I hope he's right because if there's anything I've figured out of these past few insane hours, it's that I do care about these incubus assholes.

A lot.

And I'm terrified that, like almost everyone else I've really cared about in my life, they may already be dead.

THANKS FOR READING and I'm sorry it's another cliffhanger BUT read the final book, *Darkness and Debauchery*, as soon as it's out.

If you enjoyed this book, please consider leaving a text

review. Even one line is so helpful to your friendly neighborhood author! xx

In the meantime, sign up to my mailing list to recieve a short about what Korban has been getting up to behind the scenes! (SPOILER: It's violence against everyone who's wronged Jane ... even though he hates her, right? I have a feeling Kor would burn the world for Jane even if he doesnt know it yet. #morallygreylove)

15

JANE

I had to get out of that room. Theo's emotions were an onslaught. I had no idea he feels so much all the time. He was so easy to read. It was like a flowing river. I loved it because the emotions weren't mine. It was like watching a movie.

I don't think I could filter him out like I do the others even if I wanted to. I loved feeling everything he did when he was thinking of me. I had no idea that he truly cares about me and I loved it, but I hated it as well because it made me realize how much I care about him too.

'Stupid, stupid, stupid, Jane,' I mutter to myself and I don't even bother to mute that mean voice because I deserve it.

I'm an on-call girl. That's all. They're not *mine* and they never will be. I'm a human. They're supes. Most human kids grow up with warnings from adults. The supes might be pretty and glitzy and powerful, but they aren't for us.

What's worse is that I realized how much I care about the others too even after everything and I know how ridiculous it is, how pathetic it is. But I can't help it. Aside from the fact that they're literal demons, how can I care about men who have fucked up my life so bad? After all the cruel things they did, even Theo as much as I hate to admit it.

I care about him the most. Maybe I even love him, but I have no idea because I don't know what that even feels like.

I wash my hands and pull the door, not noticing until it's fully open that Theo's room has disappeared and in its place is a long, dark hallway.

'Fuck!' I hiss, slamming it closed again and thinking as hard as I possibly can about Theo and his bedroom. I throw open the door again and, sure enough, his room is there as he said it would be if I focused hard enough.

Only he's not in it.

I shut it again and squeeze my eyes together, thinking only about Theo as hard as I can. I crack the door and I find another room that I don't recognize. There are other supes in here and I watch them from the doorway for a minute. They aren't on a loop. Maybe that means they're not part of whatever magick this place is made of. I don't know if that's a good thing or a bad thing.

I look down at myself. I'm still dressed in a bikini and I don't want to invite unwanted attention. There's a robe on the back of the door. I grab it and put it on. At least that's something.

I walk out. It looks like a regular bar. There's quiet conversation and some very light music in the background that I can't really hear above the murmur of voices. I walk around, surveying the room as I go to see if anyone I know is here. But there's no one, not even any of the guys from Maddox's crew.

I make my way to the bar and try to get the barman's attention. There's a mirror behind and I see Vic over my shoulder. He's right behind me. I twist around with relief, but he's not there.

What the fuck?

I turned back. I can still see him in the mirror. He raises a hand, telling me to wait where I am.

But what if it's not him? What if it's his weirdo dad again pretending to be Vic? Ugh that would be so nasty! I don't want to wait around for *him* to find me.

Vic (or fake Vic) looks ... concerned maybe, but without him being right there for me to actually feel him, I'm not sure.

Sie walks up to him, but a quick look behind me confirms this is all still happening in the reflection. He notices me in the mirror and looks next to him and then back at me. I can see he's as confused as I am.

He says something to Vic and I see their brief exchange but I can't hear what they're saying. Sie puts his hands up like Vic did.

'Wait there!' he mouths.

'Are you lost?' someone says from behind me, but I don't know the voice.

It's not Vic or Sie. I turn around, but there's no one there again. I pretend that I'm not afraid, but more than one supe turns their head in my direction proving that they can literally smell fear.

I am very much aware that I am the only human in a supe bar, in a supe realm. I have no protection here at all. I lock eyes with Vic and Sie.

'I said, are you lost?'

I twist again and I find a member of Maddox's clan. It's one of the two brothers who look the same. Sie told me their names are Jayce and Krase, but I don't know which one is which.

My first reaction is to feel relieved because at least I know who this person is, but have I just gone from the frying pan into the fire?

I look him over. He's tall and broad like they all are. He's looking at me strangely and I don't get a good vibe. But there's no one else who can help me here. Maybe he won't do anything bad to me. I mean, he knows I'm with the Iron I's and Vic is definitely a force to be reckoned with. Maybe the mere threat of him is enough to keep me safe.

'Yes,' I say, 'I *am* lost.'

He tuts. 'They shouldn't have left you so unprotected, little bird. This is our busiest night of the week and *everyone* is here looking for some fun.'

He takes my hand and, not letting me wriggle out of it, he leads me across the floor and through a door. On the other side of it is a gloomy room and my breath hitches. Where has he brought me? I can still feel his hand in mine but I can't see him clearly. And then he's gone as well and I'm alone.

I hear a light snap on. It sounds very much like the one from the cell in the garage, which immediately puts me on edge but the light that shines down from above is very far away and very dim.

I look around me and shriek, jumping back. But I realize it's my own reflection, contorted in a funhouse mirror.

'Hello?' I call, but there's no one there.

I walk forward down the corridor of mirrors, each one changing the way I look in a different way.

Someone laughs right behind me but when I look, there's no one there and I'm starting to see a trend.

I swallow hard. There's a reason I don't watch horror movies. Wasn't there one about mirrors where someone gets trapped on the other side of the glass and there's *things* living in there?

'Stop it,' I say out loud.

Stop freaking yourself out.

I keep walking and I see in one of the reflections that there's someone behind me again. It's a demon I don't recognize and he's walking in step with me. Another trick. I don't turn around. I watch as he puts his hand on my shoulder in the mirror and I ignore it with a roll of my eyes. But then I *feel the hand on me* and I shriek, whirling around and jumping away.

He disappears and I hear laughing.

'Stop it!' I scream, using my hands to cover my eyes, but the sounds of my words echo through the room, reverberating off the mirrors and becoming deafeningly loud.

I move my hands to my ears as I sink to the ground in distress. I call for all of the Iron I's. I don't even care if I'm a damsel in distress as long as they can take me away from this place. At this point, I think I might just pledge my undying love for them all regardless of what they've done in the past if they just help me.

The sounds fade and someone draws me to my feet. I open my eyes tentatively, hoping with everything in me that it's Vic or Sie. Hell, I'll even take Korban at this point, but it's the same guy from before.

'Why are you doing this?' I ask.

All he does is shrug.

Another one of them appears. This must be the twin, I think. He looks pretty much the same except for different clothes.

'Time to leave her alone, bro. The Iron I's won't be happy if you break their female's mind.'

The first one smirks. 'Who knew it would be so easy?'

My eyes narrow and I wipe tears from my cheeks. 'Hey, fuck you, man. You don't know me. I have medically documented sensory issues.'

He looks contrite for a millisecond before he grins like torturing me and scaring me was just a little fun.

'Are you going to help me find the Iron I's, or not?' I ask the new one.

They both look at each other and I have a feeling I'm not going to like the answer.

'Maddox asked me to come find you,' New One says.

'Is that a good thing or a bad thing?' I murmur as I look around at the 'fun' house I'm in.

'Depends on how you look at it,' he replies.

'Quit messing with the stupid human,' I say.

They look at each other again and something passes between them. I roll my eyes and turn away.

'I'm done with this.'

I go back up the hallway without them, but I can't find the door I came in. I look back. They're still standing where I left them.

'Are you going to help me, or not?'

They come to me.

'Sorry about Krase,' New One says, so I guess this is Jayce. 'He's got medically documented *psychotic* issues.' He looks at his brothers. 'You should go find Maddox. He said there was something weird going on.'

Krase nods. 'Be seeing you, baby.'

'I don't think so, *baby*.' I say to his back and I hear him laugh.

He just opens a door out of nowhere with a flourish, and both he and it disappear as he goes through.

Jayce steps too close to me and grabs my hand, doing the

same thing and I find myself back in the supe bar, except with him this time.

But now the quiet conversation has ceased and in its place are crashes and screams. The mirror behind the bar is shattered. A group of young shifter girls run past us, clearly terrified.

'They're coming. Run!' someone yells and there's a sudden stampede as more supes follow the first ones.

I get caught in the wave of bodies and I'm thrown to the ground. I hear yelling and screaming around me and Jayce pulls me up, throwing me over his shoulder.

And that's when I see them coming out of the smoke. Red robes and grotesque silver masks. They're grabbing everyone they can get their hands on ... and they're killing them.

Easily.

They're stronger and faster than the supes here and there are so many of them.

'What is going on?' I yell.

Jayce barks out a curse but doesn't reply. Instead, he pulls me through another door into a small closet.

'Stay here if you know what's good for you. They won't give a shit who you are. They'll just gut you.'

He leaves me there before I can beg him to stay with me.

I can hear scuffling outside, muffled whimpers and more screams. Someone is giving orders and cruel laughter follows.

'You supes had this coming to you,' someone chuckles from just outside the door where I'm hiding.

'Bet you didn't think this was going to happen tonight, huh?'

I can't stay here. One of them is going to find me.

I crack the door and see stragglers running down the

hall followed by more of the masked men. I gasp as one grabs a struggling shifter girl from the ground by her hair and slits her throat with a silver knife. I must make a sound because he drops her and looks me straight in the eye.

I shut the door and fumble for something to bar it with, but it's too late. He's already opening it. I push back and miraculously it closes, but then someone thuds into it hard and I'm forced backwards, my bare feet unable to gain purchase on the smooth floor.

The door opens and two of them push their way in.

'What do we have here? A supe-lover?'

I wonder errantly how he knows I'm human. He and his friend share a look and the door closes, trapping me inside with them.

I look from one to the other.

'Please,' I say. 'I don't even know how I got here.'

The first one pulls my robe apart and laughs when he sees my bikini. 'Bullshit.'

The other takes off his mask.

He's human.

He looks me up and down and steps forward, driving me up against the wall.

'I think you need a lesson on why you should stay with your own kind,' he says to me.

'How is assaulting me going to do that?' I ask, genuinely curious.

He draws back and shakes his head a little. 'We got a crazy one.'

'I like 'em like that. They have some fight.'

'Please,' I say, pressing myself into the wall as the one closest tries to kiss me.

'She's begging already!'

The other one chuckles.

No! This is bullshit and it's not going to happen to me again.

A hunger rears up inside me, something I quickly acknowledge as having always been there. I *pull* and I feel something come from them, much like I felt in that alleyway with those frat boys that time AND from all of the Iron I's when they've been feeding from me. I just didn't notice it before.

I drag in whatever it is and it tastes like *clouds of cotton candy* ... or when someone's vaping and it smells *really good*. Except that instead of being disappointed when I realize the thing is only a delicious fragrance, I'm *also eating the thing* because it's real. I can smell it *and taste it* and it's sooooo satisfying.

One of them falls to his knees.

'What the fuck are you doing to us?'

'I don't know,' I say, 'but I'm going to keep on doing it because fuck you assholes.'

I yank hard and the other guy falls too. It's only when they're both slumped over that I stop sucking them both dry like Slurpees through straws.

I don't actually care if I've killed them. At the end of the day, they're a couple of murdering rapists. I step over them and open the door carefully. The way outside is clear and I run – straight into Korban.

Relief almost makes me throw my arms around him, but this could be Makenzie Senior again and until I feel him I won't know.

'Where have you been?' he growls.

Well, it certainly sounds *like him.*

I sense annoyance and fear coming from him and I let out a breath, feeling a little lightheaded as I grip his forearm. I'm safe ... and he was worried about me. I don't have time to think about why that might be before he puts his arm around my shoulders in almost a protective gesture.

'Come on, princess,' he says, drawing me across the hallway and through what seems to be a *normal* door into a stairwell.

He closes it.

'There are more of them coming,' he says and I realize he's not talking to me, he's talking to someone *behind* me.

I turn around. Maddox is there.

'At least you found her before they did,' Maddox says, looking me over.

Not quite.

'What the hell is going on?' I ask.

'We don't know,' Maddox says, keeping an eye on the stairwell. 'But the club is under attack and they have weapons that kill supes.'

'Where are the others?' I ask, looking over the railing, hoping they're close by.

Maddox shrugs. 'They're big boys. They can take care of themselves, but the magick that keeps this engine running is starting to rip it apart. As soon as the portals open, we need to get out of here or we'll be lost in the mazes forever.'

'How the fuck did they even get here?' Korban growls from his place at the door.

Maddox shakes his head. 'It shouldn't be possible. Once the passages between worlds are closed, there's no way in or out until the portal door swings back around.'

'Could they have snuck in and have been lying in wait since the doorways were open?'

'No,' Maddox says. 'We would have known they were here, but I'll tell you this for nothing, if they could find us here, then something else is going on too.'

'What do you mean?' I ask.

'Everyone knows this is the hottest supe club. Everyone who's anyone is ... *was* here tonight. This is a coordinated attack on us.'

'They're human,' I mutter.

Maddox nods. 'The Order. There are more of them than we thought.'

'We can't just leave the others,' I insist.

'Don't worry, darling.'

Korban lets out a growl from the door and Maddox tuts.

'Just a term of endearment, Korban. I know she's yours.'

I look from one to the other, frowning. 'Not really the time for a pissing contest, guys.'

'When the doors are open, the others will go back to the house and so will we,' Korban says to me, not taking his eyes off the hallway. 'That's always the plan when we get separated.'

Maddox checks his watch. 'We have 2 minutes. Once the passages open, every door of the club will lead out for an hour ... or until the entire place collapses.'

I stare at Korban's back. Yeah this is definitely him, but is that any better than Vic's dad really? Do I want to go somewhere with him alone considering how casually cruel he's been to me ever since we met?

The lights go out suddenly and I scream. Kor's arms are immediately around me, his hand over my lips.

'Shut her up,' Maddox hisses, 'or I will!'

Kor turns me around to face him in the black, keeping my mouth covered.

'Close your eyes,' he says. 'It's okay. I know you don't like the dark. Just a sec.'

A tiny light appears in his hand and, although it's small, it's something for me to focus on.

'Thirty seconds,' Maddox says.

There's a noise from below us.

'I heard a scream.'

'They're coming,' I whisper in panic.

'Twenty seconds.'

'There!' someone shouts.

Shit!

I hear the pounding of boots up the metal stairs. We're out of time!

'Ten seconds.'

Maddox has his hand on the closed door.

The men are getting closer.

'Up here! There's three of the fuckers.'

Just as two of the masked men come into view, Maddox throws open the door and leaps through. Korban picks me up, cradling me as shots ring out behind us.

We're out in the street.

Maddox slams the door shut and I see it disappear.

They won't come out in the same spot now,' he says.

He looks past Korban and me.

'Fuck,' he mutters.

Korban turns and his eyes widen slightly. I feel a burst of fear from him, but he dampens it a second later.

I can see a fire down the street, smell smoke and hear sirens in the distance. It's night and only some of the street-lights are on. I can hear wailing, muted crying as if some-one's hurt close by.

'What the fuck is happening?' Korban says, not speaking to anyone in particular.

Maddox shakes his head. 'That wasn't just an attack on my club. It was on Metro too. The Order just declared war on the supes. Come on. We can't stay in the open.'

He takes out his phone and swears. 'The network is down.'

'It's okay,' Kor says. 'Our place isn't far from here.'

We move into the shadows, travelling quickly and silently, Korban carrying me the whole way. For once, I can't feel anger from him. There's nothing at all. He's keeping everything down, like a well-trained, compartmentalized soldier.

We get to the house without incident and Korban deposits me on the couch.

I get up.

'I'm going to change,' I say, daring him to stop me because I'm tired and scared and worrying about the others and I don't need his shit right now. I'm also still dressed in a freaking bikini and it's freezing!

'Not by yourself,' he says and I stare him down, anger coursing through me.

'I'll come with you,' he says and I step back.

Oh.

He comes up the stairs with me, a gun he grabbed from somewhere in his hand. He checks Theo's room before he lets me in.

'They're not here, are they?' I say.

He shakes his head.

'What if they didn't get out in—' My voice catches.

'Why would you care?' he growls and I feel my lower lip wobble.

I sniff hard, not trusting my voice.

'They did,' he says, looking away.

I swallow hard. 'But how do you kn—'

'Just get some clothes on, princess,' he says, brooking no argument.

I make myself nod and go into the closet, grabbing some jeans, sneakers and a sweatshirt, putting a thick jacket on top.

When I come out dressed, Korban is still there and I can tell he approves of my practical outfit.

We go back downstairs in silence.

Maddox is in the living room, eyes glued to the news.

'There have been attacks all through the city, and not just this one. Squads of humans in red robes armed with spells and magickal weapons have been taking out any supe they see. They've bombed the police headquarters and the supe hospitals in Metro and other cities are reporting the same. The Order isn't just a group of supe-hates anymore. They're an army.'

'Fuck,' Kor says. 'They've been planning this for a long time.'

'Yeah. It sounds like most of the supes have fled the cities and are hiding where they can. We can't stay here. They're going house to house and executing anyone who can't prove they're fully human.'

For the first time Kor looks lost. 'Where can we go?'

'I have a place,' Maddox says. 'But you have to come with me now.'

'What about the others?' I say just as Korban asks, 'What about Jane?'

'Leave them a message. Bring Jane with you,' Maddox says, answering us both.

'What's the price of this help, Clan Leader?' Korban growls in distrust.

Maddox smirks. 'Consider this a freebee, Enforcer. Now, come on. It's too dangerous in Metro now.'

But Korban doesn't move, staring at me, thinking something I can't figure out because he's still got his emotions pushed down deep. 'Not for a human. We could cut her loose.'

What does he mean? My heart leaps in my chest. Is he going to leave me here?

Maddox stops and turns around. 'She's not human, Korban.'

'What?' He stares at Maddox. 'What the fuck are you talking about, you British bastard? Of course she is. Look at her!'

'You really don't know?' Maddox's eyes find mine. 'You don't know either, do you, darling.'

He steps closer, shaking his head in disbelief.

'I suspected it that night at the club when you knew we were trying to lull you ... and when it didn't work.'

'Suspected what?' Kor growls.

Maddox gives me a small smile that doesn't reach his eyes, ignoring Korban altogether.

'Fate was cruel when she put you in the path of the Iron I's before my clan,' he murmurs, reaching out to caress my face, but stopping before he actually touches me.

He draws back slowly as if retreating is painful.

'You're a succubus, Jane.'

You're a wizard, Harry.

The fuck?

'That's impossible,' Korban and I say in unison.

But what if this was what Paris was talking about?

'I thought it was too, but here you are.' He turns to Korban. 'I think we can both agree that as the last of our females, she must be protected at all costs.'

Korban nods almost imperceptibly, looking dazed.

'Then we have to go.'

He takes something out of his pocket and puts in on the door to the kitchen. He presses a button and opens the door and, like in his club, it now leads somewhere else.

I look at Korban, feeling newly betrayed because he

wanted to leave me here alone. I don't trust Maddox either, and I want to find the others, but Korban picks me up.

Then he falters with a groan, falling to one knee and I look at my hand that was just on his back because it feels wet.

Blood.

The gunfire when we were leaving.

'Why didn't you tell us you'd been shot?' I shriek.

'I'll be fine,' he grunts through clenched teeth as he gets to his feet with me still in his arms and doesn't say anything more as he staggers towards the open door that Maddox has disappeared through. But he pauses at the threshold and looks at me warily.

I know Maddox has it wrong. I'm not a succubus. I can't be. But I don't want him to leave me here either, so I keep my mouth shut.

'We'll find the others,' he says as he takes me through the portal and I hope he's right because if there's anything I've figured out of these past few insane hours, it's that I do care about these incubus assholes.

A lot.

And I'm terrified that, like almost everyone else I've really cared about in my life, they may already be dead.

Thanks for reading!

Darkness and Debauchery, the final book in this series, is available on Amazon.

In the meantime, sign up to my mailing list if you haven't already to recieve a free short about what Korban's been getting up to behind the scenes …

JOIN MY MAILING LIST

Sign up to my newsletter and stay in the know!

Members also receive exclusive content, free books, access to giveaways and contests as well as the latest information on new books and projects that I'm working on!

It's completely free to sign up, you will never be spammed by me and it's very easy to unsubscribe:

www.kyraalessy.com

ACKNOWLEDGEMENTS

For everyone out there who's neurodivergent and feels
like no one understands them.

You will find your people.

xx Kyra

ABOUT THE AUTHOR

Kyra was almost 20 when she read her first romance. From Norsemen to Regency and Romcom to Dubcon, tales of love and adventure filled a void in her she didn't know existed. She now lives in the UK with her family, but misses NJ where she grew up.

Kyra LOVES interacting with her readers so please join us in the Portal to the Dark Realm, her private Facebook group, because she is literally ALWAYS online unless she's asleep – much to her husband's annoyance!

Take a look at her website for info on how to stay updated on release dates, exclusive content and other general awesomeness from the worlds and characters she's created – where the road to happily ever after might be rough, but it's worth the journey!

facebook.com/kyraalessy
twitter.com/evylempryss
instagram.com/kyraalessy
goodreads.com/evylempryss
bookbub.com/profile/kyra-alessy
tiktok.com/@evylempryss